FREAK ACCIDENT

NO ONE SEES IT COMING

Nick Jacobs
Don Jacobs

Literary Quarters
Intellectual Properties

KENDALL/HUNT PUBLISHING COMPANY
4050 Westmark Drive   Dubuque, Iowa 52002

CONTENTS

Beyond

FOREWORD

*F*reak Accident is a work of fiction. The characters and events presented in the novel are the products of the authors' own imaginations. While Mt. Kyle does not exist, the struggles, strategies, and adjustments required as individuals mature and face uncertain futures occur every place on earth. It is a natural condition of living to confront change, uncertainty, and ambiguity in any stage of life. It is part of our existence. College students are particularly at risk. Due to a lack of perspective, they may not *see what's coming* in time to adjust to life after high school.

Being unaware of *what's coming* to a young person full of hopes and dreams is disheartening, especially if the person has been sheltered from the realities of the world. Today, science knows a lot about brain chemistry—neurotransmitters and neurohormones—and, the placebo effect. Mature adults know the difficulty of living in *existential reality*—living in a world of uncertainty and ambiguity. Yet, the question remains: How can we live authentic and productive lives living in a post-modern world where nothing can be taken for granted? Brilliant insight and bold strategies must be developed to increase the chances of positive outcomes. This is the message within the message of *Freak Accident*.

At the conclusion of the novel, notes are included that reflect the authors' perspectives. It provides insight into the use of metaphor, how appearances are mostly deceiving, and how lack of preparation can completely derail the best of intentions.

Students are encouraged to make comments and ask questions relating to the novel or the college experience by logging on to the official website at Weatherford College. The address is: www.freakaccident.info.

To absent friends and fond memories...

When you're ready to feel truly "Texan" you must drive from Ft. Davis to Alpine, and from Alpine to Study Butte in the heart of Big Bend. From there your journey will take you past Terlingua to a magical place known as Lajetas, Texas. You must drive back the long way. Take the enchanting loop from Lajetas to Presidio and then to Ft. Davis. The experience changes you forever. The experience enters your soul like the melodies from Wink's Roy Orbison, or Odessa's Larry Gatlin, or Lubbock's Buddy Holly...

This novel is dedicated to first year college students who are about to embark on a life-changing journey. The feelings of uncertainty from the higher expectations of the college experience are both frightening as well as inspiring ... perhaps similar to the emotions experienced by the Sable lodgers trapped by a dangerous blizzard high atop the Mountain of the Ghost in far West Texas. Special thanks to Dr. Martha Huff for her review of the manuscript.

Nick Jacobs

Don Jacobs

Coming in through the back door

A re there foreseeable contingencies to freak accidents or is the occurrence due to nothing more than happenstance?

There are many ways to orient first-year college students to the higher expectations of the college experience. A plethora of currently available books seek to go in the front door. They seek to help students focus on what they already know they must do, which is to overcome bad study habits, avoid procrastination, become focused, and seek tutorial assistance for difficult subjects. Basically, get down to business. It matters little what authors and teachers attempt in this worthy endeavor unless students are *psychologically prepared to see what's coming.* Otherwise, they enter college with eyes wide shut.

As authors of *Freak Accident,* we decided to go in the back door. *Freak Accident* is a novel of fiction with metaphorical meaning in coping with modern problems. Education is one of those problems. The ability to see what's coming in the college experience is essential for success.

Today, more than ever before, students must be prepared to address the realities of life or face the consequences of their incredulity. Becoming *psychologically prepared* is a great advantage. Learning to look for layers of meaning in a novel that has implication to the college experience is a worthy first step. Being prepared to *expect the unexpected* and adjust accordingly is another. The novel is a cautionary tale of what can be anticipated when students enter the college experience underprepared.

Taking the first step always begins any journey. Our journey of enlightenment begins in the Rift Valley near Tanzania...

For nothing contributes so much to tranquilize the mind as a steady purpose—a point on which the soul may fix its intellectual eye

Mary Wollstonecraft Shelley

THE FIND

ETHIOPIA, AFRICA
MAIN ETHIOPIAN RIFT

In Africa's Rift Valley between Tanzania and Eritrea, most of the hominid fossils of man's early ancestors have been discovered. More recent finds exist dating from *Homo erectus* (about one million years ago), archaic *Homo sapien* (around 500,000 years ago), and the most recent *Cro-Magnon* man (circa 60,000 to 45,000 years ago).

Near Lake Victoria in the vicinity where the oldest footprints of hominids were discovered at Olduvai Gorge, Max Zander, age 49, is in the process of unearthing an extraordinary find. He disguises the location every Sunday evening with heavy foliage he accumulates from nearby overgrowths. If necessary, he returns several times during the week to replace the yellowing foliage. No one must discover the site by accident.

Dr. Zander's schedule is to work Sunday from noon until dark by himself. Ostensibly, this allows his team (two males and three females—all doctoral students) to enjoy a complete day off from the rigors of the dig. Actually, they stay behind to clean and catalogue new finds. This is the fourth Sunday in a row Dr. Zander has worked alone on his clandestine find. Since he often scouts about for alternative sites, his absence is not suspicious.

He has been working at a feverish pace to finish cleaning the upper clavicle and torso, spine, and lower body of the fossil. It is a typically hot and humid August afternoon. He mops his brow at intervals and cleans the smoky lenses of his bifocals with his red-checkered hanky. He is meticulous with his instruments, careful as he clears away encrusted dirt and aggregate rock. He finds it hard to contain his enthusiasm. He suspects worldwide implications with every swipe of his cleaning brush. Crews (interpreters) of hominid fossil finds grow close out in the field as a matter of expediency. He is more detached than usual; he must keep this find a secret. The highly respected paleontologist is entirely in awe of it.

With every bone clearly visible, the configuration of the fossil's spine, hip joint, knee joint, and foot are unique. Fragile erosional systems show limited degradation. Length from upper spine to lower lumbar is relatively long suggesting a species consistent with our own. The lumbar region of the spine is not short and stiff like a chimp's. Chimpanzees go through life with a fused lumbar resulting in an imbalance as one leg is lifted off the ground. This motion causes chimps to sway back and forth when walking, one of their most recognizable traits. Seen walking from a distance, *Homo sapiens* don't sway; rather, their heads bob up and down as they walk due to their unique lumbar configuration. This condition results in thrusting the torso's center of gravity forward producing a smooth walking motion, not a back-and-forth swaying motion. The same lumbar configuration appears in Dr. Zander's find.

Also, the pelvis is broad with a specialized hip joint. The femur angles inward and is larger at the bottom. The tibia is larger at the top suggesting a balanced distribution of weight. A distinct groove at the bottom of the femur keeps the patella (knee cap) from sliding off the knee joint. Finally, the big toe is not opposable but lined up with the smaller toes forming a natural arch for shock absorption required for walking or running, not for climbing or grasping.

At first glance, the fossil is far more advanced than *Homo erectus*. The find is more in line with *Cro-Magnon* man, the first *Homo sapien*. The creature, lying fossilized under the searing afternoon heat of the Olduvai Gorge, is distinctly larger and taller than the two million-year-old *Australopithecus garhi*. (The *A. garhi* find provided a crucial gap in human ancestry by providing evidence of a creature that butchered animals.)

Max Zander believes he may be on the brink of *redrawing the human family tree*. Quick mathematical calculation displays narrow hips in relation to broad shoulders, a human characteristic. The hands have an opposable thumb. Oddly, the fingers are much longer than in any find in the history of paleontology, including prehistoric finds dating six million years ago. The lesser toes are rounded off like *Homo sapiens* not elongated like chimps.

The fossil is not consistent with the older fossil remains such as *Homo habilis*, of a little less than two million years ago, or *Homo erectus* of about one million years ago. The cranial cavity shows a space large enough for a *Homo sapien* cerebrum suggesting a creature parallel to our own species. Dr. Zander predicts the dating of the find will coincide with *Homo sapien* chronology.

Strangely, the denser bone structure as well as the long fingers of the fossil are not consistent with *Homo sapiens*.

THE RIVAL

One month later, Dr. Zander's crew packs up to leave their most recent campsite near the Middle Awash in Ethiopia. Dr. Zander arranged with a local magistrate the use of his private twin-engine aircraft flying out of Addis Ababa to transport his crew to a commercial flight leaving the Sudan for South America and then the United States. He found it easy to lie about the urgency of his crew's return to the university.

The respected scientist believes his find will send shock waves around the world. Following Dr. Zander's publication, fellow humans may never look at their friends and neighbors in quite the same way. Working in utmost secrecy, Dr. Zander excavated the site privately and hire1 local natives to help him transport it via an ox cart to an awaiting cargo plane in Tanzania for safe transport back to his hometown.

A week later, due to his vigilance, the fossil arrived intact and unharmed at the municipal airport near his home. He hired a local courier to deliver it to his workshop in Cambridge. The fossil, along with Polaroid snapshots he took to document the find are now safely locked behind the door of his pleasantly cluttered workshop. He is on the phone calling his trusted colleague, the anthropologist Judith Lynn Lovejoy. As soon as the find is made public, shock waves will emanate through paleontology. He is not certain if he has enough energy or stamina to handle this ordeal. Somewhere in the tendrils of his thoughts, he wishes he were a younger man.

Dr. Zander's find provides compelling evidence that *two distinct sapient creatures evolved from about the same time frame in evolutionary history.* Somehow, the rival remained cleverly disguised. Dr. Zander has his own theory, and he shutters to think of

4

it. The most salient aspect of the fossilized creature is truly remarkable. Why was the head decapitated from the body? Dr. Zander found the skull, larger than a human skull, near the creature's feet, suggesting … the creature was purposively decapitated.

WELLS MCAFEE

January—Early Friday Afternoon

WEST TEXAS, USA

Geologist Wells McAfee, age 55, sits in his office on the second floor of the Hyer Hall of Mathematics on the campus of University of Texas, Permian Basin. UTPB is located on the western side of Odessa, Texas, a town once known for its oil and a football team—the Permian Panthers. Sun-weathered pump jacks litter the landscape along I-20 from Odessa to Monahans about thirty miles away. Most are idle. The legendary "Mojo"—the nickname of the once mighty Permian Panther football dynasty in West Texas—has seen better days. With two community colleges, Odessa College and Midland College, and one university, UTPB, all located within twenty miles of each other, one would think Odessa and Midland to be college towns. Oddly, they're not. They're sports-oriented towns. You have to drive over one hundred miles away to Lubbock, Texas, to find one of only three West Texas college towns—the other two are located in San Angelo and Alpine.

At a glance, Dr. McAfee is a dyed-in-the-wool West Texan. He is of medium height and has the paunch of middle age around his waist. His wrinkled and leathery face, tanned and dried by sun and wind, juts out of his neatly pressed white collar. His wavy, silver-gray hair seems always in need of a trim. He sits reading a book in his painfully cluttered office on the second floor of Hyer Hall. Stacks of papers, rock samples, and Polaroid pictures of his latest field trip litter the desk, floor, and walls. The coffee-stained Formica top of his college-issue black steel desk is ceremoniously cleaned once a semester. But he has to remember to tell one of his work-study students; otherwise, it accumulates another semester of dust, coffee spills, and food crumbs. Old test papers, yellowing newspaper articles, and dated college memoranda are in various piles across his desk. File cabinets, minus the hanging files, contain rock samples. Such is the filing system of one of the best geological minds in West Texas and much of the world.

When students visit McAfee during office hours, they must stand in the hallway outside his door and hope he is in a polite enough mood to join them. Otherwise, they crane their necks around the doorframe and hope for the best. Connected to his office in the opposite direction are two short hallways. One ends in a cavernous lab where old, dusty maps are hung haphazardly on the walls or rolled and propped up in all four corners of the room. Rock samples of all sizes and shapes litter the spaces not taken by lab students. The other short hallway leads to a large classroom of long tables with black slate tops. Sinks line the walls. The water hasn't worked in the sinks since 1985.

The need for new office space at UTPB necessitated professors of English, geology, and math to share both floors of Hyer Hall. The chemistry between the three disciplines is an obvious mesalliance. But faculties on all college campuses have features of dysfunctional families. Cordial in public, most professors are fiercely contentious of each other in private. Professional jealousy, no doubt. The popular ones, like McAfee, are detested the most. McAfee himself sits in his office hunkered down over a new hardcover book moving his lips in silent reading. Prominent crow's-feet crinkle around his eyes as he squints through his white, plastic-framed, Coke-bottle-thick lenses. He is reading a former student's recent publication, *Reinventing Myth* by Shadow Darwin, Ph.D.

McAfee is a full professor of physical geology, but his first love is paleoarcheology and, oddly, psychology—the discipline of his favorite ex-student Shadow Darwin. He has been given an advance, autographed copy of Darwin's new book. In a few hours, McAfee and Darwin will meet at the Sable Lodge in Mt. Kyle, Texas. It's an hour's drive west from Odessa for McAfee and about the same distance for Shadow Darwin driving east from Alpine, Texas. The Sable Lodge sits high atop the Chisos Mountain range next door to the vast expanse of the Big Bend National Park. Dr. McAfee is reading the Foreword to his friend's book.

Foreword to *Reinventing Myth*

With science and technology at the forefront of modern society, does myth serve any useful purpose? Myth, in times past, held the fabric—the sanity—of society together until threads of reason—cause and effect—could be teased apart by empiricism. Civilization had to survive the Dark Ages and be reformed, enlightened, and eventually uplifted by the Renaissance before the value of education eclipsed myth.

Due to brain chemistry, individual members of society have always been brilliant. But society as a whole had to get smart. The nineteenth century provided the springboard for behavioral science to convince intellectuals we could be both amid twenty-first-century modern problems.

With the rise of behaviorism in the 1950s, humanism in the 1960s, and neuropsychology in the 1990s, society shed myth like an old snakeskin. In our post-modern rationalism, we have become dismissive and impatient with myth. As science dispels myth with solid footing in neuroscience, stem cell research, cloning capabilities, and cryonics, myth has been relegated to the ranks of legend, fable, superstition, and, worst of all, fairy tale. *Are any aphorisms of truth left from myth that have not been shattered by science?*

Apparently, for myth to hold any veracity today it must be rewritten in light of new existential realities. Increasing knowledge seems to relegate myth to chapters in children's storybooks.

Once upon a time, myths existed to explain the unexplainable. Myth, legend, and superstition served unenlightened societies with cautionary tales against the supernatural and the unknown. They helped our forefathers feel more in control and less inadequate against hostile invaders. As a species, humans have been and will continue to be curious. We seek to understand the world through the phenomenological filter of perception—our own experiences and biases. Once upon a

8

time, myth existed to fill in the gaps of incomplete knowledge.

Today, with the help of the natural and behavioral sciences, we trust what the laboratory tells us. We live in the age of the expert. Yet, a large segment of society is still fragmented and striated with a sense of estrangement from the mainstream.

Those who are functionally illiterate, suspicious, unsophisticated, or paralyzed by guilt or fear must still cling to myth and legend as holding ultimate truths. Considering the number of individuals who are illiterate, homeless, living on welfare, imprisoned, or confined to nursing homes or mental hospitals, the figure may loom dangerously near 70 percent of the population. Myth has gained more than a foothold in their lives.

Historically, early founders' lives were made more predictable by myth. Poseidon, Zeus, and Hades were invented to explain the unexplainable in water, thunder, and hell. Dante's *Inferno* provided some insight for tortured souls fearing eternal damnation in the afterlife.

Feeling overwhelmed, frightened, and alone in a hostile world, ancient civilizations created the myths of Hercules and Ulysses who in dangerous odysseys across uncharted oceans fought terrible monsters and prevailed. Myth taught common men perseverance in the face of insurmountable odds. Myth became a survival mechanism told and retold generation after generation. Myth cautioned us against complacency.

Can one freak accident take away every truth and belief we once held dear? Can it destroy our faith? Living in the midst of advanced technology, are we living in the last days of myth? Perhaps the opposite is true. Are we living in an age so detached from a sense of connectedness that we must *create new myths* in order to adapt to the realities uncovered by science and the realization that we live in an unfathomable universe? In this universe the plight of individuals is uncertain: They must assume ultimate responsibility for their actions without certain knowledge of what is right or wrong. Science wields a heavy hand. Yet, science cannot explain with certainty the most fundamental of all teleological questions: Where did we come from and where are we going?

Rumor has it that a respected paleoanthropologist is suppressing a fossil find which when disclosed will cause worldwide panic. Is it true or false, myth or science? A great epistemologist once remarked that there is *a certain amount of unknowing even in knowing.* Modern science has discovered that knowledge comprises the body language of truth. Where does that leave myth with us scrambling around trying to solve modern problems?

Shadow Darwin

Sixty miles due west of Mt. Kyle and the Sable Lodge is the far West Texas town of Alpine, home of Sul Ross State University. It is early Friday afternoon. In January, the crisp, cool air and bright-blue cloudless sky are meteorological trademarks of West Texas. A contrasting front looms low in the northwestern sky as a line of dark gray clouds slung low along the horizon. The front likely brings the first snowfall of winter. The air is cold arctic air, northwesterly and gusty down from the Rockies. In this region of Texas, all wind, regardless of the compass, becomes West Texas wind—gusty and gritty—creating the well-known West Texas "dust devils" in evidence throughout the year. When they twist across roads, the dust devils can throw cars into oncoming traffic with its cyclonic winds.

Professor Shadow Darwin is driving from the campus of Sul Ross State University, a beautiful hillside campus in Brewster County along State Highway 118 in the heart of Big Bend National Park. He is behind the wheel of his 1979 black Corvette equipped with the high performance L-82 engine. SHADOW is emblazoned on his personalized plates. He is en route to the Sable Lodge located in Mt. Kyle, approximately fifty miles southeast of Lajitas, Texas. Lajitas is the sleepy West Texas town where the Mexican bandit Poncho Villa once roamed. Today, it looks like an old western movie set with a new 18-hole golf course recently constructed nearby.

Darwin's thin, six-foot five-inch body fits snugly into the cockpit of the Vette with the seat in full extension. His long, straight, shoulder-length black hair just clears the T-top of the car's removable roof. As usual, Darwin is dressed completely in black with his waist-length bomber jacket unzipped. He is wearing a lightweight, black mock turtleneck underneath. His designer black slacks have to be tailor-made to his height. He wears black boots with a rounded toe suitable to wear to a business meeting.

Darwin was detained from leaving campus immediately after his 11 o'clock Friday class. He decided to work through lunch when several grad students cornered him in the lab. He ordered Chinese take-out for the whole group. After the last stale fortune cookie had been consumed and the grad students satisfied with the data, Darwin left campus around 4 P.M. He knew his late departure would force him to miss at least one engagement at the Sable.

Shadow Darwin looks remarkably like the actor Jeff Goldblum in most physical respects. He even has a slight stutter at the beginning of some of his phonemes. The only name his mother ever considered for her son was Shadow. She named him after the popular radio program from the 1930s to the 1950s—*The Shadow*.

Throughout Darwin's childhood, she took every opportunity to make him feel he was destined to become great. Due to her reassurances, Darwin always felt he was destined to be successful and, perhaps, a bit famous. In grad school, he discovered that the great Sigmund Freud had such a mother. Perhaps due to his doting mother and the emotional distance of his otherwise caring father, Darwin found the female gender far more interesting. Yet, he never married. He thrives in the single lifestyle.

Shadow Darwin is en route to the Sable where he is meeting his longtime colleague and mentor, Dr. Wells McAfee. The Sable Lodge is a convenient meeting place about halfway between their respective campuses. The short fifty-five minute drive provides a welcomed diversion from his post as academic chair of neuropsych programs at Sul Ross.

The contrast between the bright-blue sky overhead and the line of the dark clouds appearing in the western sky provides a sense of foreboding for most desert travelers, but not for Shadow Darwin. As usual, Professor Darwin is in deep contemplation, oblivious to any meteorological metaphors. He listens with enjoyment to the Barenaked Ladies Greatest Hits CD presently playing on his custom in-dash player. He prefers music that favors the creation of lower beta to high alpha brain waves, not the headbanging high betas from heavy metal.

For the past eight years, Dr. Darwin, age 35 with a Ph.D. in neuropsychology, has built the graduate psych department at Sul

Ross into national prominence. He has published numerous articles on the neurochemical underpinnings of *revenge behavior* and the neurotransmitters and hormones believed to underlie it. His writings have appeared in national pop culture magazines, most notably *GQ* and *Discovery*, as well as in scholarly journals. In fact, his dissertation, *Getting Back: The Psychology of Revenge*, was published when he was just 27 years of age. The text has found its way into the reading lists of many graduate psych programs in North America.

Reinventing Myth is Darwin's most recent literary effort. It is a scholarly work mixing fact with fiction. The book spent a respectable time on the New York Times best-seller list. It showed strong enough numbers for his publisher to consider an additional three-book deal. Darwin's writing style is routinely compared to Michael Crighton's technique of mixing science and research with brilliant storytelling.

Amid his intellectual pursuits, Darwin finds inner peace by target practice—throwing his carbon steel Bowie knife at a bull's eye. The magnificent Bowie has a hand-finished seven-inch carbon steel blade. The exquisite knife has fire-blued steel fittings, bronze accents, and Wedgwood handle. Years ago, his father bought him his first Bowie knife, inspired by Jim Bowie in the legendary sandbar fight. It was a birthday present when Darwin turned 10 years of age. (He had requested a switchblade knife.) After seeing the movie *The Alamo* Darwin became self-taught in the lost art of knife throwing. Today, he is quite accomplished. He conceals the knife in a Velcro leg strap worn between his right knee and ankle.

Darwin practices Hatha yoga every morning at 5 A.M. Throughout the day he listens to music, chats with students, or target practices with the Bowie, usually in the afternoon. All four activities bring him inner peace. Darwin feels more at ease wearing the concealed Bowie. It's just one of his many idiosyncracies. To be able to defend oneself in the event of road rage, assault, or attempted burglary of car or habitat is smart. After all, this is the West.

Darwin is uncertain if he would actually throw it at a human unless his life was in danger. Just the dare—seeing it and the damage it could do—is the main reason he carries it. You just can't tell what people are up to these days. For Darwin, the real worth of the Bowie knife is the accuracy of finding the eye of the bull. He carries plenty of targets with him in his black leather briefcase. For

Darwin, the value of his Bowie to mental tranquility is a cold steel version of a Yogi sitting in the lotus position performing *asanas* and *pranayama*. Focusing on the target and hitting it time after time releases an inner peace of mind and body. For Darwin, it coordinates brain chemistry better than Prozac, today's drug of choice for those who struggle with living in the midst of modern problems (a euphemism for existential reality).

Yet another hobby waits in the wings. While an undergraduate at North Texas State University in Denton, Texas, Darwin was once a member of the prestigious *One O'Clock Lab Band*. He intends to dust off the black alto sax case one day soon. For the moment, target practice with his carbon steel Bowie knife and transcendental meditation through Yoga does the trick.

Darwin is not a big-city person. He prefers an informal gathering of one or two of his confidants. He likes renting movies and watching them at home. Darwin is a textbook introvert—he is territorial with his time and energy.

Unlike extraverts, his inner world buzzes with activity. Introverts avoid overstimulation by retreating to the solitude of familiar turf. Darwin loves solitude and occasionally a one-on-one informal meeting where intellectual matters can be bantered about. Darwin and his longtime mentor McAfee have translated research from collaborative sharing into respected intellectual properties. The result of one such weekend about six months ago produced the idea for hibernation studies in the grizzly bear, a project now underway in collaboration with Darwin's Sul Ross colleague, Dr. George Lennon.

In a few years, perhaps, Shadow Darwin may find his theory of revenge in general psychology texts. Dr. Robert Lemark of Johns-Hopkins University and Dr. Shadow Darwin are credited with proposing, almost simultaneously, similar theories on the cognitive and neurological bases of revenge. Dr. Lemark presented his cognitive-behavioral model in a paper entitled *Revengeful Behavior* at an annual convention of behavioral psychologists in Miami Beach, Florida, last summer. Over the same weekend at a convention of neuropsychologists meeting on the West Coast, Shadow Darwin presented his neurochemical underpinnings theory in a paper entitled *The Neurochemistry of Revenge*.

Professors, being fiercely territorial, are quick to see similarities between competing theories. Almost overnight, academic journals begin to tie the two theories together as the Darwin-Lemark paradigm of revengeful behavior. (Co-theorists in psychology are a common occurrence as evidenced in the James-Lange, Schacter-Singer, and Cannon-Bard theories of emotion.)

As he makes his way across the western Chihuahuan Desert located in the lap of Big Bend National Park, Darwin is ruminating over the salient points of the *Darwin-Lemark* theory of revenge.

In his mind, there can be no doubt that revenge is the result of a chronic personality disorder seemingly evident in all serial killers, individuals who seek to discredit others with malicious lies, and other predators comprising both human and animal species.

5

Revenge

According to the *Darwin-Lemark paradigm*, a revengeful person suffers from a severe personality disorder. An imbalance of brain chemistry exacerbates negative thinking. In internal dialogue Darwin carefully reviews the evidence for his excitement in sharing new information with Wells McAfee. By implication, a single instance of revengeful behavior (an acute episode) is not in the same category with a chronic disturbance. The *persistent nature* of the disorder is characterized by a slow, pluripotent unfolding in milieu, which is probably irreversible.

Individuals termed "impulsives" display acute episodes of revenge. They are not driven, as "compulsives" are driven—those who have the pluripotent disorder. *Powerful psychotropic medication may be required to balance faulty brain chemistry in such instances of compulsive revenge, the way Prozac has been used in the treatment of chronic depression* speculates Darwin in internal dialogue.

While it is true that the revengeful personality is not recognized by the DSM, it is nonetheless a helpful distinction because it has features of three personality disorders: borderline personality, paranoid personality, and in severe cases, antisocial personality. Perhaps, seeking revenge is the cognitive force that sets in motion the behavior that runs on the tracks of neurochemistry.

In the same way, Dr. Donald Klein's rejection sensitivity classification, which is not recognized by the DSM either, shares helpful guidelines for psychiatrists and clinical psychologists. Clinicians routinely observe, in the clinical picture, individuals who appear rejection-sensitive to the slightest remark. Rejection-sensitive individuals take almost every comment pejoratively. The prospect of observing revengeful personalities in large numbers in society is equally plausible. *Are we becoming a nation of revengeful predators?* ponders Darwin.

Clinicians who agree with the Darwin-Lemark model of revenge may diagnose clients who display revengeful proclivities with Personality Disorder NOS. This designation admits to a diagnosis of more than one of the personality traits that are "not otherwise specified" in the DSM clusters.

The severe borderline personality disorder provides the most compelling characteristics of revengeful behavior—instability of interpersonal relations and self-image; abandonment fears; impulsivity; and, the clincher, the presence of intense anger and/or difficulty in controlling anger.

Darwin believes a compelling argument exists in which all serial killers and mass murderers are actually revengeful personalities acting out in antisocial ways. Long-standing family dysfunction aside, revenge fuels the desire to act out inappropriately. From real-life serial killers like Ted Bundy and Jeffrey Dahmer to fictionalized versions embodied in Hannibal Lecter, getting revenge for the anger that twists their tortured psyches must be immensely gratifying. Once captured and incarcerated, however, there is no treatment. No perspectives in psychotherapy or protocols of psychotropics are known to effectively reverse the need for immediate gratification. And, all serial killers feel intellectually superior to those who eventually capture them. Ted Bundy, for instance, tried to dodge the needle of lethal injection by convincing authorities he was more valuable alive than dead. From his cell on death row, he sought to extend his own deranged life by acting as a "consultant" in capturing fellow serial killers. Somehow, he failed to grasp the notion that he was responsible for the savage deaths of at least twenty-nine young women and girls. Perhaps he was too focused on his own self-importance and self-indulgence. Steadily with each crime, serial killers become more self-obsessed and out of control with revenge.

"Pharmacodynamically, a Prozac for chronic revengers may be just around the corner. Perhaps it's the only medication that can derail senseless acts of violence, fanaticism, and terrorism," he says out loud as though he is lecturing his instrument cluster.

Darwin's colleague, Dr. Mary Alice Carlisle of Southern Methodist University in Dallas, Texas, recently applied the Darwin-Lemark model to a testosterone hypothesis. Given the behavioral evidence and accompanying emotional states of revenge, she proposed surging levels of testosterone with hypoactive levels of the neurotransmitters serotonin (5-HT) and gamma-aminobutyric acid (GABA). These conditions would produce ideal chemistry for the expression of revenge. Blocking testosterone with Depo-Provera, for example, would produce too many side effects. Merging Dr. Carlisle's research with the Darwin-Lemark model suggests lowering testosterone alone is not the key. But blocking re-uptake of 5-HT and GABA might boost esteem to the point of delaying immediate gratification and thereby forestalling revenge. Apparently, the "revenge cocktail" of chemistry is extremely potent and apparently highly addictive. Murder and mayhem follow, especially when seeking revenge is exacerbated by alcohol and drugs. Predators become more violent and less stable as the body count rises.

Darwin smiles to himself with satisfaction at the depth of his analysis. Darwin's retreat to internal dialogue is a deep and endearing personality trait. He frequently retreats into his intrapsychic quarters where whispers of mind exist as an invigorating intellectual oasis. In all respects, Shadow Darwin is truly an academic scholar.

As Darwin continues in internal dialogue, he has no suspicion of how his life will change over the next hours and days. The extraordinary interruption by a natural cause in the usual course of events in his life precludes a scholar's experience, prescience, and care. Reasonably foreseeing or preventing the strange occurrences coming his way is overtaking Darwin as a northwesterly front destined to become a devastating blizzard. It is gathering aloft its forces of destruction.

Glancing skyward, Darwin notices the threatening clouds practically engulfs the sky. He glances westward in his rearview mirror to verify the blanket cover. The sudden realization of atmospheric change causes a stab of claustrophobia that tweaks his nervous system. Concomitantly, the temperature outside is dropping perceptively.

As the scrubby vegetation of the Chihuahuan Desert flickers by the speeding Vette, the appearance of tiny ice crystals on his windshield suddenly reels in Darwin's attention. He disengages the custom cruise control. He snaps out of his self-imposed highway hypnosis. Quickly, the speedometer gauge falls below sixty miles-per-hour.

Suddenly, Darwin is aware of something else. He feels some-one may be watching his speedy course across the deepening gloom of State Highway 118. He trusts his intuition, and he is seldom wrong. He shudders a bit against the gloom now consum-ing the desert from horizon to horizon.

Reflexively, Darwin pushes the eject button of the CD and removes Barenaked Ladies. He plays his favorite saxophone track of all time—*Heading for the Light*, track 7 on the Traveling Wilburys' CD. The music fills the cockpit of the Vette about thirty miles from the Sable as the storm descends. The blizzard that even the supercomputers missed will eventually produce strange occur-rences often interpreted as acts of God and freak accidents. The kinds of things that always catch people off guard. No one sees them coming.

6

CRADLE OF INTREPIDITY

The mountain hamlet of Mt. Kyle, Texas, is located high atop the eastern portion of the 8,700-foot elevation of the Chisos Mountain range. This geographical region comprises a vast segment of Big Bend National Park. The Big Bend region, so named for the sudden "big bend" taken in the Rio Grande as it snakes across the desert floor, is a vast wilderness of desert, prairie, and mountain ranges in deep West Texas. In this region, the Rio Grande (known as the Rio Bravo on the Mexican side) forms the border between the United States and Mexico. The entire region sits on the lap of the Chihuahuan Desert, the highest and wettest desert in North America. Over half of the desert is above 4,000 feet elevation. The high elevation produces hot summer days and desert nights that chill the bone. In the dead of summer, during daylight, heat reigns supreme, and it can be deadly. Conversely, in the dead of winter, the single-digit cold mixed with high winds can produce hypothermia. Transition months of spring and fall provide a temporary moratorium. Scrawny shrubs scattered like pickup sticks as far as the eye can see are miracles of adaptation. Countless creatures compete for survival amid the stark splendor of this region. Water is perhaps the most precious commodity in all deserts. The trick for survival in deserts is to hang on to enough water to sustain life. To some extent, a plant has partially solved the problem by producing a natural sealing wax found only in the Chihuahuan Desert. Visually, the spirit of this region is best captured between two contrasting life forms—the beautiful white-blooming yuccas in stark contrast to the black-feathered vulture with its dead eyes and razor claws circling overhead as harbingers of death. Surviving in the desert is based upon this premise, the beauty of life struggling against the ever-present ugliness of death. Road kill littering the highway provides a constant reminder.

All deserts have long histories of struggle and conflict. Situated in southern Brewster County, Big Bend once belonged to the Mescalero Apaches and then to the Comanche Indians. By the 1920s, when the ravaging White Man had weakened the dominance of the Indians, ranching and mining developed. Times were tough. As West Texans say, the times produced "a tough row to hoe."

It is aphoristic to say that people who try to bring civilization and industry to wilderness regions struggle mightily. The desert holds on to its treasures with a vice grip. Hardly any gold or silver was found in the Big Bend. Only the quicksilver or mercury mines at Terlingua were operated into this century. Looking at the ghost town of Terlingua and the ruins near Study Butte, it's unimaginable that thousands of people once lived and worked there. Coal miners broke their shovels and backs in the Sierra Viega Mountains north of Valentine. Talc and mica miners slaved against the dirt, rock, and heat near Van Horn, Texas. No uranium was discovered in the vicinity of Lajitas, Texas, as rumors spread to the contrary in the late 1940s.

Around 1900, wax making developed as the third industry in the desert. *Candelilla,* a plant native only to the Chihuahuan Desert, produces a protective wax skin—nature's way of retaining water—a necessity for survival in a region with about five inches of annual rainfall. Originally, the recovered wax was used as sealing wax but over time, found its way into the manufacture of everything imaginable, including chewing gum. Soon, even harvesting Desert Wax would be outlawed by the Mexicans.

Unlike the Nevada and Utah deserts, the abundance of heat and water brought by summer rain brings summer-blooming plant life to Big Bend. Lechugilla (appearing like a stalk of green bananas armed with daggers), tarbrush, creosote bush, ocotillo, and a variety of white-blooming yuccas are readily seen from well-paved roads. Desert cactus plants are heavily armed, deserving of their descriptive nicknames such as "fishhook," "eagle's claw," and "horse crippler." Prickly pear is the most common cacti producing the well-known yellow cactus rose.

Similar to human personality, *appearances* are often deceiving in the Chihuahan Desert. Some species of blooming prickly pear do not appear to have thorns, but the slightest touch corrects hasty misconceptions. You have to be careful of what you come into contact with in deserts. In the winter months of January and February, desert plants struggle against the cold. Occasional snowfall signals that temperatures may plunge into single digits at night with constant northwesterly wind. Built low to the ground, a variety of trees, mostly mesquite, and scrawny vegetation struggle mightily against the unrelenting wind.

Evidence of this struggle can be observed in the angle of growth—tree trunks bending in the direction of prevailing winds. In the Big Bend region of West Texas, contrasts abound in all directions away from the oasis of wealth and influence personified in Mt. Kyle's Marx Desert Estates, and the historic Sable Lodge. Three well-paved roads lead to Mt. Kyle: U.S. 385 from Marathon, State Highway 118 from Alpine and Sul Ross State University, and Ranch Road 170 from Presidio to Study Butte connecting to State Highway 118. Roads bring people, and people bring problems, as true today in the New West as it was in the Old West.

Along the easternmost portion of the Chisos Mountains, separated by an eight-foot-tall brick wall announcing civilization's encroachment upon the wild sits the cloistered community of Mt. Kyle. This rock partition stands as a dividing line between the laws of nature and the laws of civilization. Regardless of any perceived differences, survival is the name of the game on either side.

First-time travelers to this region are surprised to discover that the Marx Desert Estates comprise the entire community of Mt. Kyle. This mountain paradise is unequalled anywhere in North America for concentration of wealth per capita. The hamlet is composed of twenty-five custom homes on approximately 200 acres of manicured lots built around a championship 18-hole golf course, which comprises an additional 500 acres. Statistics from real estate publications fix the median disposable income in the highly deed-restricted properties to hover in the vicinity of $100 million per resident. It is redundant that travel magazines and exposes on the rich and famous report the Desert Estate families to be filthy rich. Where else would you find a mountain paradise sitting next door to a National Park?

Residents commute in their private planes or helicopters from an airstrip near the Sable Lodge. Peter Marx, the principal developer of the Marx Desert Estates, owns the largest home. He has a heliport near his home and recently added one next to the Sable

Lodge. Residents fly into El Paso, Lubbock, Midland, Abilene, and Dallas-Ft. Worth to oversee their financial concerns. Muscle, brains, and the pump jacks fuel diversification so indispensable to survival in a highly competitive world.

Regardless of appearances, it is still a jungle out there.

DESERT WAX

A sharp dichotomy appears merely fifteen minutes down the mountain in the small community of Bora Flats. It is the first of several small towns scattered at the feet of Camelot. Many colorful characters inhabit these parts, including the less colorful teaching staff of the newly expanded Mt. Kyle Senior High School. In surrounding Ft. Davis, the self-appointed president of the Republic of Texas once lived in relative obscurity until his "embassy" (consisting of a small dilapidated trailer in the Davis Mountains) was overrun by federal agents a few years ago. A collection of the odd, the disenchanted, the brilliant, and the contradictory comprise the anonymous rural addresses of this region.

The residents of Mt. Kyle replaced the farmers, ranchers, miners, and wax producers who vacated the premises prior to the twentieth century. The *nouveau riche* share an uncanny prescience for knowing how to make money, something rarely learned in college. It's the way Joseph Kennedy made his fortune bootlegging whiskey during the Prohibition—intrepid maneuvering against a stacked deck.

In the early days near the region of Big Bend that would become Mt. Kyle, James Lloyd Marx purchased the region atop the Chisos Mountains in a land auction prior to the establishment of the national park to the east and the state park to the west. His fortune came from his intrepid ingenuity. Marx, an amateur geologist and plant biologist nearing 50 years of age, perfected a way to cheaply extract the wax from the Candelerra plant, indigenous to the desert. To whatever product needed moisture protection or retention of moisture, the patent on *Desert Wax* proved indispensable. This discovery paved the way to his fortune and dovetailed his love of West Texas with an ambitious, business savvy. The land upon which Mt. Kyle sits today remains in perpetuity thanks to his son, Peter Marx, not due to the elder Marx. When authorities on the Mexican side banned harvesting the Candelerra plant, the boom suddenly went bust. That marked the beginning of the elder Marx's financial ruin. His downward spiral was exacerbated by one of nature's flawless forms: Young women with bronze complexions. He lost his fortune in a series of ex-wives, an assortment of girlfriends, and a gaggle of blood-sucking lawyers.

To his last wife, a young 26-year-old Native American beauty, J.L.'s son Peter Marx was born. Twenty years later, Peter Jon Marx recaptured the land lost by his father. Peter Marx founded and developed the luxury homes of the Marx Desert Estates through his property development company, Marx Enterprises. Peter Marx did it his own way arising from a childhood of poverty with a protective single mother who died unexpectedly when he was away at Texas Tech University in Lubbock, Texas, preparing to graduate from law school.

We must prepare ourselves as best we can for the slings and arrows tossed our way by nature, the most powerful force on earth.

Not in the Forecast

By early January, weather conditions from Canada and the Northwest produced very cold air extending down into the Midwest, owing to the ever-present jet stream. By Friday, January 14th around noon in Mt. Kyle, the first frigid air descended. It had been cold enough to snow all day. The unusual accumulation of moisture was evidenced by two days of dense, early morning fog. When snow finally arrived later that afternoon, the ground provided the perfect foundation. Snow accumulated at a rate few had ever witnessed.

By all appearances, the storm was going to be a typical mild winter blast, probably not as serious as the two-day winter blast four years ago. But before long, the winds pick up and things change. It wasn't long before the roads became more suitable for snowplows. The Mt. Kyle Police Department had been given an old, broken-down sorry-excuse-for-one a few years ago during a winter storm blast that brought record snowfall to the region over a two-day period. The storm left the town's police force flat-footed. Of the two nightly patrol cruisers, the one driven by the deputy slid all the way to the end of Overlook Lake, and the other driven by the chief landed upside down in a non-injury freak accident. It seems like no one in West Texas can drive on wet roads much less frozen ones.

The chief said he was lucky to survive the freak accident. It happened near the Sable Lodge across the street from Eddie Hawkins' automotive restoration shop. Local residents, tongue in cheek, presented the ancient and dilapidated snowmobile to the red-faced chief a few days later when the snow melted. It greeted him on the front lawn of the police station complete with a red bow. He and Hawkins tinkered with it and actually made it mechanically functional. The chief swore he would use it again to the good humor of all. He had no idea how prescient his remark would prove to be.

To long-time residents, far West Texas weather is fairly predictable. On most days, wind gusts of 15 to 25 miles an hour along with blowing red sand are staples. If given enough time, West Texas wind would eventually completely disassemble a good-sized mobile home, if it didn't blow it off its foundation first.

In normally arid climates like Mt. Kyle, all that weather forecasters really need is a windsock, a directional wind monitor, a plastic rain gauge, and a decent pair of high-powered binoculars. Looking across the flat plains, storms heading your way can be observed miles away. Yet, with Double Doppler 9000s and storm-chasing vans scattered throughout the region, how could such a monster storm escape meteorological detection? Even the National Weather Service's supercomputers miscalculated this one badly. In a few hours winds will howl amid swirling snowfall around the accoutrements of the rich.

9

THE SHADOW ARCHETYPE

Naturally producing fear in the human psyche, Carl Gustav Jung, the Swiss psychoanalyst, overshadowed his entire career by Freud, explains approaching storms as events that trigger archetypes. *Archetypes* reside in a species' collective unconsciousness; they come prepackaged, so learning is less of a factor than nature. According to this theory, we share universal experiences that extend far back into our collective histories—experiences that produce recognition of our environment. This is made possible by ever-widening experiences transmitted to offspring through the gene pool. The archetypal theory explains why most of us are naturally afraid of spiders, snakes, darkness, and really bad weather. It remains one of Jung's most endearing, yet controversial theories.

Some primate researchers suggest that animals rely on their particular species' collective unconscious as a kind of early warning system in both mating and fighting. It's a built-in evolutionary survival guide. Obvious examples come from the ranks of coyotes, grizzlies, and wolves, which must avoid constant fighting. Otherwise, serious injuries or death would consistently weaken their ranks. Perhaps a species' failure to attend to its collective unconscious and to archetypes may partially explain extinction. Also, a species' collective unconscious may perpetuate evolutionary mandates taking millions of years to perfect. Between two rival species, the species more adaptable to changing conditions becomes the dominant species, according to the rigid guidelines of natural selection.

Similarly in humans, archetypes exist as an early warning system. Fear of spiders and snakes fall into the category of innate fears called *shadow archetypes*. This innate fear of animals, reptiles, and spiders acts as an early warning system in avoiding potentially fatal stings and bites. According to Jung, walking through a spider web at night is an emotionally charged experience directly related to the shadow archetype. Natural disasters that instill fear and catch us off guard qualify as shadow archetypes. They are especially deadly since they arrive with no contingencies, no predictability, and no warning.

Disasters blindside us. How can humans prepare for events that have no contingencies? Plagues, acts of God, and freak accidents fall into this category. Sometimes, they happen so fast, we don't have time to register fear, dread, or panic. Texas has had its share of blindsiding disasters.

The Great Storm of 1900 was not only the worst disaster in the state but also the worst natural disaster in United States history. The city of Galveston suffered four days of pounding rain. A vast area of Galveston stood in two feet of water. In some places the depth measured five feet and rising. When winds reached 120 miles per hour, a huge killer wave rushed through town smashing buildings and snapping trees and power lines like twigs. Six thousand people drowned. Some historians put the figure closer to eight thousand. Bodies were found in neighboring towns. With the body count mounting, the city fathers undertook mass cremations of the corpses. Over seven thousand surviving residents left Galveston for good. Economically, it would take more than ten years for Galveston to recover from the Great Storm.

In 1956, the state's worst blizzard devastated the Panhandle and the South Plains of Texas. The February storm lasted nearly a week. Entire towns were shut down as all roads were blocked with power and phone lines down. The Hale Center in Hale County recorded a snowfall of 33 inches, the most ever from a single blizzard. Twenty people froze to death while countless others lost body parts due to frostbite.

Today, on January 14th, the blizzard to match the 1956 record will cover Mt. Kyle and surrounding areas in its icy embrace. Little did the residents know such a ravenous storm would arrive as a simple blast of north wind mixed with a few snow flurries. In this region of the Chihuahuan Desert, significant snowfall can be registered in February but not in early January. This year, atmospheric conditions produced a strange commodity—moisture—unusual for most desert regions. The summer rainfall was up 24 percent over last year.

Over the next two days the blizzard will produce frigid cruelties and strange occurrences. One of the worst parts of the rapidly unfolding weather, the magnitude of the storm, wasn't even in the forecast. Nearly 33 inches of snow will fall on Friday and Saturday.

Truly violent storms seem to break the rigid laws of nature. They often usher in strange occurrences that seem to defy physics. Phenomena beyond belief are often observed in tornadoes; how can a feather be blown halfway through a brick? The same is true with the most powerful destructive force on earth, a fully mature hurricane. It is possible that blizzards, like hurricanes and tornadoes, conspire to produce phenomena beyond empirical belief.

Yet, West Texas has always been known for strange occurrences that produce wild imaginations. For instance, Native Americans who populated these regions prior to the Calvary Outposts in nearby Ft. Davis named the principal mountain range upon which Mt. Kyle sits "Chisos," meaning the Ghost Mountain. Being so close to nature, they must have perceived something in the granite and limestone formations that escaped the White Man.

There are other indicators. Less than an hour due west of the Sable Lodge is the legendary ghost town of Terlingua, an eerie reminder of nature's powerful grip on human life. Few sightseers leave their cars at dusk to explore the remains of the long-abandoned, nearly collapsed huts—an eerie reminder of dashed hopes and dreams.

To the northwest lies the city of Marfa and its mysterious northern lights. The lights have been documented since the 1800s, long before cynics suggested that car lights descending the neighboring Chianti Mountains were the true source for the "mysterious lights." However, as residents point out, no cars existed back in the mid-1800s. Where is truth amid myth and stubborn belief?

Storms are scary. A tornado can suck us up into its churning clouds like Dorothy in the *Wizard of Oz*, one of the scariest children's stories ever written. We might drown in our beds from flash floods caused by late night rainstorms, especially when our homes are near swollen creeks likely to creep up around us like a watery noose.

Our house could burn down with a lightning strike, one of nature's arsenals of destruction and frequent cause of freak accidents. Buried deeper in our collective unconsciousness resides the fear of a blizzard—one of the most chaotic storms on earth. What if we're buried alive and freeze to death in its cold, suffocating hands? What if we can't get to food or water?

Before we finally surrender to our greatest fears, we prepare our psyches with all kinds of fragile defenses and impotent rationalizations. We try to fool ourselves. We huddle around blazing fireplaces sipping hot mugs of chocolate. We put extra warm blankets on our beds—the heavy ones made by our grandmothers on quilting frames hung from the ceiling. Before we turn off the lights for the night, we double-check the doors to ensure they are locked. We don't want the doors to blow open during a storm and invade our fragile sense of security. Psychological dread lies beneath the feeling of false security—when we only pretend everything is all right. We take our mind off this deeply buried dread by reading or watching one of our favorite movies. Our children take teddy bears to bed in a universal gesture of safety and security. What could possibly happen when we hold those cute, cuddly bears? How far removed they are from their original inspirations in flesh, blood, and claw—the great brown bear family of which the grizzly is the fiercest.

As children and later as adults, we will do anything to take our minds off the worsening storm. Somewhere deeper in our psyches, however, the dread remains. We know we have succeeded in creating nothing more than fluff. We create sandcastles in the air to bolster our false sense of security. They say when we freeze to death we go to sleep first. Maybe that's why our dreams are so troubled during storms. Maybe that's why we have such a hard time going to sleep in the first place. Down deep, we know we may never wake up. The shadow archetype invades our dreams all night with nightmares of suffocation.

During a blizzard the wind reminds us of the storm's severity. Its fury conjures up all kinds of frightening images buried deep in our memories—memories that began when we learned a snowman could come to life.

10

MR. LAURENCE HARVEY

Friday Evening

SABLE LODGE, MT. KYLE, TEXAS

The blazing fireplace inside *X Marx the Spot,* the upscale restaurant inside the Sable Lodge, provides warmth to a patron who is cold as death in his interior world. Mr. Laurence Harvey, age 58, sits alone staring into his fifth drink in one hour, a double Skyy on the rocks. He is drinking a lot of doubles lately. Named after the British actor of the same name, Mr. Laurence Harvey is a thirty-six-year veteran of classroom teaching. He feels warm sitting before the fireplace bundled in his dingy gray overcoat with the faux fur lining. The coat, the best one he owns, smells of mildew and nicotine. Coffee stains litter the front of the coat almost to the belt loops. He is here to celebrate his big decision.

Mr. Harvey himself is practically dead from the negativity that dwells inside him. In internal dialogue, Mr. Harvey reminisces over the most recent waste of his students' time and energy, the ongoing celebration of the Mt. Kyle Grizzly football team's first state championship. *Now, the basketball gym will be filled to capacity with screaming morons two or three times a week until after spring break. More wasted time. More wasted effort. More wasted energy.* Mr. Laurence Harvey cannot envision a more depressing scenario.

More than usual, Mr. Harvey cannot feel the full effect of the alcohol. Perhaps he feels too sick with cynicism and negativity. Privately, he detests students, especially those students who waste time and energy on pointless pursuits such as extracurricular activities and athletics. The focus of school should be academics. The total knowledge gained by high school students should be larger than the dimensions of a football field, a basketball court, or a baseball diamond. Somehow, someway, students always find ways to make teachers (the serious ones—the ones who refuse to spoon feed) look like the dipsticks. Mr. Harvey blinks his red-rimmed eyes. Generous bags are packed under his swollen lids. He can't remember exactly when he stopped caring about the whole miserable state of classroom teaching. But it lost its allure for him a long time ago.

He has decided to retire from teaching once and for all. The last five years have seemed like an eternity, especially with the jocks— the football players, the smug "Friday night heroes" who think education is a joke.

When will school boards get the message? High school is not about academics. It's about socialization and extracurricular pastimes that counselors swear builds self-esteem.

Lately, alcohol-induced melancholia has become a dominant personality trait of Mr. Harvey. The real issue that finally crystallized in his acid heart is *curriculum modification or CM*. CM sounds rather harmless and nonthreatening. In scholastic reasoning, there are no formal guidelines for CM classification. CM is an academic "diagnosis," a subjective call made by frustrated teachers. Mr. Harvey believes by any standard CM symbolizes everything wrong with education today. It presents the final stake in the heart of all things academic. Stereotypically, if kids ride a school bus or can't keep up or seem unduly bored, the chance is great they will qualify for curriculum modification. CM is a euphemism for doing nothing all day while the teacher stands by helplessly. In reality, with the CM tag, students are exempt from any further academic challenges. *CM—what a grand idea for jocks and other assorted lame brains! Now, even the rich kids from Mt. Kyle's Marx Desert Estates have a double silver spoon in their whiney little yaps* reasons Mr. Harvey in internal dialogue.

Today, Mr. Harvey decided he can no longer, he will no longer modify curriculum for the brainless wonders of modern education. CM has squeezed the life out of his specialty—math. It no longer resembles the course he once loved. Now, students use math against him when they're not promoted to the next grade. It all boils down to a numbers game of student retention, necessitating *social promotion* to the next grade, regardless of competencies. It provides students with a loaded deck. Modify the curriculum— Modify! Modify! The word pierces his brain like a nine-inch nail. In his mind, CM lies behind something called "stay-home day."

Students who are academically challenged are actually encouraged to stay home on TAAS testing days to produce the right numbers for nervous administrators. For his part in the whole anti-intellectual mess of high school education, Mr. Harvey is on the ropes.

Once upon a time, Mr. Harvey loved math and its rules. He was proud to be a math major in college. Girls were impressed with math majors. Everybody knows you had to be a brain to be a math major. In his younger days, Mr. Harvey convinced his students to take all the steps in problem solving—work through them all to end up with the correct answer. But that was before CM.

You can live your life just like you do math, Mr. Laurence Harvey was fond of saying long ago. Take the time, and the rules will guide you through—even for students who hate math. Seems like every student hates math these days. Now, in Mr. Harvey's current frame of mind, students are no longer willing to take the time to do anything right with the exception of sex and sports. CM students, the antithesis of academicians, are all too glad to jump on the bandwagon, all too glad to sit in the back seats of the bus. CM is the ring in the belly button and the stud in the center of the tongue; it's the Cool Thing amid the chaos of Hormone High.

Mr. Harvey chuckles to himself in mild amusement at his ability for intellectual analysis, considering his current state of booze-induced melancholia. Parents could care less, too—nobody gets off Mr. Harvey's hook. If their precious little kids don't get it, it must be the teacher's fault. The whole cowardly bunch of politicians too—those obnoxious dimwits who give nothing but lip service to the national embarrassment that is education—they can go to straight to the back of the bus too.

At *X Marx the Spot*, Mr. Laurence Harvey decides to go back home to Ohio and let the numbers take care of themselves. Maybe he'll get a job as a columnist in a newspaper so he can blast politicians and educators for the sorry profession they have allowed teaching to become. It's no wonder no one wants to be a classroom teacher. Why would anyone want to modify the curriculum day after day and be nothing more than a glorified baby-sitter with a college degree?

He muses about his first article *Higher Education: A True Oxymoron*. He decides to end the article with the conclusion that education is no longer framed by insightful curricula. Take the universal "o" (symbol of unity) away from the word "course" and the true state of education is left: One curse after another miserable curse! He chuckled at his newly created twist on lexicon.

Slowly and deliberately he takes off his wire rims (the earpiece on one side was held by a ribbon of black and greasy duct tape) and rubs his red, swollen eyes. His eyes burn under his touch.

In addition to a new career, perhaps Mr. Laurence Harvey desperately needs to get a life. Suddenly, he regrets never marrying just about as much as becoming a teacher. But at least he had made a firm decision. No more whiney jocks to ruin his day with their idiotic excuses. No more CM. No more ingratiating rich kids either. But, then, he has had much too much to drink. It used to be just on weekends; now it's every evening and night. The kids have probably spotted the little silver flask he keeps in his inner coat pocket just in case he needs a snort during the day. *Things had to change* he told himself ... *starting today.* Perhaps he just wants to beat the axe he sees coming from the school board. Retirement sounds better than firing.

With Jill Frazier, the manager of *X Marx the Spot,* temporarily out of sight, and with swirling snow and darkness engulfing the lodge, Mr. Laurence Harvey exits not bothering to leave a tip. He weaves through the lobby of the Sable, bumps into a young college-aged guy at the front door leading to the parking lot. He hears laughter behind him. He stumbles out into the dimly lit parking lot, amid swirling snow and frigid temperatures, for the short drive to his modest home down the mountain in Bora Flats. The absurd notion to hum a portion of lyrics from an old Donovan song *Alone Again Naturally* tumbles across his disheveled mind. All music irritates Mr. Laurence Harvey's ravaged sensibilities.

He fumbles for his keys, drops the keys in the accumulation of blowing snow, bends over to retrieve them, and bumps his head on the door. He curses under his breath. Finally, he unlocks the door to his decrepit 1980 Buick Regal and falls into the driver's seat with a heavy thump. Normally, the drive takes about twenty minutes. It's the same route the yellow Bluebird school bus takes during the week to deliver the less-privileged kids to Bora Flats. The winter advisory has taken a turn for the worse and presents a real navigation problem for Mr. Harvey as he maneuvers out of the parking lot on four bald tires. He ignores the sign "Buckle up for safety." Beyond the lodge, the north side produces tricky roads.

And, he never makes it. His Buick Regal leaves the road on a tight curve, skids off the road, and tumbles about 500 feet down the north side crashing into trees and rock formations. The near-empty gas tank is the only thing that saves his car from becoming a spectacular ball of fire.

An apparent freak accident leaves Mt. Kyle Senior High short one bitter and disillusioned math teacher. His frozen body, which was hoisted into the back seat from the tumultuous plunge down the mountain, contains only one telltale wound from the rag doll posture of his next to final resting place. Smeared blood captured in a frozen trickle down his forehead is the only evidence of a blood clot to the brain, perhaps a fitting metaphor for Mr. Laurence Harvey's forced retirement.

11

PETER MARX, ALPHA MALE

In popular culture *image is everything,* even in West Texas. How individuals are perceived matters greatly. Just ask job applicants. Image deficits can be devastating. Image, looks, and personality are the heart of success in cultures where dollars spent on cosmetics rival drug enforcement and are greater than the national budget for education. YAAVIST is what some social psychologists call the ultimate in *au courant* pop culture. In this aphoristic label, youth, attractiveness, accoutrements (brand names), visual stimulation, success, and thin, sexualized bodies drive those not of these persuasions into isolation or insanity (the "I" in YAAVIST). Those who don't fit in sometimes become angry and seek retribution (or revenge in Darwin's view). The overweight, the schizoid, the pitiful, the depressed, the average looking, the alcoholic, the drug addict, the obese, and the anorexic pick up the scraps tossed their way from the YAAVIST mannequins with perfect body proportions. It is a depressing scenario considering all we know about neurochemistry and nutrition.

X Marx the Spot caters to YAAVIST cultists with lots of disposal income to spend on pricey menu items with four $$$$ signs printed in restaurant reviews. They think big just like Peter Marx, president and founder of *ME,* Marx Enterprises. Peter Marx has his finger in a lot of pies: a property development company and interests in a variety of concerns including Internet software development, restaurants, and health clubs. Competitors are certain that the initials "ME" are an unconscious reminder of the *individualism* encouraged at Marx Enterprises. Peter Marx thinks strong-minded, proactive individuals make a team great. Sadly, many ME employment-seeking rejects check into drug rehab centers following their interview with Peter Marx. After all, Marx was a psych major long before he received his law degree. *He privately wonders what individuals are really like beneath their carefully crafted personas.* If someone interests him, he always takes time to find out. Peter Marx's employees are carefully chosen as though bred for individualism, which always assures the best chance for survival in any context. The psychology of the icon works.

Every owner knows a collection of icons makes everyone just a little bit uncomfortable. Risk-takers watch their backsides. When everyone is a little edgy regarding office politics, the energy level is high and creativity is off the charts.

It's the same philosophy used in professional sports by successful coaches who draft those best suited for survival in an unforgiving sport. Bill Parcels and Jimmy Johnson are good examples. Between the two, they have three Super Bowl rings and a lot of less-talented admirers.

Yet Peter Marx is hard to stereotype. In some ways, Peter Jon Marx is a clone of pop psychologist Tony Robbins. In physical contrast to Robbins, Marx is three inches shorter (standing 6' 4") and built like a tall linebacker. He has long, shoulder-length blond hair framing sparking blue eyes. His many girlfriends say he drips with charisma. Peter Marx is a visionary within the fast company of billionaires in North America. In another way, he is a hybrid-type, combining brains (entrepreneurial genius) and brawn with the rugged individualism and persistence of the Texas cyclist Lance Armstrong.

As an analogy to his 25,000-square-foot estate's address brick, 3900 Camelot Court, Peter is known as "Merlin Marx." Seemingly, everything he touches turns to gold. Everything, that is, except for one thing. He shares a sweet tooth with his old man. In a convincing argument for nature, with all his positive holdings, Peter Marx is always on the chase for the young and beautiful female. *Texas Monthly* recently named Peter Jon Marx the most eligible bachelor in North America. He beat out Donald Trump for the honor. Being rich, handsome, and college-educated go well together even if Peter's numerous girlfriends always finish second to his carefully nurtured career.

Ironically, a particular cause close to his heart is animal preservation. Peter Marx is one of the leading animal activists in West Texas. Peter Marx is what pop culture calls an Alpha male. He is successful, powerful, and rich. His persona is intimidating to most. He appears larger than life.

Next to his son Jon, and his collection of "muscle cars," the thing he values most is his collection of instrumental surf rock music. The Fender reverb and staccato guitar sound fits the rhythm of his soul. His extensive collection of surf rock includes records, albums, 8-track tapes, cassette tapes, and boxed CDs. He favors anything by the father of surf rock, Dick Dale and the Del-Tones. A close second are the Ventures, Stingrays, and Mar-keys. He will argue with anyone the best surf rock tune of all time is *Miserlou* by Dick Dale, recently highlighted in the movie, *Pulp Fiction*. To Peter Marx, surf rock brings out the beastly side of human nature.

12

Animal Activist

Earlier in the day, the meeting Shadow Darwin missed due to his late departure from Sul Ross is underway in the North banquet hall of the Sable. A professionally lettered sign in the lobby announces the monthly meeting of the Mt. Kyle Animal Preservation Society. The meeting started promptly at 3 P.M. It has been held on the last Friday of each month since Peter Marx founded the organization shortly after he developed the Desert Estates. Thirsty members attend Happy Hour following adjournment to *X Marx the Spot.*

Even though the Marx Desert Estates alone dispossessed an estimated 350 species of animals, reptiles, birds, and insects in clearing the acreage for development, the group is serious about preservation. They're concerned about the future of the animals that migrated next door to Big Bend. The byline of the group's marketing efforts tells the story: "Preserving the Wilds of Big Bend."

Clearly, Peter Marx has political aspirations. He continues to make generous donations to animal preservation groups all over West Texas. Perhaps Peter Marx truly believes the development of the Desert Estates was a blessing in disguise, an act of preservation, by allowing the animals, birds, reptiles, and insects a safe haven next door across the eight-foot brick wall.

Appropriately, Peter Marx addresses the reality of predators in the wild by highlighting one of its most recognizable survivors, the gray wolf, and, by describing the significance of its social order to the packed banquet hall.

The wolf pack hierarchy and rank are vital components to communication, body language, and respect with the social order of wolves. Without rank, the very essence of the wolf pack—cohesion, purpose, and direction—are lost. The resulting breakdown leads to the disbanding of the pack in favor of a few lone wolves. No longer would there be strength in numbers. Through trial and error, wolves discovered the power of the pack as a survival strategy.

Wolf experts delineate four different classes, or ranks of wolves within the wolf pack. The first is the Alpha pair—Alpha male and Alpha female. They are the dominant "leaders and breeders" producing the pack's offspring. Alpha wolves hold their ears erect or straight ahead to threaten and they hold their tails high. Characteristics of Alpha wolf behavior indicate the body language of a cool, calm, and collected leader who demands respect. High esteem is seen in the eyes, stance, and fur; the fur is more bristled-out, never flat. The Alphas are magnificent-looking animals. They radiate importance and suggest some kind of natural splendor reserved for the dominant animals of nature. Alpha wolves often confuse humans. Humans hesitate in their presence; they are both drawn to them and repelled by them. Humans are not sure if they should pet them or climb a tree.

Second-class wolves are known as the mature subordinates. They may be the Alphas-in-waiting, but wait they must. They are lower on the wolf totem and cannot command the power or respect of Alphas. The Beta wolves, as this group is called, learn by observation, watching, and waiting. They may be the best "politicians" of any animal group due to the high stakes in the event of the loss of an Alpha. Suddenly, any one of them may become the next Alpha, if they can become intimidating practically overnight. Betas hold their tails down, the normal position for wolves, and their ears against the sides of their head when feeling apologetic. Their fur is generally flat.

Outcast wolves are routinely mistreated by the pack and hold very low status. The third class of wolves, the omega wolves, avoids many members of the pack. They eat last if they eat at all. They hold their tail between their legs; they flatten their ears and fur. Lone wolves come from the outcasts. Then last, the juvenile wolves, or pups, round out the rank of the pack members as the fourth class. They are the young wolves yet to secure themselves a position within the rigid hierarchy of the wolf pack.

When Peter Marx concludes, he glances to the rear of the standing-room-only banquet hall to see if Dr. Shadow Darwin may have slipped in late. Earlier in the week, Marx had extended an invitation to Dr. Darwin in hopes his friend would surprise the attendees with news of his grizzly bear project at Sul Ross. After all, the group is interested in protecting all wild animals of Big Bend.

13

CANIS LUPUS

Darwin regrets missing the animal activist meeting. He prepared notes on hibernation studies presently underway at Sul Ross. When he arrived late, he hoped to find Peter Marx in the lodge or in his restaurant, *X Marx the Spot*. Due to their friendship, he felt he owed Peter an explanation for his tardiness.

First, he checks the empty meeting hall. The cleaning staff is in the process of setting the room back to its original condition. Lingering perfume, hair spray, and cologne hangs heavy in the air. On one of the chairs, Darwin notices a partially rolled up handout left behind. Smoothing it out reveals a handsomely prepared souvenir program. It contains the complete text of Peter Marx's comments made hours earlier on the social behavior and hierarchy of the gray wolves of Big Bend. He turns to a section that catches his eye. He sits down on the back row of chairs and reads the section to himself. The steady hum of a vacuum cleaner does not disturb his concentration.

Human beings in the various guises of civilization systematically destroy and pillage the splendor of millions of acres of wilderness. In the process of carving up lush forests and fertile grazing land, humans essentially banish the gray wolf and the grizzly into the mountains or the frigid tundra—any place less hospitable to "civilized man."

Once upon a time, the gray wolf *(canis lupus)* was the most wide-ranging mammal in the world as well as one of the most skillful hunters. Today, vastly reduced by years of persecution, wolves still make do with what they have. The two absolute prerequisites for wolfen survival are suitable species to prey upon thereby avoiding starvation and obtaining enough water to prevent blood poisoning from the raw carcasses they ravage. Nature dictates that wolves are carnivores and predators. They cannot survive without killing other animals for food as a simple act of survival.

The creation of the demonic, bloodthirsty wolf observed in myth and legend can only be concocted from the mind of man. All the wolf myths have no basis save the primal fears of humans. Both wolves and grizzlies are animals of the wild, not domesticated animals that eat out of food bowls provided for their benefit in the fenced backyards of owners.

In reality, the wolf is a superb survivalist. Like man and the grizzly, wolves are apex predators; they are at the top of their food chain. Due to *cooperative hunting* in packs, they have carved out a niche of survival for themselves few single predators can trump. What single predator is powerful enough and smart enough to stalk and kill the ungulates—the large hoofed animals—such as bison, moose, musk oxen, deer, and caribou that wolves must eat to survive?

No doubt, wolves solved the problem of the kill through a family of wolves working together to produce a meal. Lone wolves seldom survive. Making a kill takes great skill, concentration, commitment, and willingness to work within clearly defined social strategies required by the wolf pack. Yet, less than 10 percent of the pack's hunting attempts result in a meal. Two weeks of fasting can occur when a targeted animal is missed in the chase. *The existence of the wolf is reduced to one of feast and famine.*

Yet, the sociability of wolves makes their existence viable today. They are some of the most social of all carnivores. On the plains, strength in numbers defines the wolf pack, which may range from as few as three to as many as six or eight members. Even twenty to thirty members have been documented in some packs.

Making the kill is all about separating the vulnerable from the rest of the pack. Speed, strength, endurance, and intelligence allow wolves to coordinate their efforts to this end. The wolf pack is an exercise in cooperative hunting strategies with hunger as a powerful motivator. Survival often depends upon bringing down prey many times the size of a wolf while surrounded by a herd of animals armed with sharp antlers and hoofs.

Wolves may spend eight to ten hours a day on the move. They walk and run on their toes in digitigrade manner. In contrast, humans and grizzlies walk in plentigrade (or on flatfeet). Running on their toes allows wolves to maneuver quickly, run at great speeds, or maintain a steady pace for many miles. In pursuit of prey, wolves can reach speeds of forty miles an hour (twice the speed of the fastest Olympian sprinter). They can outrun most horses as well as grizzlies. They can cover up to 125 miles in one day. Most animals cannot match the wolf paw-for-paw in survival techniques.

Adult male wolves are characterized as lean and well muscled with a recognizable narrow chest. They weigh from seventy-five to one hundred pounds and can measure up to six and half feet from nose to tip of tail. Alpha females are perceptively smaller. An old Russian proverb describes the importance of the wolf's large paws—"The wolf is kept fed by its feet." Front paws are larger than hind paws and can leave tracks up to five inches or more in width. Their legs are long and their claws are not retractable like a cat. Claws are blunt due to constant contact with the ground. Unlike the dog, the wolf's back paw prints fall exactly into the paw prints made by the front paws, a clear advantage in snow.

Wolves seek out animals in a herd that pose the best chance of a meal. If members of a herd seem healthy and vigorous, not too old or too young, wolves often pass on those members and look elsewhere. They cannot afford to waste time and energy on a herd that will not produce a kill. They seek out herds with vulnerable animals: the crippled ones, the injured ones, or imbalanced herds with too many young or old members. They look for any *sign of weakness or injury*—a limp, an open wound, massive hair loss, or inattentive adult chaperones.

No doubt wolves attend to many behavioral signs of vulnerability unknown to humans. Ironically, the wolf is doing the herd a favor. By selectively killing the vulnerable, the strategy helps to maintain healthier populations of the ungulate herds. Due to the extracting of the weakest link, the herds have a better chance of survival with the healthiest and most powerful animals populating them. The vulnerable ones only slow the herd down and expose the healthy ones to constant surveillance by predators.

More than any other climate, snowy landscapes showcase the superior physical traits of wolves. In deep snow, their endurance, power, strength, patience, commitment, and intelligence make wolves especially dangerous. Not to outshine the wolves' sheer physicality are pack strategies; superior warmth provided by thick, water-resistant fur; and the superior traction provided by large paws that function as snowshoes. Even the grizzly is no match for the wolf's maneuverability in snow. Hoofed animals have far less traction in snow and ice and can be especially vulnerable to attack by a wolf pack.

Wolves go after large prey because they offer a big meal for the vast energy expenditure and the number of mouths to feed. Hunting small prey expends too much energy with little return. Small prey is therefore avoided.

The teeth of wolves, especially the sharp canine teeth that highlight their upper jaw, are truly menacing. Their jaws are packed with forty-two teeth customized for cutting, shearing, and grinding. The four canine teeth are long and slightly curved. They grow to a length of over two inches from root to tip. They allow the wolf to seize and hold its prey like an iron vice. The carnassial teeth are specialized for cutting through meat, skin, muscle, and connective tissue—slicing pieces of meat into smaller portions for easy swallowing. Incisors are large and slightly curved, allowing meat to be stripped from the bone and torn from carcasses.

Molars help to crush, grind, and macerate bone. The upper jaw comprises twenty teeth and the lower jaw twenty-two. Fifteen hundred pounds per square inch of pressure is made possible by extra-long jaw muscles. This pressure is more than twice the pressure exerted by German Shepherds. This tremendous pressure can easily crush the large bones of the legs and hip joints. In this way, the rich marrow inside can be ingested. Consuming almost the entire carcass, the only evidence left behind for scavengers to pick over is the skull, a few large bones, and a small quantity of hide and hair.

Wolves are equipped with a large liver and pancreas for the efficient processing of meat. However, water is an absolute necessity to prevent uremic poisoning due to the buildup of toxins in the blood associated with high protein (meat) consumption. Wolves must live, breed, and travel close to sources of water. The wolf's tongue acts as a convenient ladle for lapping up large amounts of water in a short time. Even at a waterhole, the wolf does not have the luxury of wasting too much time. Following the feast of meat, the wolf may sleep for many hours due to the large quantity of meat consumed (sometimes as much as twenty pounds).

In humans, large loading of carbohydrates produces a similar sedation. The eating disorder of obesity caused by compulsive overeating results in a kind of intoxicated sleep. In a sense, all wolves suffer from a food obsession exacerbated by a binge eating disorder due to their feast-or-famine existence.

The scent of meat triggers chemistry in the pleasure pathways of the wolf's brain that transforms the wolf into one of nature's most accomplished predators. Basically, the wolf is a serial killer. The kill is orchestrated by the stark reality of survival. Charles Darwin, Shadow Darwin's distant relative, said it best in only four words: *survival of the fittest.*

14

"MUSCLE CARS"

Following the late arrival of Shadow Darwin to the Sable Lodge and Mr. Laurence Harvey's freak accident, another vehicle appears on the north side access road. The snow-covered landscape ahead lies undisturbed by the two cones of golden light coming from the headlamps of a slow-moving Ford mustang. However, it's not just any Ford mustang. It's a 1966 candy apple red Mach 1 with a 454 high performance Shelby engine. It is fully restored to showroom quality. The driver is Jon Marx, the richest kid in Mt. Kyle and the son of Peter Marx. The Mach 1 is one of seven mint-condition "muscle cars" Peter Marx keeps in each of seven garages attached to his home. (Muscle cars are the big-engine, high-performance cars from the 1960s and 1970s that became extinct due in part to catalytic converters.) The Marx men—Peter and Jon—will have nothing to do with any car manufactured after 1979 when American car manufacturers traded excitement for a flimsy excuse called safety.

"A piece of crap. I wouldn't own one," remarked Peter Marx to a business associate who asked if he had test driven a popular SUV model.

"They're too expensive, too dangerous, too confining, and as boring as cardboard. They have no character," concluded Peter Marx. Other than the Mach 1 (Jon's favorite), the Marx men have the enviable task of choosing from the following muscle cars always garaged in the Marx automotive stable. Peter is inseparable from his favorite, a 1970 black Mark II Saloon edition Jaguar. Next, there's a 1972 dark blue Dodge Challenger with a hood-mounted intake manifold—a "shaker." (The car is similar to the Challenger used in the famous car chase sequence in the 1968 Warner's Brothers movie *Bullitt*). It has two wide orange stripes over the hood for accentuation. Next is a 1969 black Hurst-shift Pontiac GTO, a 1966 orange and black, roll-and-pleat upholstered Chevelle SS 396, a silver and blue 1970 Hemi-Cuda (Plymouth Barracuda) with a 427, and, last but not least, a 1971 black Plymouth Roadrunner 427 with Holly Headers and two-inch lifters all around. Each car has a state-of-the-art Bose sound system with a 20-pack CD changer. All the cars in the stable have special front and rear shocks and a custom triple paint job. The cars are worth over a quarter of a million dollars. None are for sale.

Once a week during football season Jon and his buddies loaded up their girlfriends in Jon's muscle cars and headed across the desert to Terlingua. The players earned this privilege by playing outstanding games leading to their playoff run. Every Friday afternoon a convoy of some of the most awesome muscle cars in automotive history made the short drive from Mt. Kyle to Terlingua for a bonfire celebration amid the ruins of broken dreams. In contrast, the youthful bodies dancing around the huge bonfire captures the heart and soul of restless youth seeking a generous slice of life. The young revelers, amid the creepy ghost town celebrating a winning hand in life, is best captured in the surf rock classic "Pipeline" performed by Dick Dale and accompanied by Stevie Ray Vaughan.

Many of the residents have followed Peter Marx's lead by collecting their own vintage muscle cars. It has turned into a kind of neighborhood competition to see who can outdo the other. The current head turner is a 1969 deep purple Corvette driven by Ashley Cox. She purchased the car with ASH on the vanity plates from money saved from modeling in Europe the past two summers.

The Marx men get to see it often as she lives only two houses down from the Marx residence. On Saturday and Sunday with the cars parked in the long winding driveways of the Marx Desert Estates, the development looks like a more exciting time in our automotive history.

Jon drives the Mach 1 with the control skills of a Le Mans 24-hour endurance driver. He does not want to be the first to put a scratch on her magnificent body that, under current conditions, is encrusted in dirty snow. This is rapidly becoming a night not intended for travel, especially in a collector's edition Mach 1 Shelby Mustang. The blowing snow whistles around her sides and interferes momentarily with the rear end *posi-traction*.

Yet, the custom air-brushed, candy apple red Mach 1 cuts around the snake-like turns of the north side access road with the slow and deliberate precision of a surgeon's scalpel. The oversized tires help. A song by the alternative rock group R.E.M. is blaring on the CD player. The wipers are far out of sync with the song "Strange"; the driver's right hand on the steering wheel is not. The time is 09:07 P.M. The all black leather custom interior has a factory-fresh scent. A gold medallion with red, white, and blue ribbon hangs from the rearview mirror with an inscription: UIL 4-A State Football Champions. A similar inscription is found on the oversized silver and gold championship ring worn on the driver's right-hand ring finger.

Jon Marx is co-captain of the state champion Mt. Kyle Grizzlies. He is minutes away from meeting his best friend Ryan Trevor and some friends at the Sable Lodge. He knows from the surrounding landmarks he has only a few turns left before reaching the Sable Lodge and his father's restaurant inside the lodge, X Marx the Spot, the newest addition to the historic eighty-five-year-old lodge. Indeed, Jon Nickolas Marx lives in the lap of luxury.

For the moment, he is thinking of the burgundy upholstery and buffalo hide tables in his father's restaurant. Although Jon's father Peter Marx is the principal investor, the minority partners from San Francisco and Chicago liked the name X Marx the Spot. The name conjures up terrific images of myths, legends, and romance surrounding early scoundrels of folklore who risked life and limb in search of unspeakable riches in gold coin buried in hiding place marked by the letter X, hence the name. Local residents have settled on a more convenient moniker—The X abbreviation.

Oversized windows on one side of The X provide a generous view of the landscape surrounding the Sable. On the opposite wall, a special tribute to Native American spirit, still strong among residents in this region, hangs in silent memoriam. It is comprised of a large red commemorative shield with three Indian warriors in full war paint. Their faces are streaked in black, red, and gold. Under the shield hangs a long-handled, double-bladed tomahawk. Two silver and white feathers hang from the wooden handle, which measures about nine inches long; the double-blades of the hatchet measure from blade to blade about the same length as the handle. It is a magnificent instrument commemorating war and survival upon the plains. It is the centerpiece of *The X,* and it is priceless.

Investors commissioned the fantasy artist Jonathon Earl Bowser to paint an original oil painting of the Sable amid the Chisos Mountains. It hangs in the lobby near the hostess stand. The painting depicts a young and beautiful Native American woman who materializes from puffy white cumulus clouds to caress the Chisos. Near her right breast, carved into the mountain granite, is the barely discernible face of a grizzly. On her left side appears the face of a wolf. Along with the Bowser painting and the warrior's shield and tomahawk, the restless spirit of *The X* is captured to perfection.

The faces of the wild animals register a kind of contentment—the kind of demeanor that projects confidence amid uncertainty and unpredictability.

15

THE CREATURE

With the view ahead practically obscured by the blizzard's arsenal of wind, frigid temperature, and blowing snow, Jon Marx nears the final curve in the road that will take him to the entrance of the Sable Lodge, the warmth of its hearth, and the smiling faces of his friends. The chaos outside matches his teenage angst within. He can't wait to graduate from high school in the spring and attend college. He's just about to decide on which one it will be. For now, he can't wait to arrive at his destination. To be perfectly honest, he can't wait to snuggle beside his long-anticipated date of the evening—Ashley Cox, the hottest girl of Mt. Kyle Senior High School. Jon's been trying to score with her since midterm when she arrived as the newcomer (*newcomer* is a priceless descriptive adjective for virgins circulated around school by Jon's best friend Ryan Trevor). Model agencies have fought over her portfolio since she was a kid. Other girls should hate her for aesthetic reasons alone, but they don't. They want to be her best friend. Adolescent boys should lust after her, which they do—mightily.

Ashley Lynn Cox is a tall, blond beauty with brains. Like most beauties she looks better with no makeup than her best competitors with full cosmetic faces. At the tender age of 18, "Ash" is a study in contrasts. With the heart of a woman, the mind of a man, and the determination of a starving wolf, she has all the right moves. She has been making money as a professional model since the sixth grade. Both her parents are attorneys and well connected both locally and along the Beltway in Washington, D.C. She has determination bred into her bones. She takes her time in choosing her friends because she has that luxury. Guys wait. Even rich guys like Jon Marx. She's a virgin and intends to remain so until Prince

Charming walks out of the comic book. And, she's not even going to open the book until she's graduated from the American University in Paris. She wants to remain single and work as a model for several years to enhance her portfolio. Marry right out of high school to some chump with no job? Are you kidding? Ash's sights are much higher. It's no wonder Ashley Cox takes precedence over any weather emergencies, even ones as unexpected and serious as this one.

The newly installed efficiency apartment with the king-size bed, whirlpool, and bar behind the office at *The X* (built by his Dad with these contingencies in mind) will come in handy tonight with the storm and all.

The liquor cabinet is fully stocked, and the restaurant should be completely vacant due to the weather, and grand opening of the new *Lake Tahoe X* (accounting for the absence of most residents of the Marx Desert Estates).

Put a few logs on the fire for atmosphere, light a few scented candles, and turn on a CD by Al Green and maybe, just maybe...

Grudgingly, Jon's thoughts return to the snowy road ahead. The wind has picked up as well as swirling snowfall. The temperature is now in the low teens and feels much colder. Strangely, Jon feels a rush of cold air on his face, even in the climate-controlled comfort of his car.

Suddenly, without the slightest warning, some kind of creature looms in the high beams of the Mach 1. The driving snow obliterates the intruder's identity. The howling wind mutes all other noises including the deep throaty rumble of the huge engine displacement. For the briefest moment, Jon believes he may have fallen asleep at the wheel. But, no, the creature is actually moving right across the path of the Mustang. Reflexively, Jon closes his eyes and presses down hard on the brake pedal, not a wise choice under current weather conditions. He turns the steering wheel violently to the right. The Mach 1 simply adheres to physics, sliding across the icy road like butter across a hot skillet.

The Mustang disappears under snow-laden limbs of a gigantic mesquite tree beside the road. Jon's head bangs against the steering wheel, and he is suddenly engulfed in blackness. The deep-throated rumble, rumble, rumble of the engine goes silent. In the time it takes for the instrument panel to go black, the landscape seems undisturbed, like nothing has happened except the falling of a few broken tree branches and the swirling of snow like white dust mites on the red hood of the Mach 1.

With the winter storm intensifying and roads becoming more treacherous by the minute, it might be days before authorities find the frozen body of the richest kid in Mt. Kyle.

Two freak accidents occur in the space of a few hours. What connection could there possibly be between Mr. Laurence Harvey, the most despised teacher at Mt. Kyle High, and Jon Marx, the most popular student in the school?

Wolves, mountain lions, and coyotes, breaking curfew on the sudden need to hibernate, may find the victims before their loved ones do. How ironic is the predicament of Jon Marx? The very animals his father is trying to preserve may soon fight over his carcass.

The problem with freak accidents is that no one sees them coming.

16

MALE BONDING

At the moment in Lake Tahoe, Peter Marx is playing host to about three-quarters of "the bubble," a reference less-fortunate kids make alluding to Mt. Kyle's exclusive population. In their absence at Mt. Kyle, a handful of high school seniors and college-age students finagled their parents into letting them stay home. Well-meaning parents will soon regret a momentary lapse in judgment. Granting of empowerment sometimes overlooks possible downsides. Luckily, most of the younger kids remain safely under the watchful eyes of nannies or out-of-town relatives.

Conventional wisdom in parenting dictates you've got to let go eventually. When do you let kids make their own mistakes?

From the parents' perspective earlier in the day, loved ones left behind would be left in the good hands of three of Mt. Kyle's most recognized and trusted citizens: Police Chief Jake Munoz, the 50-year-old, heavy-set police chief with thirty years experience in law enforcement; Munoz's chief deputy Julie Quixotica (known as Julie Q), age 27; and *The X* manager, Jill Frazier, age 23. Chief Munoz, Deputy Julie Q, and Ms. Frazier are college educated but not academic types. They know full well how tenuous things really are, especially for those less privileged by socioeconomic circumstances. They learned some of their most valuable lessons the difficult way from the school of hard knocks.

The last of the college guys and girls left an hour ago for home movies and bourbon and coke. Trevor tries to act like he isn't worried. But, make no mistake about it, he is worried.

Guys in North American have limited opportunities for social bonding. If it's not through sports, girls, or drinking, other options are slim. Social psychologists contend the hole in the heart of most young males is the lack of a close bond with their fathers. Often, fathers mask their own insecurities with their sons through extended work, excessive drinking, or by overreacting and becoming too protective. For many young males, a coach is like a surrogate father, the next best thing. But fathers by proxy are not near enough. The void in a young man's life can leave scars for a lifetime.

Bonding with a buddy is another option. It's unfortunate that male bonding often requires a full contact sport. Jon Marx and Ryan Trevor have such as bond. Musically, Jon favors Incubus and Limp Bizkit. Trevor is a Linkin Park and Smash Mouth junkie. They both listen to Weezer, Flickerstick, and Phantom Planet through headphones in the locker room prior to kickoff—it helps them to get psyched for peak performance. Like all buddies, they share CDs and burn their own concoction of alternative rock music on their home PCs.

The latest bond of camaraderie was solidified in the waning moments of last month's state championship game. The two friends forged a bond that transcends other hobbies, girls, and tastes in music.

The time on the large red neon clock in *The X* reads 10:10 P.M. about the same time one of the most exciting games in state championship history ended.

17

The "Darling Dart"

The huge Diamond Vision scoreboards in both end zones of Texas Stadium in Irving, Texas, told the story.

Home: 26 Visitor: 21

Time: 00:58 seconds

Ball: 12-yard line

Down: 1st

The team designated as visitors, the Canyon Park Yellow Jackets brought to the game a remarkable playoff record. In four playoff games, they acquired a combined 120 points to their opponents 0. Plus, they went undefeated through a tough district schedule. Yet, in the final seconds of the 4-A state championship game, time was not on their side. They had no time-outs. They had marched steadily down the field. The ball was placed squarely on the Mt. Kyle Grizzlies' 12-yard line. They had the momentum, as well as the state's best all-around offensive player, quarterback Adam Riggs to steamroll over the competition. Nationally, Riggs is probably the best schoolboy quarterback since "Super Bill" Bradley of Palestine High School in the 1960s. Like Bradley, Riggs is ambidextrous, making him a dangerous rollout passer. He throws just as effectively with his right arm as he does with his left arm. He is tall (6'3") and fast (4.4 in the 40). He is a coach's dream. And, he's the Mt. Kyle Grizzlies' worst nightmare.

Yet, there existed a "fly in the ointment" with Riggs. The downside had nothing to do with his athletic abilities. In fact, he had full-ride scholarship offers from thirty-eight division I-A schools. The downside had to do with his nickname. Local fans and sportswriters in his hometown referred to their local hero as

"The Darling Dart" of Canyon Park. Yes, "The Darling Dart." A great deal of effort on Riggs's part shortened the moniker to The Dart, saving him considerable embarrassment among national scouts.

In the game of the year, the state championship football game of Division 4-A Texas high school football, enough time remained on the clock for a passer like The Dart and his all-state receiver Ash Gilbert to snatch victory from the never-say-die team from Mt. Kyle—first-timers to the state playoffs.

Across the ball on defense stood free safety Jon Marx watching The Dart like a hawk. At 6'1" (4.3 in the 40) he and his best friend, middle linebacker and fullback Ryan Trevor, 6 foot, 225 pounds, had enough adrenalin to last a week. Yet, the first state championship opportunity to come their way since moving up from 3-A ball in a two-year growth spurt was in severe jeopardy. After all, Canyon Park had been the defending 4-A state champion for the past three years! They had been there before a total of six times throughout the decade.

The game was thrilling for fans in the exciting ambiance of Texas Stadium, home of the once-mighty Dallas Cowboys. Since Texas Stadium had the hole in roof, games in there were not climate controlled. The 40-degree game time had slowly dipped into the mid-30s by 9 P.M. at the start of the second half. No one seemed to notice. In fact, following halftime, as the teams reassembled by the dressing room tunnels, Coach Jo Bob Curtis of the Mt. Kyle Grizzlies admonished his troops to roll up their sleeves—"roll 'um as far as they'll go." Seemingly, coaches stop at nothing to "psych up" their players.

In the waning moments, the game had been the kind of topsy-turvy, tug-of-war that sportswriters love to cover. Canyon Park had built a commanding lead in the first quarter thanks to The Dart and two of the reasons for his lengthy resume—his huge offensive line averaging 270 for 4-A high school ball and his speedy All-State wingback Ash Gilbert. Before their second possession of the game, the Grizzlies were down 14 to 0.

On the offensive side of the ball, thanks to time-consuming drive engineered by Jon Marx and to the power running of fullback Ryan Trevor, the lead was narrowed to 14 to 7 with three minutes to go before half time. Two series later, Trevor, from his middle linebacker position, stepped in front of the fleet Yellow Jacket wingback and raced 25 yards to score on a timely interception. This turn of events occurred just before the gun ended the first half. With the score knotted at 14 to 14, the second half was expected to be a classic high school shootout. As coaches are fond of saying, "Get the women and the children to safe places 'cause we're taking no hostages!" The mood of the coaching staffs in both locker rooms was near pandemonium. The players, huddled in strategy sessions with their position coaches, were relaxed and confident.

The first damage of the second half was provided courtesy of a strong rush by a Jacket defender leading to a blocked punt. An option rollout by The Dart provided a one-touchdown cushion as the Jackets led 21 to 14. For most of the third quarter, the game reached stalemate, the kind of back and forth possession kind of game that keeps fans wondering which team wants to win the most.

Then, early in the fourth quarter, a long punt return by "Gazelle" Jackson (pronounced "GEEzelle" by Coach Curtis), a tall and slender 400-meter track man-turned-punt-return-specialist, gave the home team excellent field position. The referee placed the ball on the visitor's 35-yard line. Then, the "the play" was called. ("The play" forever forges a bond between players in championship games. As balding old geezers, their wrinkled faces light up like Christmas trees when somebody remembers long ago heroics such as "the play," especially players who have been together since grade school and experienced a handful of losses.) Coach Curtis sent in GEEzelle on first and ten.

Everybody in the stands including Coach Mike Edwards on the visitor's bench knew where the ball was going. The ball was definitely going to GEEzelle. GEEzelle was never used as a decoy. The problem was how to stop the lanky receiver. The technical name of "the play" was too long and time-consuming to call in the huddle. For the record, "the play" was technically, end over right, strong right, fullback in motion right, fake end-sweep right, pass to the end-over. So, when Jon Marx simply called "the play ... on two," everyone knew what to do. The offensive line pass-blocked while Trevor (as the motion man) blocked the strong rush from the crashing defensive end. Jon Marx slipped into the slot at left halfback. Reserve quarterback Montgomery Tyler, who doubles as the punter and field goal kicker, stayed in the game at quarterback.

The huddle broke quickly in an attempt to conceal the numeral change at quarterback. Tyler barked the signals. The ball was snapped. The lines collided. Jon Marx took the pitch from Tyler and headed to his right. Trevor leveled the blitzing defensive end who fell to the ground clutching his right knee. The crushing block gave Jon Marx clearance for his ally-oop pass. GEEzelle feigned a block on the cornerback and ran the fly. However, the Jacket defensive backs were savvy.

In fact, when the Grizzlies came to the line with GEEzelle as the end-over, the corner, the safety, and the middle linebacker yelled in unison "Alley-OOP to GEEzelle! Alley-OOP! Alley-OOP!!" Jon Marx launched a tight spiral to the fleet end-over hotly pursued by three defensive backs.

GEEzelle sprang into the air like his agile namesake as four bodies tangled in mid-air. Four pairs of hands reach skyward. GEEzelle snagged the ball with his long, spider-like fingers as it made a nosedive into the tangled maze of hands and arms. GEEzelle simply outjumped his three competitors. The game announcer described the 30-yard pass completion as a "circus catch."

Defensive backs scouting Mt. Kyle knew the three-sport letterman GEEzelle jumped center tip-off for the basketball team as well. Although only 6′ 3," he could outjump anyone 6′ 6." The Jacket defense was simply shell-shocked. The old joke among district coaches was: How many guys does it take to defend one GEEzelle? The answer was: All eleven, but they have to want to. The very next play resulted in a five-yard TD to tight end Lowell Luman who made a diving catch in the end zone in front of the flat-footed cornerback. The Mt. Kyle crowd went wild! The Yellow Jacket boosters sat in muted silence. And then potential disaster struck the Grizzlies. The point after touchdown was miffed. The usually accurate Tyler simply sent the ball sailing toward the right goalpost. The crowd fell to a hushed silence as the ball glanced off the goalpost and fell left of center to the ground like a wounded duck. Truly, football is a game of inches, and one of miles for state champions. A missed extra point had been the difference in many state games. In the stands, the missed PAT served to add additional acid to the stomachs of the Mt. Kyle faithful. The score reflected the result:

Jackets   21

Grizzlies 20

The clock showed just over three minutes left to play. Coaching parables raced through the subconscious minds of players and coaches desperate for any advantage. "When times are tough, the tough get going! I cried because I had no shoes until I met a man who had no feet!" Coaching parables aside, The Dart warmed up on the sidelines with a crooked smile of confidence.

The game came down to a simple coaching philosophy. Keep the ball. Keep it moving. Get two first downs and take it to the house. Spoils go to the winners—in this case, state championship rings and medallions. The loser goes home with nothing but memories of what could have been.

Yet, in one grand heroic gesture of noncompliance, the swarming Grizzly defense stopped the Jacket offense before it could register a first down. Three and out punctuated by a forced punt was not what would win a championship game in its waning moments. The Dart seemed puzzled as he left the field. He yanked off his chinstrap in frustration.

In a brilliantly engineered drive with the running of Trevor and the roll-out passing of Jon Marx, the Grizzlies found the end zone for the last time that cold night in Texas Stadium. The TD came with a one-yard plunge by Trevor. The Grizzlies were ahead for the first time in the game 26 to 21. Down to every player and coach, they knew the game was far from over. In an instance of déjà vu, Monte Tyler again missed the extra point. (To this day, two missed extra points in a state championship game remains the state record across all divisions.)

Every coach who is worth his winning record knows making first downs means ball control. But, when your team is losing by six points and the clock is eating you up, a TD is the only panacea. A field goal is worthless. In the next half-minute, The Dart showed the anxious fans from Mt. Kyle why his press clippings were not exaggerated. Under his quick feet and game savvy, the Jackets moved the ball down the field with the precision of the Texas A&M Marching Band.

The Grizzly defenders who had been shadowing the antics of the Dart and his fleet receivers all evening were simply exhausted. No one should be so accurate with both hands and scramble so effectively! The Dart was already safely in the record books for most passes attempted and most passes completed in a state game. With the game's lifeblood flowing out in one-second intervals, a mere 58 ticks remained. The ever-resourceful Dart seemed energized. He smelled the end zone like a keen beagle. He was ready to win the game and add a seventh title to his school's storied past. A message from Florida State would surely be on his answering machine Monday morning.

With less than 15 seconds left on the clock and the ball on the 12-yard line of the Grizzlies, the Dart went for broke. He faded back as the clock ticked down to the game's final seconds. He spotted his tight end in the far left of the end zone covered by two defenders. He darted up the middle ready to run the remaining yards to the end zone himself. He could see the goal line stripe just ahead.

Suddenly, Trevor appeared from nowhere, blocking the Dart's forward progress with his knack of being at the right place at the right time, a mark of all gifted athletes.

In the blink of an eye, the Darling Dart, playing in his last high school game, cocked his right arm as he spotted Ash Gilbert standing wide open in the end zone. Joe Crumply, the strong safety for the Grizzlies, who had recently been cleared from rehab for a twisted knee, lay on the ground clutching his knee. The ball sailed over the outstretched arms of Trevor. The championship game came down to one catch. Make it and you're a champion, miss it and live the rest of your life second best. Every person witnessing the game in person or at home on TV focused on the flight of the ball as their minds raced to comprehend the consequences. The ball was caught! The ball was caught!

The ball drifted into the hands of Jon Marx, not Ash Gilbert, the intended Jacket receiver. It was not a reception at all, but an interception. Ironically, Jon Marx was out of position on the play. He simply drifted toward the center of the field and stood behind Trevor.

To the Yellow Jacket faithful, the interception would forever be nothing more than a freak accident caused by a player who was completely out of position. Ash Gilbert sat dejectedly in the end zone Indian-style, head down, and fists clinched. The gun sounded. It appeared to startle everyone on the field who had fallen silent with the remarkable events unfolding so fast. Of course, no one heard the gun in the stands.

The final score of 26 to 21 marked the end of a thriller. From start to finish, the game was so sensational that the sportswriters named three players—yes, three players—as outstanding players of the game. This gesture of appreciation is also a national record for high school playoffs.

For Canyon Park, the Darling Dart was chosen a co-MVP. For the new state champion Mt. Kyle Grizzlies, Jon Marx and Ryan Trevor were chosen co-MVPs.

The bond of friendship would soon be called into action and possibly save the lives of the Mt. Kyle co-captains as they face a far more vicious rival than the Darling Dart.

18

LATE-NIGHT CALL

L ate Friday night, Mt. Kyle police chief Jake Munoz is the first to learn that Jon Marx may be in trouble. He receives a late night call from Ryan Trevor who has been waiting impatiently in the warmth of the Sable and *X Marx the Spot* for his friend to arrive. Jon and Trevor have been friends and teammates since the third grade. Ashley Cox and Trevor's longtime girlfriend, the dark brunette Gable Jordan, wait for Jon's arrival. Gable, who favors sterling silver jewelry, blue denim shirts, and black denim jeans, is the quiet and unassuming girl found in every crowd. This is ironic considering her nickname, "Gabby." She earned her nickname during pep rallies and football games where she is not only the head cheerleader, but also the loudest and most acrobatic cheerleader. Classmates with low self-esteem think she's stuck on herself. Her friends know better. Beneath those brown locks and sparkling green eyes, a powerful intelligence and sense of loyalty reside.

Jon's friends arrived before the blizzard hit. In fact, Trevor bumped into Mr. Laurence Harvey as he was leaving on his ill-fated ride down the mountain. Earlier in the day, the friends planned on meeting at *The X* for a few laughs. Now, they are drinking steaming mugs of hot chocolate in the anticipation of his arrival.

Trevor spikes the drinks with a shot of Amaretto from a convenient silver flask hidden deep in a secret pocket within his bright orange parka. Impatiently, he flicks open his cell phone and dials Jon's home number. No answer. Then, Trevor tries Jon's cell phone. No answer. Not one to hesitate, the next call he makes is to Chief Munoz, a number he knows by heart. When you're one of Mt. Kyle's "Fighting Grizzlies" playing under the golden glow of Friday night lights, you require the services of the team's self-acknowledged "number one fan" on occasion. The gruff voice of Chief Munoz interrupts the ringing.

"Hello, Chief Munoz, this is Ryan Trevor, you know, Jon Marx's friend."

"Yes, Trevor the Great! Let's see, number 27 on the program but number one in our hearts ... right?" replies the chief as though he were congratulating Trevor following a Grizzly win. "Haven't heard from you for a while; what's up, son?"

"Chief, me and some friends are waiting for Jon here in *The X* at the Sable and he's not here. I recently tried to reach him at home and on his cell, with no luck."

"You're kidding? You don't think he ventured out in this mess, do you? We have a blizzard going on here, son" the chief replied in a more serious tone.

"Well, that's just it Chief. I don't know where he is ... he's supposed to be on his way here—apparently from his house. You know Mr. Marx and half the town are in Tahoe for the celebration. He was supposed to meet us here." Trevor looks at his watch. "Well, about an hour ago. With the storm and all, I'm afraid he's had an accident. Jon is smart, but it's like an ice rink out there," Trevor said with a tone intended to reflect his inexperience in these matters.

"Yes, son, it is an ice rink out there. As a rule, I don't venture out on suicidal roads. Didn't you see the 9 P.M. weather report on the news?" the chief asked clearly becoming annoyed. "They say this is THE storm of the century for West Texas. You know how protective Jon's dad is. He's going to kill him for this stunt!" *If he doesn't kill me first,* reflects the chief in internal dialogue.

"I know Chief, I'm just worried. Can you check on him, please ... Just follow the route he would be taking from his house, that's all I ask," says Trevor.

"All right! I'm leaving now. I'm on my way. You stay put; you hear me loud and clear? I don't want to have to come looking for you, too. Don't be stupid, son. I'll get back as soon as I find him." Now the chief is pissed. With the unmistakable sound of a phone being slammed down on its cradle the chief's displeasure is registered.

In his absence, Peter Marx left explicit instructions for his son to stay close to home. Obviously, what Peter and his partygoers (with an extensive guest list including the local chief meteorologist) failed to forecast was the serious blizzard presently assaulting Mt. Kyle. On regional radar, it looked for all purposes, like a mild winter cold front. The National Weather Service saw nothing in their reports to contradict regional forecasts. Apparently something unexpected happened aloft between the departure of Peter Marx's SRO charter flight for Lake Tahoe at 11:07 A.M. Friday morning and the 9 P.M. local weathercast.

How could a mild cold front suddenly become a dangerous blizzard? The West has always been unpredictable—one minute you're safe, the next minute you're not. Most of the time you don't see it coming. Life is truly scary without contingencies. For life to be predictable, it must be tied to contingencies—predictable causes and effects. One certainty—death—still seems a remote occurrence to most people, even senior citizens. Now, who could have predicted the unpopular alcoholic Mr. Laurence Harvey and the popular co-captain of the state champion football team would share a bond with a deadly storm? Why now?

19

THE SEARCH

The fierce wind of the blizzard practically rips the door out of Chief Munoz's hand. He sets his jaw against the worsening elements. He has been out in winter storms before but nothing like this. The chief has second thoughts. He slams the door hard and returns to his desk. He decides not to be stupid. He rubs his forehead hard as though trying to massage out of his skull the best strategy. He decides to call for backup, just in case. On his two-way radio, he calls his deputy, Julie Q.

Deputy Julie Quixotica is a five-year veteran. With quiet intelligence, she has become indispensable to the chief. With almond eyes and dark hair pulled back framing a striking face, high cheekbones, and dark Native American skin, she has the physique of an endurance athlete, lean and rock solid. She interned with Chief Munoz her senior year in college. Besides being an academic achiever in her chosen discipline of criminal justice, she won four letters and a conference championship as a star volleyball player. Julie's work had so impressed the chief that he created the position of assistant to the chief deputy with her in mind.

Julie's father Jack was the assistant deputy before he died in a one-car accident on the treacherous north side of the Chisos. His squad car hit a bad patch of ice in the road, flipped over once, and skidded 200 feet down the mountain on its roof in a ball of flames. Seemingly, no one knows how to drive in West Texas if it rains or snows. He was only 47 years of age.

Julie Q was promoted to her father's position. She inherited her father's steady nerves and good judgment. Her father was in line to take over for the chief when he moved on or retired.

For the past several hours, Julie has been handling some security concerns with the Sable Lodge manager, the Englishman Clint Cooper.

"Hello, Julie, come in," the chief tried to project the calmest voice he could find even though his stomach churned acid and his hands trembled.

"Yes, Chief, Julie here," came the soothing voice of Julie Q.

"Julie, we have a situation up there. I hope you are staying at the lodge overnight?"

"Yes, sir, I am. We're almost finished here. Mr. Cooper is putting me up for night. He has plenty of room. The lodge is practically vacant except for Dr. Darwin from Alpine, Dr. McAfee from Odessa, Susan Newby, and some teenagers."

"Good. Listen, Julie, as soon as possible, I want you to go over to *The X* and wait for me there. Ryan Trevor—you know Ray Trevor's kid—just notified me that his buddy Jon Marx has not arrived at the lodge as expected. He was supposed to have left home almost an hour ago. Stupid kids … it looks like he ventured out in this mess. It doesn't look good. He's probably stuck somewhere out on the north side." The chief entertains the sudden tangential thought that teenagers really do stupid things after all. And, he suspects Julie has just experienced a fist to her stomach recalling similar cond.tions in the death of her father. He quickly refocuses on the matter at hand. "I'm going up to check out the situation. I may need to be pulled out of a snow bank or something worse. Contact Eddie Hawkins at his place. He has a winch on his four-wheel drive Bubba truck. I'm starting up now. Over."

"Will do. Chief, be careful," said Julie in a voice showing concern.

The chief, a thirty-five-year veteran of protecting and serving, starts the half-mile trek up to the summit of Mt. Kyle and the Sable Lodge. From the station halfway up the summit, it is a dangerous trek up the north side. He opens the door to test the cold. Blowing snow, looking like white confetti in a Madison Avenue parade, swirls around the chief in wind gusts of fifty miles per hour. The wind whistles through the door like a freight train. The wind chill makes the temperature feel like 10 below zero. A hooded, bright orange parka covering a heavy coat on top of two layers of sweaters braces the chief against the frigid elements. Gloves are not optional. The chief's face is already red and burning when he leaves the comfort of his warm office.

After adjusting his goggles, the chief cranks his refurbished snowmobile affectionately known as "Homer." The name is stenciled in bright red letters along the side of the yellow snowmobile. The chief conjured up the name years ago when his wife worried he would wreck it just like he did the cruiser in the rollover. After all, the north side access road is treacherous when punctuated by rapid snow accumulation.

He calmed her down by saying the snowmobile was like their pet beagle, Homer, so named because he knows the way home. Funny how we try to remember familiar things to make us feel better in desperate times.

At approximately 10:20 P.M., the chief starts up the main access road to the lodge. Visibility is remarkably good considering the conditions. The upper beams of Homer make for a surreal landscape dominated by weird ice and snow frescos on tree bark and rock formations visible through the blowing snow. Squatty mesquite trees struggle against the weight of rapidly accumulating snow. It is an eerie reminder that tonight's escapades are already in the deep freezer.

First, the chief makes sure Jon Marx is not at home. He makes his way past the Jordan place and the Cox residence. Both are darkened except for motion detection lights. The quick appearance of the floodlights reminds the chief of searchlights that illuminate the yard and surrounding grounds during a prison break in old movies. His mind flashes to an image of the actor Jimmy Cagney in a popular black-and-white film noir. Any familiar images are welcome as temporary distractions under worsening conditions.

The chief knows the Coxes and the Jordans are with Peter Marx enjoying the comforts of Tahoe about now. Very little goes on in Mt. Kyle the chief doesn't know about. He doesn't bother going all the way to Peter Marx's place. It appears dark, uninhabited, and uninviting. No smoke issues forth from any of the four towering chimneys scattered along the roof. Tire tracks are barely visible in the Marx driveway. He hopes to follow them and find Jon soon before hypothermia does. Chief Munoz feels a bit of relief amid the howling and chaotic winds. Homer is on the "scent" like a bloodhound.

About one hundred yards up the incline to the entrance of the Sable, the chief observes the spot around the bend where Jon's Mach 1 left the road. It is within sight of the Sable, bathed in eerie landscape lighting, blurred by blowing snow. He spots the rear end of the bright red Mustang sticking out like a big hunk of metal playing hide and seek with the evergreens and mesquites.

It would be one of the last clear images he saw before the attack.

THE ATTACK

Chief Munoz brings Homer to a stop about fifty yards from Eddie Hawkins muscle car restoration shop just across the road from the Sable. Recalling the embarrassing rollover, he stops and gears to neutral about thirty yards from the edge of the north side.

A large snow-laden mesquite tree appears to be the only object standing between the Mach 1 and a tragic ride down the mountain. Instantly, he thinks of notifying Julie. Instead, his thoughts are interrupted by a vivid picture of her father's burned and mangled police car at the bottom of Vincent's gorge. He closes his eyes in an effort to make the image go away. He decides to help Jon first. Carefully, he trudges ahead in the deepening snow toward the perilous perch.

Suddenly, some kind of animal looms behind the chief and attacks him savagely. The chief hears the deep guttural growl of the animal. The powerful blow knocks him to the ground with a muffled thud. Immediately, the snow turns red. He feels a stinging sensation on his back and neck. What he doesn't realize at the time is the presence of a gaping wound marked by four deep incisions producing a rapid flow of blood.

The chief turns over on his back with great difficulty. His life's blood trickles down his neck and back from the wound. The blowing snow and its rapid accumulation saves his life. It constricts the blood flow. Great puffs of his breath condense into the cold wind and blowing snow. He cannot distinguish his own moaning from the sounds of his attacker. His body feels heavy and useless to him like dead weight. His head throbs; his vision blurs.

In an instant, the creature standing over him vanishes from his field of vision. As if he were looking through the small viewfinder

71

of a camera, all the chief sees is a picture of snow-drenched tree branches, swirling snow, and black sky. In some small sector of his brain, he wonders if he is dying. He feels a strange sensation as though drifting away from familiar surroundings. He is either too cold or too weak to get up. He can't distinguish between sensations, yet he feels the strange sensation of losing the fight inherent within all animals—the fight to stay alive. He wonders if a large mountain lion, well known to inhabit the Big Bend along with wolves and coyotes, might simply eat him alive.

He had read about such attacks. What is left of human victims wouldn't fill a "to go" bag at McDonalds.

The chief's mind races for answers. For a split second, the creature moves back into his small viewfinder. What he sees is not a mountain lion, a coyote, or a wolf. The chief blinks in amazement. It appears to be a huge grizzly standing tall on two legs. Failing to appreciate what his mind registers, the chief is in a near comatose-state. Certain of his own death at any moment, the chief feels the absurd notion to laugh. *There are no grizzlies in Big Bend! They left decades ago,* the chief observes in internal dialogue. He closes his eyes in disbelief with the anticipation of death.

Now, the creature stands silently beside the door of Jon Marx's hood-mangled Mach 1. The creature's exhaled breath billows like steam from a locomotive climbing a steady grade. The grizzly is largely shrouded by darkness and blowing snow amid the low limbs of the mesquite tree. Suddenly, the grizzly lets out a monstrous growl heard all the way to the Sable. Then, the sound of a big car engine intrudes on the howling winds.

21

REVERSE

_____

_____

_____

Jon Marx regains consciousness and turns the ignition key. Shaking off nausea and a splitting headache, he prays for the ignition to spark the engine. The sudden impact of the head-on collision with the mesquite tree rendered Jon unconscious for an undetermined time. Strangely, the first conscious thought entering Jon Marx's mind related to his car. How much damage had his car sustained? The speed on impact was about 20 miles per hour. The impact was forceful enough for Jon to bang his head on the steering wheel. The newly installed seatbelt was engaged. The unearthly growl of the animal a few inches from the driver's side had provided the stimulus for awakening him from his trauma. He quickly forgets how pissed he is over the suspected mangled front bumper when reality bites ... well, almost.

Jon's body feels slow and unresponsive on the hard, cold seat of the roll-and-pleat upholstery. Apparently, the heater had been off for some time. A glance in the rearview mirror discloses Jon's face as colorless. His lips are a light blue color. Looking to his immediate left he turns the key. Due to the excitement, he unconsciously interrupts the flow of urine before it could stain his boxers. Wetting one's pants is a perfectly natural thing to do when a thin sheet of window glass separates a giant grizzly from devouring your head.

Good thing the Mach 1's electrical system is much simpler than the idiotic tangle of feedback sensors available on new cars. The ignition sparked the first time, even in subzero temperature. After all, a grizzly is not the animal you want to give a second chance of ripping your head off. At the precise moment the reverse gears of the Mach 1 engage, the creature's right paw crashes into the safety glass of the driver-side window. The indention caused by the force of the animal barely misses Jon's head. The sudden reversal of direction and the churning tires cause the creature to fall forward directly in front of the Mach 1's headlamps, which had been shattered by the collision. The Mach 1's back wheels narrowly miss the chief as he struggles to his feet. His bleeding wound has temporarily slowed due to the cold. Jon glimpses "Homer" in the rearview mirror. In the next instant, the chief's wide body bumps against the driver's side rear quarter panel practically scaring Jon to death. He is sure any minute the creature will devour him.

In the next instant, Jon recognizes the chief out of the corner of his eye in his bright orange parka. *Police Chief* is stenciled in black letters across the front.

"Get in Chief....Hurry!" screams Jon in a voice he does not recognize. He reaches over the console to unlatch the door as the chief lumbers over to the passenger side. With a strong push from Jon, the passenger-side door swings to full extension. Miraculously, the chief falls through the door landing on the passenger side with a thud. As Jon maneuvers his car into gear, the chief is able to clear his feet from the door as it slams in conjunction with forward motion. In plain sight, the eerily lit Sable is just around the curve.

"Chief, my God ... are you all right?" Jon Marx screams in a hoarse voice.

In a fog of unconnected thoughts, Chief Munoz can only manage a faint whisper. As far as Jon knows, the creature is moments away from crushing the car like a tin can or shattering the windshield and devouring its contents.

22

WEST TEXAS GRIZZLIES?

Good thing grizzlies don't exist in West Texas, the chief ruminates as he drifts in and out of consciousness. Going against a hungry grizzly is the last thing a human wants to do with the lone exception of confronting a great white shark. The Sable seems an eternity away as Jon's mind races with the possibility they won't make it. His warm breath hisses against the cold windshield making visibility even more difficult. At any moment, Jon expects the grizzly to crush the car with its terrible strength.

Presently, scientists do not have a clear understanding of how to measure bear intelligence. Rivaling human curiosity, bear curiosity extends far beyond food strategies to virtually any new object or event in its immediate environment. For example, through the well-established principles of classical conditioning and the law of association, very young bear cubs learn the precise location of a particularly rich food source and the route back to it. Predictably, the cub returns to it later even without an adult chaperone.

Without the slightest hint of detection, bears are known to strategically place themselves in locations allowing for maximum camouflage so they may observe humans. Bears are voyeuristic when it comes to observing their next meal. They stand practically motionless for long periods while completely hidden by trees or bushes. In the polar region, white polar bears place a paw in front of their black noses to prevent detection. Some scientists are convinced this strategy of self-concealment suggests conscious awareness and therefore some *level of self-awareness.* Numerous examples are recorded of bears pursued by humans who outfox the fox. Bears modify their paths to avoid leaving tracks. Similarly, bears have been observed using sophisticated strategies to either avoid or deliberately trigger the mechanism of traps to foil the best-laid plans of trappers.

Bears live in a world of diversion, a world of the *constant dare*. Using what they have as physical gifts of nature, they live to fool others. Otherwise, bears would be forced to live most of their lives severely injured from constant fighting. Through dare, grizzlies are able to focus on what's important—food strategies, hibernation, and mating. Blessed by nature, the creatures' height, massive bulk, and speed offer the perfect combination of fear-inducing cues and means to capture whatever they want.

It is well documented that grizzlies can outrun, outclimb, outmuscle, and outswim any man. The menacing size and razor-sharp claws of the grizzly provide the visual cues of the ongoing dare. In water domains, only the dorsal fin, dead eyes, and razor teeth of the shark rival the grizzly.

Grizzly bears are very agile and swift creatures. They are capable of outrunning a horse at speeds of 35 or 40 miles an hour. All bears are very capable swimmers, and nearly all bears climb trees with skill and dexterity until they get too heavy. Unlike most carnivores, the lips of bears are not attached to the gums; they are protrusible for a variety of biting and eating strategies. For those unlucky enough to be in sight of the grizzly, this feature more than any other, exacerbates their menacing look. Bears walk as humans do in plentigrade manner. Heels and feet are placed flat on the ground, which explains how bears can balance on their hind legs with such dexterity. Some grizzlies measure over eight feet tall. Increased height adds to the dare.

Ursidae comprises the family of eight species of bear, including the American black bear, the polar bear, the giant panda bear, the Asiatic black bear, the spectacled bear, the sloth bear, the sun bear, and the brown bear. The brown bear is synonymously known as *Ursus Arctos*—the grizzly bear. The grizzly bear is so named for its silver-tipped grizzled hairs that develop with age.

Approximately 30 to 40 million years ago during the Oligocene period, tree-climbing carnivorous mammals appeared in the mountains, tundra, and practically everywhere else. Today referred to as *miacids,* this small family of animals developed special canine teeth, which enabled them to tear the flesh of their prey. Carnassial teeth are located in both upper and lower jaws. They aid in shearing meat from a carcass into easily eaten smaller chunks of meat. The first bears evolved from a heavy, bear-like dog that developed from the *miacids*. Approximately two and one-half million years ago, the direct ancestors of modern bears appeared in wide circulation. Members of the genus *Ursus* (Latin for bear) divided into three distinct evolutionary lines. Two lines developed in Asia leading to what are now known as the black bear and the brown or grizzly bear. The third line developed in Europe producing the *Ursus spelaus*, often referred to in literature as the "cave bear." Today, the European brown bear has taken over the habitat of the *Ursus spelaus*.

Most bear species have excellent eyesight and hearing. Since their eyes are set so close together, they have excellent depth perception. They can detect very small movements several hundred yards away. In the wild, young, strong, and agile bears are plentiful; bears older than 30 years of age are rare. Sense of smell is so acute that it rivals the bloodhound. Bears appear to use all three senses (smell, eyesight, and hearing) very well in surviving the wilderness and tracking their prey. Bears sniff the air repeatedly as they zero in to make a kill.

Grizzlies are able to detect their next meal many miles away, even in adverse weather conditions such as ice and snow, wind and rain, or under blizzard conditions.

23

TAHOE X

Saturday afternoon in Lake Tahoe, Nevada, the *Tahoe X's* grand opening is in full swing. A gathering of beautiful people naturally brings out the "people persons." The psychiatrist Carl Gustav Jung theorized that people who are energized by other people have certain characteristics of personality known as *extraversion*. They are the recognizable "people persons" fawned over by the hedonists who gather to rub against each other in cocktail party *frottage*. Intrapsychically, extraverts do not have the internal buzz of activity that characterizes introverts; hence, the extraverts need of other people to jazz up their internal world. Their opposites, introverts, are characterized as shy and territorial. They naturally shy away from such spectacles, their internal world is already buzzing with activity. The common perception of introverts is not true; they are not party-poopers. Rather they are pooped by parties. They will attend a party if they can make an exit after a few minutes. In contrast, extraverts are drawn to social interaction like moths to flame. Many of Peter Marx's friends and colleagues are consummate extraverts. They love center stage. The *Tahoe X* celebration is just such a venue.

Minority partners from San Francisco and Chicago arranged the Tahoe trip as publicity for the opening of the second *X Marx the Spot* restaurant in the Lake Tahoe Grand Regent Hotel and Gambling Casino. Peter Marx seized the opportunity to impress his investors—mainly his neighbors. What better place to appease investors?

Not a single celebrant is aware of the blizzard and its affect upon loved ones at home. With all the excitement, no one thinks to call home; it wouldn't have mattered. Under blizzard conditions phones and power are temporarily in blackout. No phones, no fax, no e-mail. Mt. Kyle remains disconnected from the rest of the world just as Alzheimer's disease effectively disconnects the hypothalamus from the rest of the brain.

It is nearing 11 P.M. in the Grand Ballroom of the Lake Tahoe Grand Regent Hotel on Saturday night. The party is not winding down from the 7 P.M. start time. In polite society, it is a *faux pas* to arrive too early. The revelers beginning arriving around 7:15 P.M. and things got underway in earnest about an hour later.

Sam Mannerly, the San Francisco partner, opened the proceedings. Keeping the program lively, he provided a near-perfect balance between facts and figures from the substantive side of the ME portfolio and the sizzle of the prospectus for future sites.

He concludes his remarks with a virtual reality tour contrasting the interior decors of the original restaurant in Mt. Kyle with the Tahoe unit. A Bowser painting and replicas of the Warrior's Shield and twin-bladed tomahawk will grace the walls of the Tahoe unit. Next, he provides an overview of menu selections, wine listings, and other sundry items. Thoroughly convinced of their own investment genius, attendees raise glasses of champagne. Around 9 P.M., the agenda dictates the guests to proceed directly into the Tahoe version of *The X* for a sampling of the fare. Of course, drinks are on the house.

Celebrants surrounded by such tempting diversions have yet to consider the danger back home. Could anyone have foreseen the impending danger—the blizzard or the grizzly attack on Chief Munoz and Jon Marx? TV reception (certainly CNN or any of the twenty-four-hour news channels) is off-limits amid the celebration underway in the Grand Ballroom. What a stark contrast between this gala proceeding and the unnerving events transpiring in Mt. Kyle. Wealthy partygoers often feel insulated from personal harm whether to themselves or to their loved ones by a sense of false security like Prospero in Poe's *Masque of the Red Death*.

Sam Mannerly stands in the center of the crowded ballroom. Beside him stands the inner circle of minority partners, men and women of stature and fame. A strategy session is clearly impending. Only one person is missing. Sam Mannerly scans the crowd for the person of Peter Marx.

He is nowhere to be found.

24

RESIDENT GRIZZLY

Presently, back at the Sable, both Darwin and McAfee are pleased with the productivity of the meeting just concluded; the plethora of information has been dissected and further insight into the analysis of the *psychology of revenge* has been ascertained. (In academia, Darwin and McAfee view their collaboration as intellectual prospecting. In the process of mining topics, information is converted into the bounty of intellectual properties such as books, articles, and theory.)

Darwin is in the final editing stages of his most recent project, a kind of sequel from his doctoral dissertation *Getting Back: The Psychology of Revenge*, published eight years ago. His latest effort, entitled *Neurochemistry of Revenge*, provides a convincing argument that revenge is related to cognition (most likely angry or jealous thoughts) with neurochemical underpinnings that drives *chronic obsession*. Low levels of 5-HT and GABA, of course, account for the nasty mood providing the platform for acting out and harming others. The springboard to action is testosterone, the hormone of aggression, twisted by negative and vengeful thoughts. A glitch in adaptation has suddenly turned aggressive with a result not intended by natural selection. *The action of the revenger, armed with a chronic revenge obsession, does not to multiply the species, but, rather diminishes it.* Darwin's book ends on a scary note: Vengeance could wipe out the human race given enough revengers existed.

The racket outside quickly changes the sedate, academic climate inside to one of anxious anticipation.

"Good thing grizzlies don't exist in West Texas," remarks Wells McAfee offhandedly, "because that sounded just like one!" Both scholars are brought to their feet by the commotion outside the lodge. They hurry over to the large double windows of the lodge. The blizzard produces poor visibility but jazzes up the imaginations of the lodgers nonetheless. Susan Newby, a 30-year-old PRN nurse and part-time Mt. Kyle historian; Julie Q; Jill Frazier; and Jon's friends, Trevor, Ashley, and Gable, press toward the front windows in hopes of getting a glimpse.

"It's probably just the howling wind," remarks McAfee, not an alarmist. He knows these parts like the back of his hand. McAfee is an interesting character among many known to inhabit West Texas. He is a skeptic and practically deaf in both ears. He was born and raised in the Permian Basin, a vast stretch of prairie extending from Big Spring, Texas, westward to Big Bend and the border of Mexico. He is not bothered in the least by the sound of high wind. Like the movie character in *Blues Brothers*, Elwood Blues, who is forced to live next to a railway track in Chicago, long-time West Texans are so accustomed to the wind they barely notice it.

Clint Cooper, the manager of the Sable, runs into the lobby from his office just behind the main check-in counter.

"My God," exclaims Cooper with a surprised, worried look. "What on earth?"

"Settle down, Mr. Cooper, it's just the ghost grizzly" replies Shadow Darwin without even as much as a wink.

Scattered smiles and knowing glances, from everyone, but no laughter. The teenagers are too busy peering into the mouth of the blizzard to take note.

"Ghost grizzly? What do you mean?" asked Cooper, his eyes narrowing as though squinting.

"Just what I said. Legend has it that since the giant grizzly once heavily populated the mountains, the animal spirits left a ghost grizzly behind as a reminder to all the kindred spirits who perished though the centuries due to the excesses of man. As the legend goes, once ever so often the ghost is transformed into a physical presence, sort of an archetypal bear. It's a reminder of how overcivilized we have become. How we have lost touch with the essence of nature and have become a burden to each other."

Darwin's remarks seem timely considering the wilderness abuse with the Marx Desert Estates encroaching on the wildlife of the national park. Remembering his own residence, a sprawling 200-acre ranch outside Alpine, Darwin continues, "Discounting, of course, the Mt. Kyle development and my little spread, we are sensitive to the natural forest and wish it to remain untouched," concluded Darwin with a wink, obviously pleased with his slippery rendition.

"That's bloody absurd! Who in his right mind would buy such fabrication," replied an annoyed Cooper in his proper British accent. "It's rubbish!"

Now McAfee throws in his two cents worth. "Lots of folks around here don't think the legend is rubbish, Mr. Cooper," in his matter-of-fact inflection. "You see, Mr. Cooper, those of us who call West Texas our home know you can't completely tame something that is naturally wild. Geographically, the desert and the mountains are pretty much the way they were millions of years ago when the Great Permian Basin Sea dried up. The wilderness is wild and untamed, except for the small, civilized part—Mt. Kyle and its surrounding towns. Deserts produce all kinds of unexplained events. We accept this fact; it's our birthright. Why do you think the Indians named this very mountain range Chisos?"

Unable to make out anything unusual through the bay windows of the lodge, McAfee nonchalantly parks himself on one of the overstuffed sofas near the hearth. Shadow Darwin stands by the window and continues to peer out into the night, stroking his black shoulder-length hair. Presently, he returns his gaze to the lobby. He continues with McAfee's explanation.

"Mr. Cooper, Chisos means ghost. A storm such as this might be an announcement by nature of the ghost grizzly's return. Residents in these parts say, if you listen when the wind dies down, you can hear the grizzly growl on nights of the full moon." Besides being a brilliant scientist, Darwin is well versed in all kinds of West Texas legend and lore, the stuff of speculative logic. He may be the only person at the lodge willing to support the sound heard moments before as coming from a ghost instead of howling wind.

The good nurse and part-time historian Susan Newby, the kind of woman who is both attractive and bright with no specific identifiable characteristics to account for them, adds her perspective by first clearing her throat. "Gentleman, it is possible the sound you heard is due to some aspect of paranormal auditory hallucinatory experience. Furious storms have been known to produce both auditory and visual hallucinations due to heightened sensibilities, possibly akin to conditions known as 'cabin fever' or 'highway hypnosis.' It's all a matter of perception. When people peer out into the night while a storm is raging, imagination may cause objects to materialize out of trees and blowing snow. Late-night drivers who may have had too much to drink and who venture out of the warmth of their homes may be particularly affected," continues Ms. Newby.

Darwin and McAfee have enjoyed Ms. Newby's interesting comments through the years. They always invite her to their intellectual retreats. She offers explanations to conundrums that are completely novel. No one knows for sure what's going to come out when she opens her mouth. It's not boring and is mostly insightful.

"What the weather is doing is playing tricks with our perception," Susan Newby adds. Apparently, her psych rotation in nursing school produced a *psychologizing* devotee.

Following amused and puzzled looks from the group, Cooper remains more skeptical than amused. It is now way past the bedtimes of most of the lodgers, and tempers might start to boil over any minute.

"Incidentally, esteemed friends, what McAfee said about there being no grizzlies in West Texas is not necessarily true. *There is one grizzly in West Texas I am aware of.* In fact, it's right down the road at Sul Ross," Shadow Darwin announces like a proud father.

You could have heard a pin drop on the floor had it not been for the howling winds of the raging blizzard.

RESEARCH IMPLICATIONS

Chyler Haden, an aspiring actress and model living in North Hollywood, California, is in a local treatment center for the life-threatening eating disorder, anorexia nervosa. In this increasingly diagnosed disorder, patients starve themselves dangerously thin. If the disease continues, it becomes a chronic psychophysiological disorder. In severe cases, death ensues as the body literally eats its own vital organs in a last attempt to survive. Internal bleeding and organ dysfunction leading to heart failure are the usual causes of death.

Across the nation in Atlanta, Georgia, a routine procedure occurring thousands of times daily across North America is underway in the new ER at City Hospital. The patient Willis Zimmerman, age 49, is being wheeled into surgery for the removal of gallstones. Medication failed to dissolve his problematic stones. The prospect of surgery has upset family members.

At the same instant in Bangor, Maine, a jogger, out for a morning run is hit from behind by a drunk driver. He is taken by Care Flight helicopter to Metropolitan Hospital. During routine lab work following surgery to set his broken leg, advanced kidney disease is discovered. According to his wife, the patient had thought he had a slight kidney infection. Due to the trauma of the accident, he took a turn for the worse. Family members were called in.

All three patients might have experienced far different fates had the hibernation studies at Sul Ross State University had been funded years earlier. Instead, the studies are just getting underway. Those in need will have to wait—if they survive long enough.

Shadow Darwin's colleague, Dr. George Lennon of Sul Ross University in Alpine, Texas, is smiling as he sits down at his desk on Monday morning (prior to the events at the Sable Lodge) to contemplate the delivery of his research project—a female grizzly bear, affectionately known as "Bonzo." Dr. Lennon intends to unlock the secrets of hibernating grizzly bears. Their specimen is a healthy female grizzly standing almost 76" by Yellowstone records. She is tall for a female brown bear. She weighs a mere 458 pounds, minus the expected weight loss due to her cross-country excursion in a covered cage atop an 18-wheeler. In person, such dimensions would make her appear too tall for her weight; she would look emaciated.

The Lennon-Darwin research project was given the green light almost six months ago courtesy of funding provided by the Bear Conservation Group of North America (BCGNA). Now, with funds in place, research guidelines laid out, and a trained staff in animal psychology ready to begin upon the arrival of Bonzo. Bonzo has been loaned to Lennon and Darwin courtesy of the Greater Yellowstone Ecosystem's "loan" program. She arrived Monday afternoon and the staff have been busy ever since. The Greater Yellowstone Ecosystem consists of 18-million acres of wilderness situated in Wyoming, Montana, and Idaho. It is a sanctuary for grizzly bears. Since 1975, grizzlies have been listed as "threatened" under the Endangered Species Act. This conservatory is one of the few remaining areas where these animals live and flourish.

An ecosystem can be the size of a few animal droppings or as large as a planet. For endangered grizzlies, their ecosystem is the vast expanse of Yellowstone. Bear management specialists from the Ecosystem were enthusiastic about Bonzo's transfer to Sul Ross. A team of neuropsychologists may unlock many secrets of human development. Hibernation studies may provide long-sought-after answers as to why patients suffer from an array of dysfunctions including eating disorders, gallstones, and kidney failure. Hope for future health may ride on research like the type recently funded at Sul Ross. Formerly a nationally recognized Bear Management Specialist at the Yellowstone Ecosystem, Dr. Lennon realized a dream when he was able to return to academics for a sabbatical, and to author a study with Shadow Darwin.

The one grizzly in West Texas represents the newest addition to Dr. Lennon's neuropsychology lab. The national alliance of ecosystem conservationists, along with the BCGNA, and a private stipend from Peter Marx, funded a three-year study centering on the physiologically adaptive characteristics of a pregnant grizzly. West Texas is cold enough for hibernation studies in late December, January, and February.

Intriguing questions surround the physiological mechanisms of hibernation in the grizzly. For example, what biochemical mechanism allows bears to hibernate up to seven months without voiding body wastes such as urine or fecal matter (humans would die of toxicity caused by a fraction of these accumulated wastes). In pregnancy, what mechanism allows the fertilized egg, a mass of cells known as the blastocyst, to float in the uterus for up to six months without implanting in the endometrium? Then, what neurochemical process does it use to detect enough accumulated body fat to support pregnancy during hibernation? How does the conceptus (the fertilized egg) survive, apparently in suspended animation? These questions will shed light on a myriad of human medical complaints. The bear must be in uninterrupted hibernation for as long as possible along with state-of-the-art monitoring equipment to record physiological states.

Bonzo was not supposed to escape the Sul Ross conservatory during a blizzard. Was it nothing more than a freak accident caused by lack of experience in handling a guest with such a large appetite? How long had the grizzly been missing? Did the monitoring system malfunction for days? How could security have lapsed so drastically? Unfortunately for those in the Sable Lodge, it has long been known that grizzlies travel fast and their range is wide and far even when they should be hibernating. Especially, when they're hungry.

Grizzlies are intrepid creatures. They have no natural predators. They fear nothing inclement weather throws at them, including blizzards. No door of a lodge will prevent a grizzly from barging in, sampling the human buffet, and using a sliver of wood from the splintered door as a toothpick to remove human leftovers.

26

SOMETHING STRANGE

Deputy Julie Q walks across the lobby into *The X*, joining Trevor and the two girls at the four-topper inside the vacant restaurant. Courtesy of Jill Frazier and the discourteous blizzard, patrons vacated hours ago. Jill is making preparations for the teenagers to stay in the lodge thanks to Marx Enterprises. Privately, she fears the worst for Jon Marx. She reads the same fear and uncertainty in the faces of Jon's friends. Julie fakes a broad smile as she pulls up an extra chair and sits between Trevor and Ashley. Once upon a time, Julie dated Peter Marx. In their whirlwind relationship, she met all of Jon's friends. Their breakup produced a good, solid friendship. Unlike most of his previous mésalliances, both Julie and Peter still like and respect each other. Neither one elected to burn bridges. She wonders if Jill has enough maturity to follow in her footsteps when Peter decides he has little in common with a 23-year-old.

"Hi guys," Julie says flashing her best demeanor. "I know you guys are worried, but, any minute, I expect to hear from the chief regarding Jon's whereabouts." Speaking to Trevor she continues, "He told me you called … you're right to be concerned about Jon, but don't worry, Trevor." She pats his hand on the table. "The chief is a good tracker; he and Homer will find Jon in no time." She forces another trademark smile. Trevor could not find one to return.

The Mach 1 fishtails away from the attacking grizzly on the slick road as though wagging the state championship sticker affixed to the rear bumper at the creature's naughty antics. The large tires grip a portion of the road not completely encrusted with ice, giving Jon Marx and the grievously injured police chief a relatively speedy escape. Jon hears the earth-shattering growl of the creature once again. The howling wind precludes the exact sounds emitting from the creature. His mind races slightly ahead of his heart. Both are pumping with adrenaline's fight-or-flight response and therefore neglectful of acoustic specificity.

"Chief, are you OK?" yells Jon Marx with difficulty. His lips and mouth are still cold enough to make speech difficult. His voice appears to come from a deep well.

A distinct moan issues from the chief.

At least he's alive, thinks Jon. "Hang on Chief, we're almost to the lodge!" Jon cannot determine through the rearview or sideview mirrors whether or not the grizzly is in hot pursuit. Is the creature ready to leap on the roof of his car at any moment? This is his greatest fear. Jon glances up as far as he can toward the roof. He sees nothing but falling snow and black sky. He drives straight through the Sable's front entry flowerbed, crashing over and destroying Clint Coopers's newly covered bushes around the small fountain disarmed due to winter. It is the straightest shot possible from his position in the entryway to the front door of the lodge. Jon presses hard on the horn to announce his emergency to anyone who might render aid. Unfortunately, the horn competes with the howling winds of the blizzard. Visibility is near zero.

The time is 10:43 P.M. in *The X*. As Jon's friends contemplate Julie Q's remarks, the sudden blaring of a car horn brings everyone to a standing posture. They rush into the lobby of the Sable. Clint Cooper, the lodge manager, emerges from his office behind the front counter with one arm in his robe and the other trying to find the remaining sleeve. Shadow Darwin races around one of the huge support columns. He has been throwing his Bowie over by the hearth trained on a bull's eye he taped to an oversized log he leaned against the wall next to the hearth. Carefully replacing the Bowie in his Velcro leg strap, he joins the others. McAfee joins Darwin near the front door. Susan Newby retired to her room for the evening and is presumably asleep. The raging wind of the blizzard most likely muffs all extraneous acustica.

"What on earth?" cries Clint Cooper. "Who is this at this hour?"

"It's Jon, I know it is," replies Trevor in a voice that rings with certainty and conviction. The group presses toward the front door.

Suddenly, Jon Marx bursts through the door like the Jim Carrey character in the movie *The Mask* with his stolen bank loot. The cold winds of the blizzard blow into the lobby like an Alaskan freight train over frozen tracks—powerful and loud. The Arctic wind tunnel seems endless.

The doorknob slams against the wall knocking a hole clear through the sheetrock. The scene is instant chaos. Both Ashley and Gable grab each other and scream in unison.

"Jon, you're safe, thank God! I knew the chief would find you," cries an excited Julie Q.

Almost passing out from his frightful experience, Jon collapses on the lobby floor. Clint Cooper hurries to close the door behind him.

"Don't close the door! The chief's in the car; he's hurt badly," gasps Jon in the general direction of Clint Cooper. Momentarily, Jon has forgotten about the creature that may have devoured the chief by now.

"Let's fetch him," replied Shadow Darwin looking directly at Trevor. The two dash out into the night, fresh on the tracks of adrenaline. Neither one wears a parka, nor are they aware of the potential presence of the dangerous grizzly lurking somewhere outside the door in the mouth of the blizzard.

Ashley, Gable, and Julie Q attend to Jon Marx who appears close to shock; they half-drag and half-carry Jon to the hearth, perhaps his last resting place on this earth. Moments earlier, Shadow Darwin had replenished the fire with several logs. The heat is intense. Jon responds slowly to the healing warmth of the flames. The girls make him comfortable on one of the sofas. He appears unhurt except for a large red whelp on his forehead. His face registers the color of parchment paper, appearing drained of blood. His lips are still a light blue.

"Jon, what happened?" exclaims a wide-eyed Julie. Ashley and Gable are pressing close to his side hugging each other and nearly in tears.

Just as Jon is about to answer, the door bursts open allowing the blizzard train to enter. Reflexively, Jon screams in the direction of the door "Quick, it's the grizzly, he'll kill us!"

The tall stature of Shadow Darwin appears in the doorway. He emerges from the blizzard carrying the front half of Chief Munoz. Trevor follows carrying the rear half. Fortunately, they are carrying the whole person between them as though the chief is on a stretcher. Trevor manages to close the door with his powerful back and legs. They bring him to the sofa nearest the fire. Darwin observes frozen blood on the chief's hood.

"Quick, wake up Newby," cries Darwin to Clint Cooper. "The chief has a nasty wound. Quick now!"

Cooper sprints away. The group huddles around Jon Marx and the unconscious chief. Fear hangs heavy in the lobby on the faces of the lodgers.

"A grizzly attacked us … it nearly killed both of us … it was right behind me … it's out there now. It's the most bad ass thing I have ever seen," Jon said in a stream of barely connected words.

"Slow down son," said Shadow Darwin. "You said a grizzly attacked you, just now … a grizzly?"

"Yes, a grizzly," said Jon shaking from limb to limb.

Julie Q's criminal justice academy training kicks in. Without a word to the others she draws her sidearm and leaves the group to check the front door and entryway to the lodge. A quick surveillance of the front entryway and the front lawn produces nothing but the outline of Jon's wrecked car with both doors ajar and blowing snow spilling into the car from all directions. The sound is almost deafening from the raging winds of the blizzard. Can it get any worse?

Susan Newby arrives in the lobby dressed in a terrycloth night robe and slippers. Her auburn hair is pulled back exposing a freshly washed face. She has known Chief Munoz all her life. She kneels down to check his wound. She discovers a very nasty gash to the chief's neck punctuated by four, deep claw-like incisions about a half-inch deep encrusted in frozen blood. It is one of the deepest and nastiest wounds she has ever witnessed.

"Quick, get me some warm water and any topical antiseptic you can find, anything … STAT," said the nurse reverting to her emergency room training. She knows a wound of this kind almost always means instant infection.

Briefly, an out-of-breath Clint Cooper returns with everything Newby requested. In the excitement of the moment, Shadow Darwin dashes through the lobby grabbing his parka on the fly. He disappears around the long corridor leading to the side entrance of the lodge. The chief remains unconscious and presumably near death.

Fear grips the lodgers as the storm continues to build momentum. No measly wooden door can prevent the ravaging grizzly from ripping through at any moment and killing everyone.

A thought races across Darwin's mind from a graduate course in existential psychology: The existential author Jean-Paul Sartre might suggest the chaotic scenario in the lobby is fast becoming a real-life *No Exit*.

27

GLASS-EYE EDDIE

In the Sable lobby, events are unfolding quickly. Susan Newby is attending to the chief. After a few tense minutes, she cleans and bandages the near-fatal wound. Now the chief is resting comfortably following an injection of a strong sedative. She fears he may have lost too much blood to survive. How can the grievously injured chief be airlifted with no way to communicate to the outside world? The blizzard has disconnected the lodgers from life-saving outside intervention.

Jon Marx is recounting his recent scare with Trevor and the girls. With the help of Trevor's flask of Amaretto, Jon slowly regains the blush on his cheeks. Darwin, McAfee, and Julie stand by the desk plotting strategy with Clint Cooper.

Suddenly, the supposedly locked door flies open followed by the blizzard train blowing snow into the lobby like trash swirling over a playground. Instinctively, Julie draws her side arm. Everyone braces for the appearance of the grizzly. Their eyes are riveted on the door expecting a rampaging bear to barge into the lobby intent on consuming a late night supper. The figure that emerges from the wind tunnel of snow is the local "heavy Chevy" mechanic and part-time handyman "Glass-Eye" Eddie Hawkins.

No one is positively sure of anything regarding one of Mt. Kyle's most colorful characters. The one thing they are absolutely sure of is his nickname. He does have a glass eye for all the world to see. As far as Peter Marx is concerned when a mechanic has the skill to restore both the bodies and engines of "muscle cars" to mint condition, who cares about the sordid details of their past or if they happen to have one good eye or two. Eddie refuses to wear an eye patch over his eye, so the glass eye is obvious in the tradition of Peter Faulk, the TV detective in *Columbo*. One eyebrow is slightly upturned and the other—the one over the glass eye—is downturned.

Glass-Eye Eddie manhandles the door and turns around to greet the anxious lodgers. He is dressed in green camouflage, black high-top boots, and a bright yellow parka with no hood. He is carrying a large-caliber rifle, possibly a Winchester scope model.

Peter Marx met Eddie at a "muscle car" exhibition last year in Midland, Texas. Right away, he offered to pay Eddie's moving expenses to Mt. Kyle. Eddie agreed. The first car Eddie tinkered with upon his arrival was Shadow Darwin's '79 L-82 Corvette he purchased in an auction. Glass-Eye Eddie became the new tenant of the defunct automotive repair shop left behind by Carl Wright, the former tenant who died suddenly last summer. His shop is a mere stone's throw from the Sable. Glass-Eye Eddie doubles as the Sable's groundskeeper, and as general maintenance man for the residents of the Desert Estates. Like Riff Raff in *Rocky Horror Picture Show,* he is an odd-looking specimen of humanity, yet he is an effective handyman. He is known as Mt. Kyle's "lone wolf"—he lives alone, eats alone, and works alone. He wears a certain grin on his face as though he knows something others don't.

Once, Clint Cooper observed Glass-Eye Eddie stepping off the distance around the side of the lodge property for the construction of a fence (the plan was later dropped). On an earlier visit Cooper remarked to Shadow Darwin how Eddie's mannerism appeared more characteristic of the *Australopithecus*, the species of ape prior to the more commonly known "missing link." Clint Cooper's observation has to do with the way he walked around the property. Eddie craned his head forward ahead of his shoulders, and his long arms swung up and down like an ape. Darwin agreed with Clint's assessment. Good naturedly, they concluded Glass-Eye may have more roots in *Australopithecus* than *Homo sapien.*

Glass-Eye Eddie hurries through the door and braces his wide body against the door and succeeds in closing it the first time. He appears to be in his mid-thirties and is built like a fireplug, short and sturdy. He is dressed as though he's heading to a deer blind.

"Eddie, you almost got yourself shot," says Julie Q.

"I thought the door was secure. The lock must have broken when the young man smashed the knob against the wall," replies Clint Cooper. He disappears through the door of his office.

Julie Q returns the .38 to her side holster. "Perhaps we should double-check it this time or shove something heavy against it," Julie suggests.

"I don't think a table, no matter how heavy, is going to hold a 700-pound grizzly at bay," remarks a slightly amused Shadow Darwin. "Just keep your gun handy, Julie. A bullet should be more than enough to discourage a grizzly ... if there is one."

Momentarily, Clint Cooper returns from his office carrying a sawed-off, over-and-under Winchester hand rifle. Everyone looks with surprise at the illegal weapon. It has short twin barrels that are configured over-and-under and connected to a worn wooden stock just long enough to fit snugly into the palm of the hand. "I've had this little guy for years. Just in case of robbery or some bloody West Texas redneck comes in looking for trouble. The actor who played Josh Randall on the old TV western *Wanted Dead or Alive* once slept here. Steve McQueen, rest his soul." Clint Cooper looks upward in a universal gesture of respect for the dead. (Many years ago when Clint Cooper first became the manager of the Sable, he let it slip to a local resident that his parents named him after the American actor Clint Eastwood. This bit of information, plus his fondness for Western movies may explain why no one has ever observed Cooper wearing any type of shoes except exotic leather, Western cowboy boots.) "Yes, sir, Mr. McQueen slept in the celebrity suite, top floor. He complimented me on the privacy we afforded him during his stay. When he left he said he would send me a gift. You could have knocked me over with a feather when this arrived by special courier about a month later. I thought it was a replica, you know, a play gun. The note signed by Mr. McQueen made it clear it was the real thing. It was one of the many similar guns used on the set. Apparently, this one was getting too old to be useful any more. Immediately, I had a gunsmith work it over. It really works. And it's priceless. It might come in handy tonight," remarks a proud Clint Cooper.

"Just keep it pointed down" Shadow requests nervously.

"I'll pretend I didn't see it," said Julie Q, aware of its illegality.

Eddie speaks after dusting the snow off his parka and stomping the snow off his boots on his way across the room to the inviting hearth. "Heard someone laying on a car horn pretty hard and some kind of commotion. I just came over to see if y'all need any help. I thought the lodge would be vacant except for you, Mr. Gary Cooper." (Eddie's remark is in obvious reference to the actor

Gary Cooper, who became a star playing in Western movies.) Glass-Eye has never called Clint Cooper by his real name. Cooper doesn't seem to mind.

Shadow Darwin fills in the details of the chief's wounds and Jon Marx's claims.

"You're kidding!" remarks Eddie with a look of surprise from his one good eye, the right one. " A grizzly in these parts? You're kidding, of course."

"Don't make light of it, Eddie," replies Darwin. "For your information, there is at least one grizzly in West Texas. If fact, it is—or was—down the road in Alpine. My colleague, Dr. Lennon, acquired her on Monday. Her name is Bonzo, for heaven's sake, not Cujo. She's part of our hibernation studies."

"Dr. Darwin, the chief's injuries are not play-like boo-boos," remarks the prissy-mouth of Clint Cooper.

"No way!" is all Glass-Eye Eddie can manage.

28

ONE-EYED SENTRY

"Shadow, shouldn't we at least try to verify the bear's where-abouts with your colleague?" asks Julie Q.

"Brilliant deduction," states a suddenly serious Clint Cooper.

"The phones have been down for sometime as you know. A cell phone is useless, due to the discourtesy of the blizzard out there. Mr. Cooper already tried to call out when we discovered Jon's emergency. We may not have any way to communicate for hours, perhaps days. Since it's almost midnight now, the phone crews from Bell can't make it out of the driveway, much less up here; not in this storm. We better prepare ourselves for a long night and the worst possible scenario," Shadow pauses (a trademark pregnant pause he uses to let his words sink in, calculated for effect). "Until we know more we must assume the grizzly somehow escaped, and she's hungry and disoriented. In such a state, she attacked the chief and Jon. And, something else—we may not have lights for much longer. The transformers and power lines are attached to poles, which are becoming more pendulous with the weight of snow. Power has not been converted to the underground type, which is not in our favor."

"I suggest we make a big fire that will last throughout the night," added Julie Q.

"Good idea, Deputy," Darwin adds.

"It's Julie," replies Julie Quixotica, eyes blazing in Darwin's direction.

"OK, Julie," Shadow blushes as he speaks her name. He then turns to Clint Cooper.

"Mr. Cooper, round up all the candles you can find and bring them to the table. This table is our command post." Darwin indi-cates the intended location to the others by pointing to a large coffee table set in the center of the four overstuffed brown leather sofas. Shadow Darwin is displaying the behavior expected of a leader; he has always been perceived as a leader since he was a kid.

The arrangement of the low-flung table in relation to the sofas works nicely as a conversation pit. It is directly situated on top of an expensive ornamental rug in front of the huge fireplace. Plenty of logs are stored in wide slits on either side of the hearth constructed of Granbury stone brick. It makes sense to use this spot as a strategic site due to its location and configuration.

Glass-Eye Eddie prepares to make his exit. "Y'all seem to have everything under control. I may be more useful to you by keeping watch from my place across the road."

The lodgers fail to see how a one-eyed sentry could make much difference one way or the other, but no one is prepared to say otherwise. Besides being a loner, Eddie has the additional reputation of being a little slow upstairs. None of the others seem surprised by his suggestion. Eddie continues, "that way, if I don't get him first, maybe one of you will. When you hear Winny (referring to his Winchester no doubt), it is a signal that he's dead or he's on his way here. If you need me, just pull the trigger on your .38, Ms. Deputy."

Eddie has a detached look about him as though his mind is always predisposed. Clearly, he is not the sharpest knife in the drawer. Never married, he is a confirmed bachelor and a workaholic. It's probably a good thing. Most women want someone with a bit more electricity than a 60-watt bulb and one good eye. After the attractive Jill Frazier spurned his advances when he arrived in Mt. Kyle last year, Eddie lost his manly courage to approach other females. Now, his love of hunting and tinkering with automobiles dominates his somewhat gloomy life.

At any given time, he is knee deep in restoring numerous vintage 1960-1979 "muscle cars" for the residents of Mt. Kyle. In addition, he does general maintenance work for residents. He is handy with nail, hammer, and saw. "Odd Job" would be a good nickname for Glass-Eye Eddie.

Truly, Glass-Eye Eddie Hawkins holds a unique place in the Mt. Kyle community. He is not wealthy, nor does he own land there. Eddie's story is simply not being afraid of hard work, being in the right place at the right time, and loving "muscle cars." He completely restored the love of his life, a midnight blue 1970 427

Olds 442. She is his constant companion. He talks to the car like the car is a real person. At times, he pats her doors, side panels, and hood as though he is affectionately fondling a lover.

Residents wouldn't know he existed if they didn't see his car or hear music coming from his shop. He favors two "Hanks" in country and western music: the original Hank Williams and Hank Thompson and the Brazos Valley Boys. He owns every record made between the two Hanks. He hums along with the lyrics as he piddles with the big engines. Mt. Kyle residents accept Glass-Eye Eddie for what he is, a rare find, and a utilitarian interloper with an apparent heart of gold, even though he has only one good eye, talks to his car, and listens to Hank Williams and Hank Thompson rockabilly from dusk to dawn.

Eddie made a small residence for himself with an add-on room connected to his shop. It works perfectly for sleeping and eating quarters. The fact that he's a loner and a dimwit, and possesses only one good eye does not distract from the practical logic of having someone with his abilities around.

On this night, having a least one eye and two strong legs to scout around in the darkness for a return visit by a dangerous grizzly is, in a nutshell, the value of a man like Glass-Eye Eddie Hawkins.

29

THE PLAN

Glass-Eye Eddie leaves the Sable for his post across the road leaving the lodgers ill at ease in having one good eye for a sentry. Shadow Darwin assembles the group around the large coffee table. The lodgers sit on the four overstuffed sofas configuring the points of a compass. The table is adorned with about forty candles of all shapes, sizes, and colors. It looks like some kind of pagan ritual intending to ward off evil spirits. A blue plastic cigarette lighter and several gray fold-over match containers inscribed with *X Marx the Spot* in navy blue letters litter the table.

Jon and Trevor are sitting with their girlfriends on the sofa facing the others. McAfee, Darwin, and Clint Cooper sit on the opposing couch facing *The X*. Susan Newby, attending to the chief's wounds at random intervals, sits on the sofa directly facing the fireplace. Julie and Jill sit on the remaining sofa in idle conversation. With her head tilted, Jill is staring at her own waist-length raven hair as she examines strains of it with her thumb and forefinger as though contemplating its protein content. Random conversation is brought to a silence by the voice of Shadow Darwin.

"Let's decide our strategy for the night—who is on watch and what procedures to follow. I don't know about you, but I would like to survive the night in one piece," says Darwin matter-of-factly. Darwin checks his watch. "I have a quarter past midnight, the same as the lobby clock over there. I'll take the first shift from now until 2:30. Clint, I'll need your Josh Randall." Shadow casts his eyes in the direction of Clint's sawed-off over-and-under propped against the sofa. Shadow is not confident his Bowie would be effective against such a formidable foe. "The rest of you try to get some sleep."

Clint Cooper provides pillows and blankets for everyone from the Sable's large walk-in linen storage. Next, Clint Cooper suggests an elaborate exit plan. Shadow sums up the value of Clint's suggestion in the lodgers' one, life-saving oasis—an impenetrable spot even for an agitated grizzly. Behind a masquerading heavy oak door just to the right of the entrance to *The X*, a storage closet appears complete with the words "Storage" inscribed on the door. Actually, the façade masks a two-inch-thick steel door behind it. Most residents in Mt. Kyle have witnessed for themselves, or heard about the charade, but visitors haven't, which is the point.

The small floor-safe in Clint Cooper's quarters behind the front desk never contains more than a few hundred dollars. On the other hand, the walk-in vault, a seven-by-twelve-foot steel room fits snugly behind the oak door façade. The antique Union Pacific Railroad vault often contains thousands of dollars in sales from the Sable and *The X*. It also contains valuables lodgers leave for safe keeping during their stay. Some larger items of value such as Peter Marx's European antique purchases are covered in drop cloths or bundled in their original packing material. It is rumored that infamous Old West train robbers including Billy the Kid and Butch Cassidy and the Sundance Kid had no luck robbing the UPR vaults.

Clint Cooper makes the necessary left and right turns on the large calibrated dial o unlock the walk-in vault. Next, he set the access handle to the down (or open) position assuring a speedy entrance. Now all the lodgers have to do is pull on the access handle and enter, affording themselves a safe haven. Fortuitously, the vault can be opened from the inside as well. The downside of the vault is formidable—it has no exhaust fan or way to get circulating fresh air from outside. Yet, in the dire situation facing the lodgers, they take what they can get.

Calmed somewhat by their newly hatched exit plan, the lodgers finally begin to settle for the night, except for the teenagers. They are simply too wired, too jazzed, partly because of danger and partly due to hormones. Fear kindles lust in the thin sexualized bodies of teenagers; they adhere to a universal anthem of adolescent sensibility: *We are the bulletproof, we are the fearless, and we are risk-takers. We face danger and laugh.*

Forget what lurks outside.

The "D-Spot"

Hollywood producers have long known that teenage guys like to watch scary movies with their girlfriends. Being scared is roughly in the same league with dancing, kissing, drinking alcohol, and smoking the illegal "cigaweed." Sometimes, talk alone does the trick. Showing off "your stuff" at the beach also helps. When guys see girls dressed in skimpy outfits, they think of sex. (When they see chalkboards, trees, or clouds, they think of sex too.) Foreplay is the point of teenage movie themes. It might be true that males think *everything* is foreplay. To some extent, the aforementioned activities have aphrodisiac qualities; they work as sexual stimulants, which unleash a mix of powerful neurochemistry.

Neurotransmitters in the brain and hormones of the body prepare audiences who watch scary movies for the well-known physiological condition of fight-or-flight. In the case of teenagers, it can lead to more serious foreplay before they ever leave the theater. The almost identical condition of being scared sitting in a dark theater is the jazzed-up, highly excitable state of foreplay that must exist prior to consensual sex.

Partners destined for sex, experience heightened libidos with biochemical underpinnings in a predictable scenario. This is especially true when a natural amphetamine in brain chemistry known as PEA brings the participants together in the first place. PEA (or phenylethylamine) is known to trigger the "romantic rush" behind physical attraction. It acts as a natural brain stimulant and is almost impossible to ignore. Individuals who are drawn to each other by virtue of PEA likely become intimate. When a female is convinced a guy is cute enough, smart enough, and worthy enough, she may consent to what comes natural. In other words,

101

girls need a good reason to have sex while guys just need a place. PEA provides a new spin on the expression "PEA-brain." This ubiquitous neurotransmitter, acting as natural brain "speed," works as well on young brains as on older ones. With couples high on their own PEA, they feel both arousal signals and pleasure signals in the brain's pleasure pathways of the Medial Forebrain Bundle (MFB). This region in the anterior hypothalamus is rich in dopamine, the neurotransmitter of pleasure, sexual behavior, and libido (sex drive). Now we know why summer movies (as well as midnight movies) are replete with fear-inducing or libidinal evoking themes.

In the 1960s, experimental psychologist, Dr. James Olds made us aware of this region when he implanted electrodes in the brain of a dangerous psychiatric patient. One of the electrons passed directly through the center of the MFB and could be stimulated to produce a powerful message of pleasure when activated by a button (connected to the electrode) worn on the patient's belt. The patient had to be disconnected when it was discovered he had practically worn out the button by constantly pressing it all day long—day after day. The patient received perhaps the best therapy in the world, the equivalent of one orgasm after another! Yet, he was doing nothing to regain his grip on reality (or perhaps he didn't want to).

Since that time, the "spot" in the MFB—the spot where dopamine flows like a fountain—has been christened as the "pleasure pathway." It works in this way due to the ubiquitous pleasure neurotransmitter, dopamine. It has been suggested that neuropsych call this spot of pleasure *The D-spot*.

Norepinephrine and dopamine are prevalent in the brain while adrenaline does its magic as a blood messenger in the endocrine system. Add the powerful androgenic hormone, testosterone, and the sexual urge is no more than an overpowering drug. At this point, a strong elastic piece of latex rubber is probably the only thing likely to come between the "wheel" and "road."

Such are the conditions surrounding Jon and Ashley, Trevor and Gable, on this night of strange occurrences, exacerbated by the fear factor—the impending appearance of the dangerous predator at any moment.

They might as well be in the balcony of a multiplex watching yet another teenage movie.

This time there is a real serial killer somewhere just beyond the theater doors not thinking of popcorn and Coke.

A-N-T-I-C-I-P-A-T-I-O-N

A t about 1 A.M. Jon taps the knee of Ashley who is snuggling close to him with her head on his shoulder. She only pretends to sleep. Actually, her pulse indicates something else.

"Let's go!" whispers Jon.

"Where?" answered Ashley in muted tones, typical of the coquettish behavior expected of females raised in North American culture. Young females act forever clueless by the advances of males; yet psychological research into the mating game suggests, increasingly, that females know exactly what's happening scene-by-scene—even before it happens.

The great Swiss psychoanalyst Carl Gustav Jung was ahead of the curve in his theory of the archetypical anima and animus. In this theory, each sex inherits gender qualities of the other. In an insightful look at human nature, he concluded that males and females really do understand each other's libido-driven behavior more than they admit. It's just a convenient ploy to pretend they don't. Even "acting dumb" or clueless can be stimulating (as witnessed in the "ditzy" blond stereotype). The traditional gender divide—males as pursuers and females as objects of pursuit—provides convenient stereotypes and pigeonholes for behavior.

Basically, social psychologists know why the 1960s failed as an exercise in role-reversal. It's not the nature (or training) of females to be the pursuers; they feel more comfortable being pursued. Great job if you can get it. And, they have it now as an exclusive gender property. Simply, the societal experiment that occurred in the 1960s and early 1970s did not fit female brain chemistry. Females set the rules and the boundaries. Males must learn to take "no" for an answer, cool their jets, and that's that. Most males get over this delicate relationship mandate by the time they become college freshmen. They keep asking. They keep pursuing. We're not sure if the saying, "the old college try," relates to the archaic male pastime of engineering "panty raids" on campus or just prowling around the dorms trying to find an intimate partner. Time changes meaning.

Jon continues. "You know, silly, to my Dad's office behind *The X* ... we can get more comfortable there ... stretch out ... not be around these old farts."

"Sure we can," replies a wide-eyed Ashley. You could cut a-n-t-i-c-i-p-a-t-i-o-n in the air with a dull butter knife. Even girls who have planned out their lives far in advance regarding nights such as this have immense trouble disengaging a brain and body surging with PEA.

Working simultaneously, PEA-brains plant erotic thoughts that lead to action, while testosterone manhandles the body's thoughts into action. This chemical cocktail makes participants shortsighted and stupid. Perhaps Freud was correct regarding hedonism. Guys and girls really do the dumbest things under the influence of PEA-brains.

"OK, but no funny business" replies Ashley knowing full well what's on the agenda.

"Jon," asks Ashley as she interrupts his efforts to stand up. "Do you think it's safe to be so far from the others? You know whatever attacked you is still out there."

"It's OK. We haven't heard anything for hours now. We probably scared it away. We'll be OK," replies Jon in the most confident voice he can find. He completes his efforts to stand and pulls Ashley to her feet. The blanket is tossed aside revealing the curvaceous figure of a young woman, who perhaps desires the same intimate embrace as Jon, but by convention, may not admit it.

Neither Trevor nor Gable missed one sentence in the exchange between their two friends.

"We're coming too," said Trevor on Gable's behalf. Trevor helps his girlfriend to her feet. The young and the restless head for a rendezvous in romantic cocoon of *The X*.

However, Shadow Darwin, listening to the muted whispers of the teenagers, isn't buying any of it and intercedes. Before the teenagers can advance one more step, Darwin emerges from the shadows. "Where do you kids think you're going?"

"My Dad's place, Dr. Darwin," replies Jon in hushed tones. "It's just as safe as it is here. In fact, it has no doors. It's only accessible through the lobby here."

"You're forgetting the windows," replies Darwin.

"Well, sir, I thought of that, too. The windows in the apartment are so small no bear could ever wiggle through it. By the time you hear breaking glass, you can be there to protect us from Smokey the Bear."

"Don't make light of this son. After all, you were the one that barely escaped death. You know more about what's out there than any of us, except the chief," replies Darwin.

The girls do not make eye contact with Darwin.

"I know, sir, but it's obviously gone somewhere else. Do you think Smokey is going to hang out in a blizzard like this? And besides, weren't you young once? We're all 18."

Then act like it thinks Darwin in internal dialogue. "All right, damn it," replies an annoyed Darwin. But, officially, I don't know anything about this. I'm going to stand here in the middle of the hall so I can get a good look into *The X* just in case. Are you girls OK with this?" asks Darwin rhetorically, not expecting to get a response. Ashley and Gable look at each other and nod affirmatively with their heads down.

"We just want some time alone to talk, that's all," Gabby says in a soft voice that almost sounds convincing.

In such cases, girls must give the green light to male advances. That's the way it works in civilized society. In parked cars with hands groping in all directions and breaths fogging windows, girls are the harbingers of sex in all its varieties. Guys know this beforehand. They must play by the rules. For example, girls often help less-experienced guys who fumble with the latch on her bra strap by undoing it themselves. Other guys are so good at it they would make excellent safecrackers in the New West. They can "pop a latch" on a bra strap in seconds flat.

But, when it gets down to the nitty-gritty, the panties must take a slide off the girl's derriere as the final barrier. Girls have to raise their behinds just a little for the material to the clear the upholstery of the car seat. This is the unmitigated green light. It's downhill from there. For all intents and purposes, this highly anticipated event marks the male entry into manhood.

With the green light to proceed, Jon's group disappears into *The X*, leaving behind Shadow Darwin shaking his head and reminiscing about his own youth far removed from this time and place.

Freud's *theory of sublimation* is therapeutic to older males once intoxicated by the sights, sounds, and smells of the young and the restless libido. In this theory, libido (sex drive) is refocused into more *cognitive* (rational) domains allowing males to actually concentrate and focus on more creative endeavors. They can write books, create art and science, and become a role model for those who seek career success.

The downside of this rechanneling of libido is the loss of the visceral fun of sexual anticipation, tactile stimulation, and all the libidinal accoutrements appertaining.

The time of a male's youth where he has little to answer for may be gone, but not forgotten, in his young-as-ever psyche. Sublimation is a benchmark of middle age. The phrase "middle-aged" crazy suddenly makes sense. Corvettes and motorcycles become the mistresses of middle-aged males full-blown into libido-taming sublimation. It's also a handy device for saving marriage, family, and one's standing in the community.

With hormones raging in the lair of Peter Marx, the air is supersaturated with pumping testosterone. The heat in the room stands in sharp contrast to the frigid cruelties of the blizzard. Yet, before the first touch or the first embrace, a sudden noise interferes with surging PEA-brains. Hormones recede. PEA-brains clear for rational thought somewhere in the vicinity of the perception of fear, superego (conscience), and the startle response.

The small reading light Jon left on for navigation to the bathroom blinks on and off like it has a short. Jon had no idea where his father keeps the candles. Suddenly, a dull, thud-like noise rattles the wall just behind them. Both girls scream. Jon and Trevor practically run into each other trying to get to their feet. Is it a manly gesture of defending their women, or is it due to sheer fright? We'll never know.

"What the hell was that?" Ashley cries.

"I don't know. I think Smokey's out there," says Trevor who looks directly at Jon.

"You know, buddy I think you're right," confirms Jon.

The "thump thump" sound outside the window returns.

A voice from the other side of the door answers, "Get out here, it's Darwin. Hurry up! We're going to lose power any minute. The grizzly has returned."

Momentarily, Jon opens the door. The girls grin sheepishly amid tasseled hair. Their necks are mottled red—the mark of foreplay known appropriately as the sex flush, one of the more obvious findings of Masters and Johnson.

Darwin is aware of what he just interrupted. But survival is one emotion more powerful than foreplay or sex. But not by much. Just ask anyone under the influence of PEA-brains.

32

SECOND WATCH

The blizzard gets its second wind just after 2 A.M., close to the time designated as Julie's turn on the second watch. Darwin is concerned that things are coming to a head with the stress of the storm and the grizzly lurking nearby. With Jon and Ashley and Trevor and Gable in tow, Darwin enters the lobby. He looks twice his age. His thick, black hair looks like a grease filter. His clothes are wrinkled. His eyes have beginnings of red rims and dark circles underneath.

"You kids park it over there on the sofa," Darwin demands in a tired voice. "Don't wander off again or I'll tie you up."

"Promise," replies the smart mouth of Jon Marx.

"Promise," confirms Darwin with a look of disdain.

The kids plop down on the sofa like they have been busted and face a week in the alternative center. Shadow Darwin returns to *The X* to further investigate the source of the noise. He is carrying the Josh Randall in one hand, a flashlight in the other, and his ever-present security blanket—the Bowie—strapped to his leg.

Julie wakes up. She stands stiffly from her position on the sofa. She yawns and stretches her ripped body and walks over to the front counter. She pours herself a steaming black cup of coffee from the server on the check-in counter. She stretches a second time before lifting the hot liquid to her lips. A sip is all she can stand. "I'll take us to morning," she says in a voice that still cracks from light sleep.

Momentarily, Shadow Darwin returns. He is the next to speak.

"I don't know if I'm hearing things or not, but our friend may be back. I can't tell what I'm imagining from what is real. The sound of wind modifies every sound and makes detection difficult. The noise from the bedroom could have been a branch rubbing against the wall, I don't know. I guess I'm just tired." He turns to Julie. "Keep an eye on the kids, they like to wander off. They think this is Big Tree." Shadow smiles faintly.

Big Tree is a favorite parking spot for all teenage licensed drivers in Mt. Kyle. For a while, adulterous middle-aged husbands from Bora Flats took their girlfriends up there only to be busted by next-door neighbor's kids. Julie and Chief Munoz regularly patrol the area as a community service for worried parents. They pretty much leave the kids alone unless someone looks distressed.

Usually, the kids just look sheepishly into the powerful beams of their flashlights all the while grabbing any article of clothing larger than underwear to shield naked body parts. Julie smiles. Darwin reads her smile as having fond memories of the same place.

Darwin drops like a brick on the sofa. Susan Newby, who had not slept more than a wink, checks the chief. He is resting peacefully under sedation, exactly what his traumatized body requires. Clint Cooper appears to be the only one asleep.

All the trouble and all the planning seems so pointless in the face of what looms like a nightmare outside. Darwin doubts if unloading all the rounds in both guns and burying the Bowie to the hilt into the creature would save any of their lives.

The lights fail again. They blink on and off like a scene from the conclusion of the movie *Alien*. The storm continues in intensity.

Suddenly, the lights go off … and stay off.

33

THE CREATURE INVADES

Julie braces for her shift by refilling her coffee cup with strong cappuccino, a Clint Cooper trademark. She sits on the brown leather sofa recently vacated by Darwin. She places several candles and the lighter on a small oval table next to the hearth Darwin used as a makeshift ottoman for his long legs. She lays her .38 special on the table and fixes her eyes on the door. Finally, the wind has died down. She feels a chill, no doubt, due to the fire burning low and the bitter cold encompassing the lodge. If darkness had a temperature, it would register single digit cold. Without saying a word, she glances in the direction of Shadow Darwin. He is ahead of her glance. He appears momentarily with an armful of logs to replenish the fire. In a matter of minutes, the fire roars again. Swirling snow is still visible through the large front windows of the now-darkened Sable. Truly, if the entire world is a stage, this one could use a cheerier lighting scheme.

Julie glances over at her fellow lodgers with a sense of sadness. Ashley and Gable with so much of their lives ahead are snuggled in blankets with their heads resting on their boyfriends' shoulders. She wonders how sick with fear their parents must feel if they even know of their plight. Sometimes it seems we live our lives in one big shadow. The shadow can only be a giant's foot posed to squash us like an insect we never see coming. Yet, we have to get over it and live life to the fullest even though at times we feel hollow and unsure with a sense of false security.

Clint Cooper sleeps alone with an intermittent snore. He has one hand close to the Josh Randall. Susan Newby dozes fitfully beside the peaceful chief whose sleep is the most peaceful of all. Shadow Darwin is pacing slowly back and forth in front of the giant fireplace in one of his pensive moods. He could be in a hospital waiting room anticipating the birth of his first child. She wonders if he will resort to yoga or his Bowie knife to relax his jangled nerves.

Julie feels alert and remarkably rested considering the few hours of her catnap. The blaring light from the magnificent fireplace cast ambivalent images on the walls. *Shadows exist because something real lies behind them.* Plato, in his theory of the cave, suggests we live in world of illusion; unreliable images swirl around us. When we see truth, we may not recognize it. Wundt, the father of psychology, said it right in the mid-1800s: We interpret the world solely as a function of our own perception. The writer A. Nin observed: We don't see the world as it is, we see it as we are. The real exists behind the false; to be psychologically healthy we must see behind the shadows. If the weird configuration of shadows cast on the wall of the Sable merely hints at the reality behind it, it may well be over for the lodgers, except for the screaming.

Now, Darwin, looking more peaceful than ever, stares hypnotically into the fire; he bends down to retrieve his Bowie from his leg holster for a little target practice. Julie reaches for the lighter to light another candle. The chief stirs momentarily from peaceful sleep. Susan Newby feels the chief move and opens her eyes to half slits. The teenagers' deep, even breathing suggest delta, slow-wave sleep—just what they need to replenish the energy to tired bodies. Julie leans forward to position the lighter over the wick of the candle.

She never gets the chance to flick her Bic.

Suddenly, the heavy front wooden door of the lodge shatters into a thousand pieces. It literally explodes off its frame as though a stick of dynamite ignites it. Cognitively, in slow motion, lodgers seek to connect with reality as though they have spent much of their lives in Plato's cave. The cognitive part of their brains attempts to grasp the intensity of the moment. Brain synapses work fast to allow perception, the organized part of sensation, to make sense of the exploding door amid the chaos of the moment.

The frigid elements of the blizzard enter the lobby like water from a busted damn bringing in the cold, stinging winds and 10-degree-below-zero temperature and swirling snow into the lobby. The flames in the hearth skip and jump to the intrusion of the wind like the fast feet of a flyweight boxer. Everyone scrambles off the sofas in a mad rush for the vault—the only safe place in the Sable.

Who's coming for dinner?

Instinctively, Susan Newby tries to protect the sedated chief by throwing her right arm across his chest much like a mother would do for her infant strapped in the car seat upon a sudden stop. Julie's .38-caliber pistol slides off the overturning table. It lands on the floor with a dull thud in the semidarkness.

Most likely it would have discharged had the safety not been engaged. Total chaos engulfs the lobby in the proverbial Chinese fire drill. Then, just as suddenly, the trapped lodgers stop dead in their tracks. Not a soul breathes even a sigh.

The gaping space where the door once stood is now filled with the body of a giant grizzly. It belts out such a thunderous growl that the terror in the room could melt a ton of invading snow. Everyone stands paralyzed.

Slightly hunched over in the attack posture, the huge animal appears ten feet tall. The creature's jaws are foaming white with saliva (the first stage of digestion). His eyes appear to glow blood red. The long, black claws attached to his paws, which are the size of a catcher's mitt, accentuate his menacing appearance. Blood appears to color the ends of both claws like demonic fingernail polish. He steps further into the lobby as though he is surveying the dinner menu. The light from the fireplace casts strange images on the floor as everyone in the lobby stands perfectly in place with frozen stares. The creature looks worse than any *tableaux vivant* lodgers could conjure up in REM sleep.

The giant creature lunges at Julie. With one powerful motion of his long right arm, he decapitates her as clean as a recently sharpened French guillotine. Her truncated body drops to the floor in convulsions, blood sprays from her neck like a recently opened fire hydrant. Nothing from the surreal brush of Goya could rival the realism.

Then, Julie awakens from her nightmare clutching her neck, screaming and screaming and screaming.

CABIN FEVER

Saturday

Ominous clouds greet the lodgers on Saturday morning. The blizzard train came to a screeching halt sometime before 5 A.M. But would more be on the way? Julie Q's nightmare a few hours earlier unnerved everyone in the lobby to the extent that not a single person slept in the remaining hours before daylight. Now, every lodger, except for the injured chief, is in full-blown REM-rebound, a condition triggered by sleep deprivation, well known to college students on the verge of flunking out of college.

Before the rooster crows, the smell of coffee and pastries wafts through the lobby like the pleasant smells in a croissant café. The lodgers begin to stir about from restless sleep. Shadow Darwin shuffles over to the window to survey the blizzard's wrath. Snow stands around every structure perpendicular to the ground in three-foot drifts. Trees are bent double with their burden of snow. The surreal landscape looks frozen to the bone. Having been without electricity for the past several hours, Darwin wonders if Eddie Hawkins survived the night. Yet, he observes a steady stream of smoke issuing from Eddie's fireplace just across the road. Shadow senses that Eddie has survived—his one good eye and all. Glancing over to the Sable hearth, he sees the glowing embers will soon cool. Wood is what they need, and they need it now. The real possibility of hypothermia enters his stress index.

A few things seem obvious to Darwin as he peers outside across the frozen landscape. First, everything as far as his eyes can see is frozen solid in a West Texas deep freeze; dangerously falling temperatures are likely to continue after nightfall. Second, the electricity is probably out for good, which means the hearth is the only source of heat. It is their lifeline. The prospect of freezing to death is not such a remote possibility. Third, there will be apparently no communication with the outside world for some time. Fourth, the creature that stalked them earlier may return for another try at a late-night buffet feast.

How could they be better prepared? With its inborn survival skills, the chance that a mature grizzly froze to death last night is remote. Grizzlies are too smart to get caught unaware even in a blizzard. Finally, he must rally the lodgers against these realities before depression or panic sets in, or the kids bolt and run in a foolish attempt to thwart cabin fever.

Darwin rests his head against the window frame. He feels his body quake under the pressure of impending reality. He glances back at the lobby. The lodgers will soon come to the same conclusion. He suspects Julie, McAfee, Newby, and Clint Cooper have already come to the same conclusion. Due to the suspense of coming nightfall, the teenagers, and Jill Frazier, who is only 23 years old, are probably getting a kick out of their hormones ignited by suspense. They haven't figured out yet the most difficult task facing them in their lives is to figure out their own minds.

Making motions to unwrap herself from a gray wool blanket, Julie appears to be unwrapping herself from mummy bandages. She stretches beyond her natural height on tiptoes and arches her athletic body backward, a body made stiff by troubled sleep. Observing her, Darwin wonders why he has been so cool to her friendliness. She heads for the coffee urn without a word or a glance his way.

Chief Munoz rests peacefully beside the ever-vigilant Susan Newby. He has not regained consciousness since his injury. Newby wonders if he will suffer some degree of brain damage. She is in the process of applying a new dressing to his slow-healing wound that appears will not become infected. The chief's breathing is deep and steady. Jon and Trevor are talking in muffled tones by the fireplace. The girls are most likely in the lobby powder room using everything at their disposal to combat "morning mouth" and "rack hair."

Presently, the lodgers choose their sweet rolls and cereal and gather before the inviting hearth drinking coffee and orange juice. They exchange worried glances. McAfee appears lost in thought. The girls appear from the powder room with a youthful bloom that belies their increasingly dire circumstances.

Darwin is the first to speak. "Attention, everyone, please ... let's have a little meeting." Once again Darwin's slight stutter returns. "It is past time to lay bare the facts. Reality is boring in like a powerful drill. No time to dodge what lies before us tonight. Our first order of business is to find more wood, hopefully cut and ready to burn. Mr. Cooper, do you know if there is a woodpile out back?"

"Yes, there is more wood around here than we will ever use in our lifetimes. Also, Mr. Hawkins has more wood behind his shop just across the way," replies Clint Cooper.

"Okay, guys I suggest we bundle up as best we can, dig our way out, and recruit Eddie to help gather more fuel." As soon as these words leave his mouth, a sudden and heavy "thud" echoes against the front door bringing everyone to an abrupt standing position.

Clint Cooper grabs his Josh Randall off the sign-in desk and points it toward the direction of the noise. Julie draws her .38 in one swift motion. In the predetermined drill, everyone else heads for the UPR vault. Shadow Darwin races over to the window for a quick look. What Darwin sees outside the door brings a smile to his face.

Glass-Eye Eddie is standing in knee-deep snow, draped in a bright yellow parka and armed with an army-issue shovel. He is hacking at the three-foot drift blocking the front door.

"It's just Glass ... it's just Eddie Hawkins." Shadow reports in his trademark stutter, careful to avoid the words Glass-Eye. "OK, calm down ... he's just digging us out ... everybody calm down."

Shadow knocks on the window glass with his knuckle. Eddie acknowledges with a wave and continues his dig. Eddie's efforts provide a welcomed reprieve from cabin fever.

For the lodgers to romp outside in the snow provides a temporary moratorium on the impending gloom of nightfall and the sense in every lodger's mind the creature will surely return.

35

SURVIVAL PLAN

As soon as Glass-Eye Eddie digs his way past the snowdrift and enters the lobby, Shadow inquires about his night. Eddie tells the group he had experienced the same electrical outage and loss of his phone. He built a huge fire in his hearth after fearing the worst from the storm. He retrieved his Winchester from its place above the mantel, made a soft pallet, lay down before the hearth, and slept like a child. After the initial commotion, he did not hear so much as a peep from the grizzly that caused so much fear in the lodgers.

Darwin observes that Eddie looks remarkably rested in contrast to the others. He looks as though he has had two full nights of sleep rolled into one. No one in the Sable has been so fortunate. Apparently, some people can sleep through anything. He wonders if Eddie slept with one eye open.

Shadow gathers everyone together to summarize his plan for survival as daylight slowly and inexorably turns into shadows. "Eddie, we need you to stay here with us in the lodge. Considering the intensity of the storm, it's anyone's guess what will happen tonight. We don't know what the grizzly has in store for us."

Eddie nods in agreement. Shadow continues. "Mr. Cooper tells me we have enough food and water for three days. Our most urgent need is to stay warm. Here's how we can remedy that. Here's the plan. Eddie, McAfee, and I will make a run to the woodpile. Mr. Collins will cover us from the rear window with his Josh Randall. Jon, Trevor, and the girls will gather by the fireplace with Newby and the chief. Julie will stand guard there. Don't hesitate one moment if our friend returns. Keep an open ear for the phones. I doubt they will come back before some degree of thaw. We don't have a lot of time to get prepared for another round of whatever may come our way tonight. We have been forewarned, now we must be forearmed."

With the plan in mind, Darwin, McAfee, and Eddie bundle up and emerge from the back door of the lodge. Prevailing northerly winds bring with it a bitter cold that had not been felt in these parts for a very long time.

The men sink almost to their knees in the deep snow. Retrieving the wood takes the better part of four hours punctuated by frequent visits to the Sable hearth for warmth, the most precious commodity of the moment.

Now, it is late afternoon. Plenty of wood rests in the wide slits of the hearth. The lodgers are quietly mingling, when suddenly the lobby phone rings loudly. It startles everyone as though they had never heard a phone ring before. Who could it be?

36

BONZO

Checking supplies behind the counter, Clint Cooper is closest to the phone. *Thank God,* Cooper whispers to himself as he picks up the black cordless phone, cold when it touches his ear. *If the phone works perhaps the electricity will kick on the heaters,* he reasons.

Shadow Darwin and Julie have been warming their hands by the fire and chatting in muted voices. They interrupt their conversation and hurry over to the counter. Cooper half expects the caller to be Peter Marx. As soon as Cooper says "hello," a voice he does not recognize speaks.

"Yes, may I speak with one of your lodgers, Professor Shadow Darwin?" the professorial-sounding voice inquires. The voice belongs to Dr. George Lennon from Sul Ross State University.

"It's George Lennon, Dr. Darwin … from Sul Ross."

Retrieving the phone from Cooper, Darwin speaks enthusiastically into the receiver. "George, thanks for calling, I was beginning to wonder if we had been transported through time into the midst of the Overlook Hotel." For the first time in days, he actually felt like himself.

"Just checking to see if you made it through the night. The weather forced me to stay all night at the college. No more long hours for me on Friday evening, I can assure you of that," stated the tired voice of Dr. Lennon, a bachelor.

"It's been quite an experience here as well. Wells McAfee from UTPB, Deputy Julie Q, Eddie Hawkins, and four teenagers spent the night here. Chief Munoz was injured by some kind of animal attack last night. Susan Newby looked after his wounds, but he's going to need more medical attention as soon as we can get him down the mountain."

"Attacked by an animal ... what kind of animal?" asked Dr. Lennon.

"I was getting around to that, George. Can you tell me if Bonzo is there on campus?"

"Yes, of course. I'm looking at the big girl right now courtesy of our remote monitoring camera. She is sleeping like a baby, and all the instruments are humming along collecting data," Dr. Lennon assured Darwin. "As I speak, live, and breathe I'm looking at her now on Video Cam 3 ... I've been here for no telling how many hours observing her and reading data the whole time." Dr. Lennon sounded a bit like a proud father. "I can also confirm she is pregnant. We expect to monitor all her life functions until she emerges from hibernation. We should have a mountain of data by then."

"Well, well ... that puts a completely different spin on our problems here," Darwin replies.

"What do you mean?" asks Dr. Lennon.

"I mean .... (the stutter returns) since Bonzo is not our intruder—I was kind of hoping she was—we better get serious about identifying the creature that attacked the chief and stalked Peter Marx's kid. We need to find out all we can. It'll be dark soon."

37

SERIOUS CONDITIONS

No sooner than Darwin replaces the phone to its cradle, it rings again, and steadily for the next hour. The voice on the other end of nowhere is one of the many repair crews heading their way, if weather permits. Clint Cooper handles the numerous calls from service companies. Static interrupts conversation and adds to the confusion and desperation of calls from repair crews and separated loved ones who have since learned of the lodgers' plight.

Closer to home, the surrounding towns dig out of their front doors and garages. Life is attempting to return to some degree of normalcy. Since the electricity will be restored (hopefully before nightfall), lodgers experience a faint stab of hope the worst might be over. As the electricity and phone service comes in drips and drabs, TV reporters paint a serious picture of the almost-complete whiteout and the near record snowfall and blizzard conditions that caught West Texas meteorologists (as well as the National Weather Service supercomputers) flatfooted. The weather is blamed for several deaths from Ft. Davis to Mt. Kyle. Some individuals are missing from their homes while anxious relatives fear the worst.

News flashes starting Saturday morning keep large viewing audiences glued to the TV. Nothing like this ever happens in West Texas. According to the newscasts, individuals are encouraged to stay inside their homes while emergency vehicles render aid if possible. Unfortunately, snowplows don't exist in West Texas (neither do storm sewers for water run-off when the snow melts). Helicopters are called in from nearby air bases. Electrical crews are slow in arriving to Bora Flats, Ft. Davis, and surrounding towns. Most residents lack underground power just like the Sable Lodge, over 8,000 feet higher up. It doesn't look good for restoring service until sometime Sunday or Monday, if by then.

Daylight hours pass like an out-of-control carousel. The lodgers make the best of a bad situation. In *The X*, the guys try to persuade the girls to play strip poker. The girls are sure the boys will cheat or make up the rules as they go. Anyway, the girls are far too modest to sit around in the cold in their underwear. With this no-win situation, the girls retreat to Peter Marx's efficiency, the scene of Friday night's short-lived attempted seduction.

They exchange makeup knowledge and idle talk geared toward the future. The same thing happens, in principle, when adults facing uncertain financial futures run to the bank and get an installment loan; it makes things seem better for the moment.

The guys play a few hands of poker and talk about girls they know—other than Ashley and Gable. Darwin, McAfee, Cooper, and Newby spend time sitting at the Pine table reviewing their options in the event of the creature's return. Jill and Julie drink steaming mugs full of hot chocolate by the fire in idle conversation. Julie brushes Jill's waist-length hair and suggests new ways she might wear it. She pumps Jill for juicy details of her relationship with Peter. As females are inclined to do, they giggle over some of the more torrid parts. Jill is fully aware of Julie's prior intimate relationship with Peter Marx. So what? X-rated descriptions of romantic interludes shared by females would make guys blush. In reality their locker room talk is on par with the male variety.

Soon, the evening marks a swift return to gloom for the lodgers. Daylight has passed with no rescue vehicles traversing the north side of the Mountain of the Ghost. The phone goes dead again after only a few hours of airtime. If family members in Lake Tahoe are watching CNN, they can see evidence of the devastation left by the blizzard. Now, how could they communicate their fears and worry with no way to connect?

Shadow decides to share his knowledge of Bonzo's whereabouts. The burning question must now be addressed: What kind of creature is still stalking the lodgers? Is the creature some kind of a hybrid mix cooked up by someone with nothing else to do; someone like Glass-Eye Eddie Hawkins?

Glass-Eye Eddie is the first person Jon and Trevor suspect. Do others share their suspicion? Questions, questions, questions.

No answers.

38

FOUR FACTS

This is not a time for complacency—the kind of self-satisfaction that blinds one to ineptitude. The temptation is great, however. Shadow Darwin believes complacency is a drug; its effects are robust in underachievers, slackers, and individuals whose only joy left in life is dispensing misery to others. Sadly, complacent individuals are blinded by their own deficiencies. Someone should tell them. Complacency is both anti-intellectual and pitiful, especially when observed in the last profession on earth anyone would conceive it to exist, and that would be in higher education. Professors who contribute little or nothing by way of innovation or creativity to their profession are a disgrace. Taking their frustrations out on students is a handy rationalization. They are the ones who complain how bad students are these days. They puff up like a frog with low retention rates as proof of their constipated mind-set. Unfortunately, many Mr. Laurence Harvey type exists in academia today—the disgruntled and unimaginative who take paychecks under false pretenses. And, they can't even spell the word r-e-t-i-r-e-m-e-n-t. Thankfully, most professors are both inspired and inspiring, teaching the already brilliant to be smart.

Complacency can get the lodgers killed at the Sable Lodge. Shadow Darwin is one the verge of solving the Sable conundrum by use of both *a priori* reasoning (speculation) and *a posteriori* logic (analyzing facts). At Sul Ross, he likes nothing more than sitting in his office, advising students on curricula choices. For a brief moment, he gets to touch the future. Now, what a sharp contrast as he sits alone in the lobby of the Sable with the future of every lodger in doubt. He gazes intently into the crackling fire that partially illuminates the lobby. He seems oblivious to the fact that darkness is rapidly descending. With phone service out and darkness seeping in all around, the lodge sits high atop the Mountain of the Ghost victimized by a stranglehold of ice and snow tentacles.

Will the lodge ever return to the friendly ambiance evidenced in her inviting lobby of dense indoor foliage, wood paneling, soaring archways, and marbled columns? Hope for a better tomorrow seems strangely remote to Darwin, a born optimist. For perhaps the first time in his life, Shadow Darwin, Ph.D., distant relative to the great Charles Darwin, appears completely baffled.

Only a few hours earlier, Darwin's colleague, Dr. George Lennon, confirmed from his lab on the campus of Sul Ross that the new resident grizzly never left her lair.

At least this confirms what Darwin suspected all along.

Now, Darwin can face facts and his uncanny ability at speculative logic. The chance that another grizzly appearing out of thin air on this particular weekend during a raging blizzard is completely out of the question. He dismisses the "grizzly theory" as a moot point.

Trudging through three-foot drifts of snow earlier in the day Darwin, McAfee, and Eddie Hawkins were unable to identify footprints of any kind in a fifty-yard circumference search of the Sable grounds. Unfortunately, the blizzard erased all indentations in the snow. The drifts left nothing out of the ordinary except evidence of the attack on Chief Munoz (faint splashes of his blood frozen captured in ice and snow) around the vicinity of the tree that saved Jon Marx's life.

A part of Darwin's mind appears to house a high-performance cerebral booster, a kind of hyper-cerebral function not found in all sapient brains. To Darwin there may be shadows of doubt in accounting for the events of Friday night, but no hypothesis is too outlandish or too improbable to pass muster in his mind—a mind not boxed in by convention or the need to please others.

If it wasn't a grizzly that attacked Jon and the chief, then what was it? Where could the creature have gone to survive the blizzard? As shelter from the driving winds and subzero temperatures, to what den could the beast have retreated? Jon, Chief Munoz, and some of the lodgers distinctly heard sounds made by an angry animal. But what kind of animal? The grizzly theory is dead.

Also, the beast stood upright on two legs like a man. Other than species of monkeys and apes, what other animal is capable of standing upright on hind legs and appearing as tall as an NBA center? Conventional wisdom is running thin. Conditions are ripe for Darwin's intellect to admit to alternative explanations, not necessarily quantifiable by science.

In part, the miserable weather conditions are responsible for the sketchy evidence. Darwin shifts his weight in the overstuffed sofa and continues his "postmortem" in the vast mental lexica of his mind.

In his mind, four facts are indisputable. He proceeds to re-assemble the cognitive puzzle. If facts are not supportable by quantifiable contingencies, then so be it.

One—some kind of powerful animal standing upright on two legs attacked the chief, nearly killing him. The same animal stalked Jon Marx all the way up to the front door of the lodge. With the fierce blizzard consuming the noise, no one could say definitely what kind of animal was responsible for the attack. At intervals, it had returned to threaten the lodgers.

Two—Clint Cooper and lodgers McAfee, Jill, Julie, Trevor, Ashley, and Gable heard the sounds of an animal attack. Eddie Hawkins and Susan Newby were the only ones unaccountable in the lobby as they were elsewhere.

Three—The bloodstained snow, the chief's terrible injury, Jon's whelp on his forehead, and the sound of the attack all exist as physical proof. Tangible evidence trumps imagination every time.

Four—Until now, Darwin kept one important detail completely to himself. He has shared this information with no one. Now, it's time to connect fact four with the existing evidence and share it with the lodgers. Especially, since nightfall is approaching and Darwin is sure the creature will return.

Darwin is now prepared to speculate on what the creature is and what it wants. In internal dialogue, he is preparing to unveil his new theory of evolution.

39

INSPIRATION

Julie joins Shadow by the blazing fire in the lobby of the Sable. She finds him staring intently into the flames in one of his many pensive moods. She approaches him from behind as stealthily as a cat and gently lays her hands on his shoulders as softly as the touch of a lover. She gently messages his shoulders and neck with her strong hands. Darwin acknowledges her presence with a deep and pleasing sigh.

"I'll give you all night to stop doing that," he whispers.

Possessing an insightful *anima*, he confides to Julie in body language and in words how much he misses the attention of a confident female. He touches the tops of her hands with his. Darwin smiles in satisfaction. The power of tactile stimulation! A close relationship with Julie that has only been suggested in the past seems to be brewing. Darwin's facial muscles soften for the first time since the events of Friday night. Prior to present circumstances, Darwin and Julie have been only casual acquaintances, having crossed paths a few times in *The X*. Darwin's smile registers a flirtatious demeanor. There's just no accounting for events that mark a transition from acquaintanceship to a budding romance. The light from the burning logs cast a romantic glow on the faces of Darwin and Julie.

Julie finishes her massage and takes a seat on a small table across from Darwin. "A penny for your thoughts," she asks in a soft voice.

Darwin shifts his gaze from the hearth to Julie's beautiful face, which is accentuated by an exotic mix of shadow and soft light from the flames. A kind of sensuous glow penetrates her inquisitive eyes. Truly, Julie is a remarkably attractive woman in any degree of light. Her intelligence makes her even more physically attractive. Shadow starts to say something ... pauses ... and then appears to change his mind. Suddenly, his whole facial expression changes to a more serious demeanor.

It is impossible to say from what remote part of Darwin's intellect the sudden occurrence of an insight drifted into cognition. It may have been building from his dreams of troubled sleep. It may have crystallized from the flirtatious mood set by Julie's proactivity and by his receptivity. Inspiration can result from romantic attraction growing from flirtatious behavior, according to psychologists and confirmed by poets. The saying *talent can, genius must* derives from inspiration and its root word meaning "to breathe, " suggesting inspiration is the breath of creativity.

Shadow Darwin's insight occurs as quick as a flash of lightning; it locks like a cerebral vice into cognitive awareness almost ready for verbal expression. It continues to gain momentum even while Darwin sits across from Julie's seductive charm. Intellectual insight must be closely related to sensuality just as the appetitive drive is next door in the brain to sexuality. Fact four is seconds away from being cracked open like a coconut. Darwin is ready to speak what he considers to be the truth amid the intoxicating presence of Julie Quixotica, her maiden name reflecting a playful capriciousness, a trait often producing an intoxicating inspiration.

"Julie, our search this morning produced not one hint of an animal track around the lodge. We found faint indentations in the snow too large to be an animal's; no substantive clues were left from Friday night's attack. I want to share with you what I am now convinced is the identity of our unwanted visitor by revealing information I have thus far kept a secret. So, go with me on this just for a moment."

Julie braces herself as if preparing to hear really bad news.

Shadow Darwin does not disappoint her.

40

FACT FOUR TAKES SHAPE

"What if our troublemaker is not an animal ... at least all the time? What if it has a human side? What if the creature can change its shape at will from animal to human form depending on what shape best serves its needs? I am certain what attacked the chief and stalked Jon is a shape shifter. I'm certain the facts are pointing in that direction," Darwin speaks the words without the slightest stutter.

"A shape shifter? Shadow, you're not serious. You mean a werewolf?" Julie asks as though she misunderstood him.

"No, not in the sense we perceive a werewolf from the movies or literary fiction. *I mean the real thing.* From literary sources, the shape shifter is a fierce archetypal specimen from another species such as grizzly bears, coyotes, or wolves. I suspect the creature's ability to change—known as morphing—is dictated by the species' genotype—the neurochemical laws of growth, change, and development, not unlike our ability of adaptation. The possibility of shape shifting has been in our myths for ages. Why not? A shape shifter is a creature of natural selection, a species who has mastered the ability of transformational morphology by degrees over a long time span—perhaps over millions of years. If that's true, the creature is self-aware regardless of the form it takes—human or the most extreme animal form. Many researchers suspect the wolf and the grizzly to be self-aware as an animal species. With self-awareness, dodging detection and staying hidden would be one of its strengths." Who knows, it might be another species unknown rival?

He pauses a moment to see if Julie is still following. When she appears completely transfixed by his theory, he continues. "I believe an unforeseeable event, the blizzard, precipitated an unintended morph in one of the new recruits. Being somewhat familiar with the literature, I believe new recruits are called beta shifters. A beta shifter is a subordinate wolf-human, learning to change—learning to morph. Considering what we know today about neuropsych, the placebo effect, and the ability in some species to reanimate lost appendages, the shifter theory is very possible," concludes Darwin.

Julie ponders the words and analytic ability of one of the world's most scholarly neuropsychologists. By his demeanor, principally through his eyes, she knows he is dead serious.

"Look Julie, every single culture in the history of the world has some mythology surrounding shape shifters. In my research for *Reinventing Myth*, I ran across plenty of references in literature from as far back as cultural histories take us. We may be in this predicament because we have ignored one of the most persistent myths in all literature—the myth of the shape shifter. Perhaps, it's not a myth at all. Traditionally, vampires and ghosts have gotten all of the attention, but references on the web to shape shifting will blow you away."

"But, Shadow, you're a scientist, trained to think logically. You're not a fictionist," Julie interjected.

"Actually, I'm both," replies Darwin sheepishly. "Privately, I adhere to my own *cogency principle*, as I call it. I won't bore you with the details of a dry epistemological theory, but my perspective requires a certain degree of empiricism mixed with a willingness to embrace observable events that appear to have no contingencies—no cause and effect. We must trust our gut regardless of where it takes us. I call it *speculative empiricism*. Facts and reality can go beyond science and what is observable, as long as they contain strong elements of possibility from perspectives that seem plausible. In physics, the most mathematical of all sciences, look at black holes, quirks, and subatomic particles for examples," Shadow lightly stutters. Watching Julie carefully, Darwin is pleased she is seizing his idea as something entirely plausible.

"Julie, we know some kind of creature is definitely out there. Science does not have to understand or explain it in empirical terms for it to exist. Otherwise, if everything had to be quantified, all of the religions of world would cease to offer teleological explanations. Sometimes, you have to trust what adds up—what emerges from the total picture."

Julie slowly shifts her faraway glance to meet Darwin's eyes. "So, we have a shape shifter? Great, what do we do? I don't think wolf bane grows in Big Bend, and I'm fresh out of silver bullets," she sarcastically remarks.

"Well, you won't need silver bullets; the regular ones will do fine on the beta shifters—the new recruits trying to bring morphing under conscious control. Essentially, the lower order shifters, like the one I believe to be in our midst is just an animal, not a poltergeist. They bleed and die just like us." Darwin's expression changes to a more serious demeanor. "Of course the alpha shape shifter is another story. Unlike the betas, they have really tough skin and strong, fibrous muscles. They are really hard to kill. I suspect they display *morphallaxis*—the ability to reanimate tissue, which means they may be practically unstoppable. But, for the rest, the regular garden variety betas, whatever kills a human kills them."

"Practically unstoppable?" Julie replies. "Then something must kill an alpha. What it is?" Julie asks earnestly.

"Decapitation," replies Darwin. "The problem is outwitting their superior animal instincts to get close enough to severe the head from the body. And, you don't want to get bitten. Chances are great the bite transfers wolfen DNA. The literature suggests wolfen DNA is more potent than pure testosterone. If my theory is true, it is ironic that human fetuses become masculinized due to the action of testosterone upon, of all things, embryonic ducts known as Wolffian ducts."

Darwin pauses momentarily to determine if this bit of wolfen irony sinks into Julie's vast store or mental lexica. When he is certain it has, he continues. "Lower order werewolves are very savage. Apparently, subordinate shifters—the betas—go through some kind of intense psychophysiological process in the struggle to become alphas. No one knows the protocol. No one has captured an alpha lately," concludes Darwin.

"Shadow, you owe it to the others to tell them. As you know, in all probability, the creature is coming back tonight."

"I know it's coming and I know what it wants," concludes Darwin.

41

PREPOSTEROUS

Freaky shadows extend through the Sable Lobby like an ancient sea monster's long tentacles threatening to squeeze the life out of the lodgers. The flickering fire mixes with twilight amid the large windows producing weird images spurning wild imaginations. The time draws near for the creature's return.

Since morning, the weather has become more stable, about as stable as the chief's slowly improving condition. Due to Newby's swift action and knowledge, he will survive his injury. He has been moved to room 102 right off the lobby and is resting peacefully in earshot of the lodgers. Newby administered antibiotics and sedatives around the clock that saved his life.

Now, Shadow Darwin and Julie join McAfee at the nine-foot pine table across from the overstuffed sofas. The table has chairs for twelve guests who often wait there to meet their arriving friends and associates. McAfee looks up from his two-day-old paper. He senses something is brewing and stares directly at Julie who looks away.

Clint Cooper, Jill Frazier, and the teenagers are huddled in Clint's office. They are going over the agenda for nightfall. Glass-Eye Eddie is making repairs to the door and checking the windows for damage. Time draws near for the lodgers to hear Darwin's new theory of evolution. He summons everyone to the table. Momentarily, with everyone seated and looking on with anticipation, Darwin speaks, no doubt, with the authority of his distant relative.

"Until a few moments ago, I have not been on the level with anyone regarding my suspicions of the events of Friday night. Now, the time is right. I am as certain as I can be that my suspicions are correct, as unbelievable as they're going to sound. To my friend and colleague Dr. McAfee, who may think I have lost my mind, believe me, the reality of my theory, I fear, will soon be demonstrated." Wells McAfee stares directly at his prize pupil. Straight through the eyes, a kind of knowing seems to pass between them that only they feel.

No one seems to breathe or blink. They sit staring like wax figures.

Darwin continues. "I caught a glimpse of the creature the night of the attack. I was the first one to rush to the window when Jon arrived with the injured chief." Darwin seems to be looking at an internal projection device replaying scene-by-scene Friday night's episode of chaos. "I saw a tall creature. Yes, it resembled a grizzly. But, I suppose it did because that was what I expected to see. The Gestalt psychologists—Wertheimer, Kafka, and Kohler—showed how our minds fill in gaps of incomplete perception as occurs during time compression, or during disorienting conditions such as a blizzard. Also, as you know, my colleague, Dr. Lennon and I have recently taken delivery of a grizzly bear at Sul Ross. And, since we are in the midst of Big Bend, I half-expected to see a grizzly anyway; I must have created it, rather my brain created what I expected to see. I know from my research that covering the distance from Sul Ross would be no problem for a bear, even in adverse weather. Anyway, after Jon's arrival, I saw the creature running into the woods on the north side of the lodge. Certainly, blizzard conditions and darkness made identification impossible. I'm saying I saw a grizzly because I expected to see a grizzly. Later, when things calmed down, I tried to recall in as much detail as possible what I had seen. If it had been a grizzly, it was the most anorexic one on record. It was as tall as a grizzly but not nearly as heavy. The creature definitely stood upright on two legs. Later, after we attended to the chief and Jon, I stood by the window and distinctly saw the creature reappear under the perimeter lights near the west side of the lodge. *It had changed appearance.* It looked more like a human than an animal. I couldn't make out much of anything except that the hair on its head was practically shoulder-length. The face was distinctively human. I'm sorry, but the creature looked like Wolverine in the movie, *The X-Men.* It's the best analogy I have. There is no question in my mind what I saw. From the time it attacked the chief and ran into the woods and reappeared no more than 30 minutes later, *it had changed.* It looked more like a man than animal. One thing for sure, it had long hair like a rock star."

The lodgers sat in silence. McAfee blinked like an owl. He spoke next. "Long hair, like yours?"

"Yes, exactly like mine," said Darwin with a dismissive look.

"Why haven't you said anything before now?" asked Susan Newby.

"I wanted to wait until I knew more ... until I could be sure," said Darwin. "Here's the kicker. Later that night, I heard a disturbance near the back of the lodge. It was shortly after the time Jon and Trevor tried to seduce their girlfriends in *The X*." I went to investigate. I guess I scared off the intruder. It was lurking near the backdoor. As it retreated around the corner of the lodge, it appeared even more like a man and less like an animal. I know that what we all heard here in the lodge and what Jon heard was definitely an animal. The blizzard's high winds make sounds that mimic howling wolves—we use the expression 'howling winds' all the time. So, you see where I'm going with this. We heard an animal, but I observed what looks like a man running away—not once, but twice."

Darwin pauses a moment and takes a deep breath. The lodgers looked as though they expected something to jump out at them.

Then he continues. "Without question, I think we are dealing with a shape shifter. You may not be familiar with the term, so I'll speak in simple terms. I believe we are dealing with a modern equivalent of a creature once steeped in myth as a werewolf. I believe this were-creature may be in the process of perfecting the mechanics of morphing—of changing. Accidentally, the blizzard acted as a kind of stimulus of a classical conditioning that elicited—that caused—an involuntary morph. I suspect the creature is a new recruit—a beta, trying to control morphing. Morphing, like our ability of adaptation, allows the creature to adapt to or conquer hostile surroundings the best way it knows how."

The lodgers sit and can only blink in amazement. Darwin continues.

"When shape shifters first change, or morph from human to wolfen form, they look remarkably like wolves. They can morph on two or four legs and acquire body hair, pointed ears, and paws—any semblance of wolves they conjure up. Basically, it's mind over matter. When betas reach alpha status, they become superhuman—they possess the minds of humans and the strengths and instincts of wolves. They resemble tall linebackers in the NFL with long hair and bodies like Greek statutes, "ripped" with long arms, legs, and fingers. They have a special armored skin like a rhinoceros. They look nothing like hairy wolves. As leaders of the pack, the alpha shape shifters achieve that status because they learn to control all aspects of the morph quickly and efficiently. I suspect the failure rate is rather high. Few make it. When they achieve alpha status, they can call up at will any wolfen characteristic in any context that gives them the advantage. Then, just as quickly, they can morph back to anthropomorphic characteristics. They retain their remarkable strength, speed, agility, and, of course, sense of smell as alpha shape shifters. How many times this is possible in a twenty-four-hour period no one knows. I just hope we are not dealing with an alpha. The alpha shape shifter is a real badass wolf. I don't think we have a terminator for this bad boy."

Extended silence. Then McAfee speaks. "Preposterous. I think you've been reading too much of your own fiction."

42

The Alpha Has the Scent

Wells McAfee, the crusty ex-politician turned geology professor is aware that just a few months ago Darwin completed research on myths and legends in conjunction with his manuscript, *Reinventing Myth*. He respects Darwin as a truly gifted scientist and colleague who does his homework and knows what he's talking about long before he opens his mouth and complicates things. But, still, how can his proposal of shape shifting be reconciled with any empirical methodology? After all, this is the twenty-first century; it is not the Middle Ages.

Darwin paces back and forth in front of the lodgers as he prepares to recite the pertinent section of his text as though he is reading it line for line. He speaks with authority and is not interrupted. "A distinction must be made between *shape shifters* and *lycanthropic episodes*. A true morphological transformation—from man to wolf or to any creature and back again—occurs in shape shifting, hence the 'shift in shape.' By contrast, the term 'lycanthropy' refers to a psychiatric condition where individuals imagine themselves to be wolves in mind only. There is no shape shifting. However, the afflicted person may display behavior consistent with wolves such as running on all fours, experiencing an imagined heightened sense of smell, or howling at the moon. By contrast, a true shape shifter morphs from man to animal and then back again at will. Alpha shifters have solved the evolutionary riddle of morphing, while beta shifters are trainees who hope to become alphas as soon as they learn self-control. Betas have less experience and are subject to morphological faux pas—unintended morphs—which I believe characterizes our intruder. In an animal wolf pack, the alpha male is the leader along with the alpha female. In shape shifter species, the alpha male is at the top of the apex all by himself; apparently, it is not possible for a female to attain the status of alpha. She reaches her peak as an accomplished beta shifter, a mature subordinate. The lack of testosterone may explain why female shifters do not become alphas. The male alpha shifter displays the best assets of both human and wolfen characteristics. Who could stop alpha shifters from displacing humans as the dominant species if they were organized and have support from enough betas? Remember, all shifters are cleverly disguised as either humans or wolves. Since alphas control the morph transformation at will, they can be what they want to be when they want to be it and never be detected. This strategy is as old as the written word involving survival: Take what you have to get what you want but don't have.

"Beta shifters are new to the morphing process and are much more vulnerable to *outside influences* in initiating morphs such as full moons, violent weather, or strong sexual stimuli. As betas, the morphing process is highly unstable; they cannot dictate when they morph to wolfen morphology or when they return to human form. Alpha shifters and alpha wolves have attained apex status because they have learned to use more gray matter, patience, and skill. And, they have mastered the placebo effect—mind over matter.

"Alpha shape shifters must select a new recruit from the human population—a person who promises to be an excellent candidate for alpha status. Otherwise, their ranks grow thin.

"In the beginning, the new recruits are clueless. I believe our creature falls into this category. I suspect the blizzard precipitated the unintended morph. If we had killed him at the time of the attack, we would have found a large wolf. We would have all gone to our graves believing we had killed a wolf. We would never have known the truth.

"Apparently, the myth is all wrong. Wolves don't suddenly morph back to humans at the moment of death. They die as a wolf and no one knows their secret. Apparently, they have to be farther along in the morph for a human corpse to be found," concludes Darwin.

He pauses to pick up the next strand of thought in his seamless mental lexica. "I think some missing persons are in reality unfortunate individuals who were bitten by shape shifters and became juvenile, omega, or beta shifters. Since the pack leader, the alpha shape shifter, refused to take the new recruit under his paw, so to speak, the pack ignored the recruit. In such a state, the new recruit might wander off a lone wolf—an omega. Later, somewhere in the morphing process, farmers, ranchers, or hunters kill the wolf. The missing person is never found. Instead, a dead wolf is found.

"As I mentioned to Julie just moments ago, were-creatures have appeared in all ages across all known cultures. Coincidently, shape shifters and lycanthropic episodes began to appear in literature about the same time as tiny villages sprang up amid forests and woods. As civilization spread into towns and cities, wild animals were forced to compete with mankind for survival along uncivilized frontiers. Naturally, the focus is on bears, mountain lions, wolves, and coyotes since they are the fiercest. They populate the shape shifter literature.

"The appearance of were-creatures has been interpreted metaphorically for the fear associated with change, competing for food, and not feeling safe in hostile surroundings. Ironically, the same conditions—not feeling safe, fear of change—are the most commonly observed reasons for individuals seeking psychotherapy. They fear the unknown or they fear changing. Being bitten by a werewolf, characterized by the Lon Chaney, Jr. movies, depicts more of a creation of Hollywood than myth or legend. It's a logical assumption that weather conditions play a major role in animal survival; hence, animals and weather share an uneasy alliance. Wolves and grizzlies are perhaps the most accurate weather forecasters alive. They make the National Weather Service supercomputers look like tinker toys. I believe our mysterious creature is no longer a mystery. Whoever the shape shifter turns out to be, his brain chemistry has been altered by wolfen DNA, and, like the epileptic watching a blinking light at three cps, seizure is elicited. In this case, it wasn't a blinking light or a seizure; it was a blizzard and a morphing episode. "

Darwin pauses. He glances around at the faces of the lodgers. They are completely caught up in his explanation. He continues.

"Apparently, the stronger the catastrophizing event, the quicker the morph occurs and the shorter it lasts. And, the creatures must be seething with revenge on humans," Darwin concludes, taking advantage of the opportunity to interject his revenge theory.

"So I'll be the first to ask the obvious," remarks Susan Newby who startles everyone with her intrusion. "Who among us fits the profile of an alpha?"

Laughter erupts from everyone but Shadow Darwin and McAfee. The two colleagues stare at each other without a word. Then, Darwin speaks. "That's what we must find out before nightfall. I think the alpha is among us and will make his move tonight to recruit one or all of us. *The alpha has our scent,*" says Darwin in the most serious voice he can find.

"What's more, the alpha could be right here in our midst and we wouldn't even know it, because he looks human."

No one blinks an eye or seems to breathe. The lodgers look at each other in careful analysis as though trying to detect any clue as to the identity of the alpha who has their scent.

43

Homo Morpholupus

CAMBRIDGE, MASS.

It is Saturday night in the Cambridge, Massachusetts, home of Dr. Max Zander, professor emeritus of paleontology at Harvard University. A lifelong bachelor, Dr. Zander is bursting at the seams to tell someone what he no longer suspects to be conjecture. He is running full-throttle on adrenaline tonight. He has waited for this night nearly four months since his return from Rift Valley, Ethiopia. You would think he is entertaining a high-priced call girl for the evening, not a matronly anthropology professor ten years his senior. All day he has been a whirling dervish of activity preparing for this evening.

Even the day before, all day Friday, he could scarcely contain his jazzed-up behavior leading some of his students to believe he had found the woman of his dreams. Was an announcement of his engagement eminent? Some of his more assertive female students ventured to ask him pointblank if there was a woman in his life. What else could cause such a change in the laconic habits of a stuffy, middle-aged bachelor?

Since that cold October morning when he delicately and piece-by-piece unpacked his fossil from the delivery truck, he had not experienced a normal night's sleep since. He assembled the fossil over one weekend. He had a bounce in his step the entire time as though he were an expectant father putting together his first child's baby bed. First, he carefully cleaned, assembled, and catalogued the find. He checked it and rechecked it. Then, he ran comparison studies. He retreated to an inner playground reserved for grown men who began collecting things as kids. How he managed not to mention a word of the find to anyone reflected his professional discipline and the profundity of his discovery. He pictured his find in various stages, angles, and textures in *tableaux vivant*. What better place to admire his discovery than in the living pictures of his dreams? For the past three months, he had lived up to his reputation of being one of the most meticulous cataloguers of fossil finds in the world (it sometimes takes him years to publish information related to one of his finds).

Promptly at 7 P.M., the doorbell rings—Dr. Judith Lynn Lovejoy, age 59, a world-renowned scientist with Ph.D.s in both anthropology and paleontology. She stands shivering on the stoop. Dr. Zander makes it to the door before the second ring and invites his long-time colleague in. Musk perfume hangs in the air like a helium balloon.

In light drizzle, Judith made the short drive from her home near the Harvard campus. Her husband, Dr. Brannan Lovejoy, is chief of orthopedic surgery at Harvard Medical School. In their younger days, he and Max had thrown a few back in just about every pub in town. After the exchange of pleasantries, Dr. Zander can no longer contain his excitement.

"When I found out you were in Paris and wouldn't return until now, I wasn't sure I could contain myself. But I'm glad I did. No one has seen this find, not even my crew."

"Well, Max, let's not waste any more time. Let's see it. Let me see the find of the millennium." Judith fluffs her stylish, graying hair in Max's small hallway mirror and removes her coat and gloves on the way down the hall to his study.

Max Zander fumbles with the lock. He drops his keys and tries again.

"Relax, Max, this is not good for your blood pressure," Judith says. In the next moment, they are standing inside his pleasantly cluttered study and staring at the find assembled on top of an old ping-pong table, absent the net.

Max Zander stands silently, admiringly.

Judith stands by his side with her mouth wide open. She cannot take her eyes off the fossil. Zander glances first at the fossil and then back at Dr. Lovejoy. He bites his lower lip in anticipation. He has traveled half way around the world and dug up enough dirt to fill the Grand Canyon to reach this moment in time. After an extended silence, Judith Lovejoy speaks barely above a whisper.

"Max, you're not going to believe this, but I saw one so similar to this one, it could be this guy's brother." Dr. Lovejoy spent the last week in Paris on invitation from a mutual international friend and colleague, Dr. Carlo Martine, chairman of paleoanthropology and prehistory at the College of France. She had not told Dr. Zander the reason for the trip. Sending the explanation by fax or mail was out of the question as she now reveals.

"Max, Carlo is preparing to publish his discovery by his French and Kenyan cooperative on what appears to be an almost identical find as yours. He invited me there to help edit his manuscript. These discoveries may qualify as twin finds of the millennium. You have found Romulus, and he has found Remus ... or vice versa. Max, you must call Dr. Martine immediately ... tonight. Compare notes and co-publish and take your place in the annals of paleoarcheology. My opinion is this: I believe you and Carlo have discovered a parallel link to *Homo sapiens*. More disturbingly, from the looks of things, perhaps our rival.

"What do you call him, Max?" inquires Dr. Lovejoy.

"Magnificent ... phylogenetically, he's *Homo morpholupus*," replies Max barely above a whisper.

"Brilliant ... 'man morphing to wolf,'" translates Dr. Lovejoy.

"Incidentally, was Carlo's find decapitated?" Max inquires.

"Yes, the head was found on the ground near its feet as though someone lopped it off on purpose," Judith replies.

Max paused a moment. "I think I know why the head was lopped off."

44

GIRL TALK

Saturday Night

MT. KYLE, TEXAS

Outside the Sable Lodge, the snow-draped landscape appears surreal. The deep snow glistens under the bright light of the full moon against a cold, cloudless sky full of twinkling stars. Night descends on all creatures. The scene from afar appears picturesque, perhaps from a Norman Rockwell painting. For the poor souls inside the Sable, the mood is somber and fearful. At any moment now, perhaps the dangerous shape-shifting creature would return seeking a meal. The feeling is similar to walking through a spiderweb at night. The spider is on you somewhere; you just don't know where and when it's going to bite.

Presently, a CD by the group Nickelback is playing softly in the lobby thanks to a small boom box provided by Clint Cooper. It's the same one he uses to play his extensive collection of Hugo Montenegro music adapted from Ennio Morricone instrumentals. The music is from Sergio Leone's *Dollars Trilogy*—*A Fistful of Dollars* (1964), *For a Few Dollars More* (1965), and *The Good, the Bad, and the Ugly* (1966). The Sergio Leone directed movies and its music form the basis of the European-made "spaghetti westerns" that launched Cooper's hero, Clint Eastwood, into stardom. The collection of the *Dollars Trilogy* reached number one in the United Kingdom in 1968 shortly before Cooper left for the United States. The typical Eastwood character makes the best amid world-weary skepticism. In this way, Eastwood's characterizations appeal to Clint Cooper; an attitude that may be the common thread that weaves together the experiences of individuals who huddle amid the wilds of the Chisos Mountains in far West Texas.

Gable and Ashley sit on one of the sofas talking and laughing, a strange thing to do considering the danger that lurks about. Yet, youth insulates with a bulletproof armor. Levity in the face of danger is a distinct luxury of youth. Of all things, the girls are sharing their future collegiate plans. Prior to the current conversation, they spent the last hour listing all the reasons they could think of why young guys are afraid of commitment.

"I can't believe I have four years of college ahead of me," says Gable punctuating her remark with a smirk.

"Time will pass anyway; we might as will be doing something that has a future to it, don't you think?" replies Ashley.

"Yes, I guess so … if I can get a full-ride scholarship and cheer the whole time, maybe I can tolerate all those boring classes," replies Gable. "I can't believe I have such a bad attitude about college. I have had so much fun in high school, cheering and all. I have dated some cool guys—before I met 'nit and wit' over there (she nods her head in the direction of Trevor and Jon). Seriously, though, they're fun guys. I hate to get serious for college. My parents didn't graduate high school, so I have plenty of time before I have to buckle down. I just don't think college can possibly top the good times of high school."

"I just hope I get my chance to go to the University of Paris and model," states Ashley. A beat of silence and Ashley changes the subject. "Gable, I know I'm the new girl on the block. I really appreciate your friendship. I mean, being a cheerleader and being popular, you could have really treated me like a disease. I guess I'm trying to thank you for being a regular person."

"Thanks. You're only the best-looking girl in school, plus, you seem prone to more mature thinking than most of my friends. I seriously think you're good for me," says Gable earnestly. "Let's agree to write each other every day. Maybe I can come over to Paris for a visit. Maybe you can set me up with a hot French guy model!" Gable's hazel eyes blaze, clearly getting into the possibility.

"No problem…" Ashley's voice breaks off and then her mood hits rock bottom. "I just hope I have my chance at life," she says in a way that brings tears to Gable's eyes.

"You will Ash, you will," Gable replies without much conviction in her reply.

Spontaneously, the girls hug each other. Suddenly, college doesn't seem so bad when compared to their immediate situation. Somewhere deep down, both girls wish their guys were as emotionally accessible.

45

DARKNESS DESCENDS

A cross from the girls, Darwin sits with Clint Cooper, Julie, Jill, Susan Newby, and Wells McAfee. Without actually casting lots, Darwin suspects the others feel Glass-Eye Eddie is the most natural alpha shifter suspect.

Before he begins checking the agenda, Darwin glances at Clint's Josh Randall, Julie's holstered .38, and Glass-Eye Eddie's Winchester. "We don't have much firepower. Besides, I'm not sure what drops alphas. I believe their skin and bone are dense and armored like rhinos." Using the words *shape shifter* no longer seemed nonsensical to Darwin. It rolled off his tongue as easily as if he had spoken "serial killer" instead. "According to my research, unless we have an elephant rifle, silver bullets are about as effective as regular lead bullets. It might buy us time to get inside the vault. As you know, we cannot use our cell phones inside the vault. Oxygen won't be available very long there either.

"If I am correct regarding the morphs, Jon saw the same creature I saw but in a different body type. The unknown factor here is wolfen strength and sensibilities. Do they retain wolfen strength as humans?" Darwin states rhetorically. "Next, why is the shape shifter here to begin with? Is it due to some freak accident that he turns up here of all places, and on this particular weekend? I suspect the alpha is up to something." He glances almost with humor at his friend McAfee whose physical appearance seems the least likely of all to morph into a beast. But, truly, no one looks the part. No one, that is, except Darwin himself.

"I guess I fit the profile better than anyone here," concludes Darwin.

To the person, every lodger wonders what they would do if Darwin suddenly became an alpha shifter right before their eyes. It is just too far-fetched to be entertained as more than a tangential thought. But ... there's always the possibility that lingers in the back of the mind.

46

THE REAL GLASS-EYE

It is 9 P.M., and time to survey the blizzard's wrath. In a large radius around Mt. Kyle, destroyed or damaged transformers, crooked telephone poles, and downed power lines mark the devastation. The massive storm dumped three inches of snow on Abilene on its easterly exit before petering out in the Parker county town of Weatherford, Texas, over 200 miles away.

Inside the lodge, adolescent fires burn brightly. Jon and Trevor are sitting at the pine table near the front desk playing poker, but thinking of the girls. For the moment, the creature is on the back burner. Ashley and Gable are in the lobby powder room in a makeup session of fluffy hair and sweet-smelling perfume. Big date tonight?

"I'm not sure any of these old farts are up to tackling anything bigger than a breadbox," Jon says. He studies the remainder of the cards in his sorry hand as though he expects to actually win the hand. He is down 5 to 0 to Trevor. (Before his retirement last year, Trevor's grandfather had been the sheriff of Brewster County for over thirty years. He played a few hands of poker, blackjack, and any other game with a pot at stake. It didn't matter on which side of the border either. Obviously, he passed on a few tricks of the gambler's trade to his grandson.) With Trevor on the verge of winning another hand, Jon speaks.

"Look, Ash and Gable will be at least another hour in there no matter how much we try to hurry them up; like we can walk out of here and go downtown for dinner and a movie. We don't know any more now than we did last night. Let's you and me go for a little evidence gathering, what do you say?" Trevor looks over his hand and tosses it on the table. It's a royal flush.

"Lucky bastard," Jon remarks as he glances at the hand.

"That Shadow dude will kick our butts," replies Trevor. "He may be old, but he looks like he's in shape. I think he's serious about our welfare." Trevor arches his back in a long and satisfying stretch. "All things considered, what do you make of our predicament?"

"I'll tell you what I think. I think Glass-Eye is one weird dude. He probably created some kind of weird-as-hell hybrid animal by crossbreeding wolves, coyotes, and no telling what else. What attacked us was probably one of those freaks … I'll bet you. You know what else, I bet we can find it. And, I know where to look. We'll be back before the girls finish and anyone misses us."

"Don't you think we would have heard some kind of sounds if this creature existed?" asks Trevor, who coincidently is heading to Texas A & M University, the animal husbandry capital of the world. "Do you know how corny what you just said sounds?" Trevor adds.

"Come on, I'll show you how corny it is," Jon replies.

The boys round up two large flashlights, grab their parkas and gloves, and move as quietly as possible past the other lodgers who are preparing to defend themselves for yet another night. The boys are not willing to press their luck at taking the Josh Randall. The Winchester is not in its usual place, somewhere in the vicinity of Glass-Eye Eddie. The boys deduce correctly that Glass-Eye has run home on some unknown errand.

Ironically, the best exit at the time is the front door. Their elopement is completely undetected. The wind has subsided completely so wind noise does not call attention to their hasty exit. On the large wraparound front porch, Jon and Trevor duck low as they make their way down the steps and across the deep snow covering the front lawn. The night is bright, cold, and clear. The clouds have completely vanished leaving a brilliant starry night punctuated by a ripe, full moon. The landscape is bathed in silvery moon glow reminiscent of the meeting between Jonathan Harker and the three voluptuous vampires at Castle Dracula in Bram Stoker's *Dracula*. Amid the silent splendor of the snow-draped Sable, there is a sense that the cork is about to come out of the bottle.

Eddie's residence is just down the hill on the two-lane blacktop that provides a northerly entrance to the Sable. Jon believes the hybrid animal is kenneled in the makeshift two-car garage behind the add-on. The boys keep their lights low to the ground. They

148

make steady progress. Jon and Trevor pass the section of the house Eddie uses as his sleeping quarters. All the lights are out suggesting Eddie might not be staying with the others for the night as originally planned. The two young detectives appear as Sherlock Holmes and Dr. Watson upon the moor.

In plain sight about ten yards to the back of the property the two-car garage stands, leaning slightly out of plumb, no doubt due to prevailing winds. The boys creep slowly and silently through three-foot drifts of deep, powdery snow toward the double doors. They find it to be padlocked with a heavy, rusty chain.

Then, noticing the ground just below their feet, the boys spot large bones littering the immediate area. Due to the recent snowfall, the bones must have been recently deposited.

"Look at all these bones. How corny is my idea now?" asks Jon in muffled tones. Jon and Trevor creep around the side of the garage looking for another entrance.

"Jon, come over here," shouts Trevor in a slightly muted tone. He points to larger bones and what appears to be a human skull. They find much larger footprints that appear more human than animal. They appear to be freshly made. "Those prints look more human than animal. I think we better get Dr. Darwin." The boys shudder at their discovery.

Suddenly, a hideous sound brings Jon and Trevor to a freeze-frame. It is the unmistakable blood-curdling howl of a wolf. It seems like it came through a megaphone from the back porch of Eddie's add-on, no more than fifteen feet away.

"Let's get the hell out of here," shouts Jon, who no longer cares if anyone hears him.

The boys trudge away from the garage in knee-deep snow. Just as they move past the back door of Eddie's add-on, waddling like ducks in the deep snow, the door suddenly explodes off its hinges as though rigged by a bomb. The boys duck low to the ground to avoid the splinters of wood that sprinkle around them like toothpicks. What they see in the doorway of Eddie's home, brightly illuminated by moonlight, is a wolf-creature of some kind—tall as a man and filling the doorway to the top. The creature looks directly at the boys as though it has been watching them for some time. The werewolf is upon the boys in one stride and towers over them. The star athletes of Mt. Kyle Senior High School cower at the feet of the predator like mistreated pups.

The physical presence of the beast is truly ghastly. The face of a half-human and half-wolf looms out of the neck of Eddie's recognizable work shirt. Hairy claw-hands with long fingers and nails protrude from the sleeves. The nails are long and sharp like claws; his long fingers move constantly. The red-black wolfen mouth drips saliva in spoonfuls. The sharp, white teeth appear protrusible from the lips like a grizzly adding to the hideous disfigurement of Glass-Eye Eddie Hawkins. The werewolf's good eye glows red, the sign of an omega looper—a shifter in training. The glass eye is colorless and dead like the victim's eye in Poe's *Tale-Tell Heart*. The werewolf moves with a fluid motion that leaves but one conclusion: The boys are seconds from being devoured alive. Now, the werewolf is rising on tiptoes ready to crush Jon and Trevor with its terrible strength and savage desire to survive. The omega looper is confronting its human rival.

Then, the sound of a gunshot.

47

THE JOSH RANDALL

The next instant, the werewolf is knocked backward by shots from the twin barrels of the Josh Randall. Shadow Darwin emerges from behind a large mesquite tree. He breaks open the smoking double chambers at the stock, drops two shells into the twin chambers, and walks out into the full blush of moonlight looking like Clint Eastwood in a black trench coat. The sight would have produced goose bumps on the arms of Clint Cooper.

"Jon ... Trevor, let's get the hell out of here" yells Darwin at the two dumbstruck buddies lying flat on their backs on a mound of snow.

All Darwin can see are two pairs of wide eyes glaring at him. The boys are speechless. In unison, they look back in the direction of the werewolf. The awful creature is crawling toward them with a massive head wound! Two holes in its forehead are blood red toward the center, outlined in black circles, and gushing blood from twin two-inch wounds in the werewolf's head. Blood-red saliva drips in gobs from the wolfen mouth. *These things are messy,* Darwin reasons in internal dialogue.

Darwin rushes over and grabs Jon by the collar of his yellow parka and yanks him back to reality with one swift pull. Jon lands sideways on both feet and struggles to regain his balance. He does not immediately trust his legs. Trevor snaps out of his temporary *fugue* with the hoisting of Jon. Almost comically, he rolls over and over in the snow away from the wounded wolf. Darwin stands directly over the werewolf. The creature is dressed in Eddie's clothes and red suspenders. Eddie's black boots would have never fit over the gigantic paw-feet. He watches the head of the wolf bob back and forth like a big, bloody apple.

Then in a flash, the huge claw-hand of the beast grips the ankle of Darwin in a vice grip. Just as fast, Darwin unloaded both barrels of the Josh Randall point-black into the face of the agonized werewolf. Following the blast and the blue white smoke, the beast falls silent.

"My, my, what big holes you have in your head Mr. Wolf," says Darwin, with his slight stutter, paraphrasing a well-known story. He frees his throbbing ankle from the grip of the monster and steps back—and back again, retreating one more step for insurance. The near faceless werewolf lies in a pool of blood-soaked snow and twitches in spasms of death. A chorus of howling wolves ensues.

Darwin wheels around to gather the boys who are puking in unison onto a mound of snow. Suddenly, the silence is broken by the shrill sounds of girlish screams back at the lodge. The Sable looms just over the hill in the bright moonlit night.

Between the howling of hundreds of wolves and the screams of the girls, all Hell is breaking loose.

48

PANDEMONIUM

B ack at the Sable amid long shadows cast in the lobby by the blazing fire, three werewolves on all fours surround Ashley and Gable. Twice as large as full-grown German shepherds, the werewolves show sunken sides indicative of desperate hunger in exposed ribs and flat fur.

Minutes earlier, Darwin had knocked on the door of the powder room to tell the girls to stay put and tell Julie to come out and stand guard while he gathered up the absent boys. Unknown to Darwin, the girls subsequently emerged without Julie. She had not been with the girls in the bathroom as Darwin had suspected.

Expecting to see Jon and Trevor playing cards at the pine table, what the girls found instead are three werewolves snarling at them no more than five feet away. Where are Julie and Jill and the rest of the lodgers? Have the wolves already stripped muscle and skin from their bones, eating them alive in the process? Have Clint Cooper and Wells McAfee met similar fates?

Moments tick away as the girls sense they are going to be torn limb from limb by the hungry predators. Like Glass-Eye Eddie, the werewolves display long white teeth protrusible from their lips adding to their hideous appearance. The beta loopers inch closer and closer toward the helpless victims with jaws dripping saliva. Gable and Ashley grasp each other and fall down in a fetal embrace. Suddenly, the three werewolves morph into two-legged beta shifters standing upright. In less time than it takes to scream, they had morphed from creatures three feet tall on-all-fours to creatures six feet tall on two legs. The front legs and paws morph into two long arms and long claw-hands with long, sharp nails. The girls wait in anguish as the horrible creatures draw inches from devouring them. There is no way out.

Then, the front door of the lodge flies open.

Shadow Darwin appears in the doorway with the Josh Randall followed by Jon and Trevor. The boys have regained their composure. A bad scare followed by a good puck works wonders, adding years of maturity to boot.

Fearing he will hit one or both girls with the ammunition, Darwin points the Josh Randall straight up in the air and pulls the trigger on one barrel. Startled, the beta shifters freeze and turn in unison. Now, Darwin and the boys face three six-foot-tall werewolves. They seem to be in the process of morphing, apparently for purposes of retaining the full effects of wolfen strength.

"Jon … Trevor, get yourselves and the girls in the vault, NOW!" Shadow shouts in a hoarse voice.

The boys move on command as though their coach has just sent them into the game for a desperate goal-line stand. They scoop up the girls just as the beta shifters turn in the direction of Shadow Darwin.

Darwin must be living right. He glimpses Julie's service revolver in its holster slung over the back of one of the wooden chairs arranged around the card table.

"Thank you, Julie," Darwin whispers.

Effortlessly, one of werewolves jumps once, then twice, and reaches for the barrel of the Josh Randall. But, it's too late. Darwin pumps the remaining shell into the werewolf's exposed side. The creature doubles over in pain from the massive wound and falls grotesquely to the floor. Since beta shifters are without tissue regeneration, the werewolves can be killed just like humans.

The athletic Darwin turns a somersault over the floor and in one motion pulls the .38 from its holster, and flicks off the safety. The gun only clicks as the empty chamber turns. The gun is empty! The two remain werewolves start to work as a pack and press forward ready to leap on Darwin. They hem Darwin in from exiting to the left down the hall or to the right up the center toward *The X* with a clever strategy. Apparently, reinforcements are moments from arriving!

Suddenly, the night comes alive with the sound of wolves. The howling of a thousand wolves pierces the night. In a flash, Darwin's mind pictures the lodge completely surrounded by wolves. In the next instant, he sees his only way of escape and takes it. Darwin dashes to the right before the werewolves can close rank on that side. Darwin is the last to disappear behind the iron vault door preceded there by the teenagers. One flick of the locking mechanism and the locks shoot home with a satisfying clang. The werewolves run head-on into the wooden façade. Scratching on the door continues for many minutes. Then silence.

Inside the vault, candles are lit, nerves are jagged, and pulses are racing. Darwin and the teenagers look at each other in disbelief. How did they survive what they just encountered? All five sit on the cold concrete floor of the safe. In the dim light, they try to catch their breaths and make some sense of the chaos spinning around them. The biggest mystery of all might prove to be the biggest horror of all—where are Julie, Jill, Newby, Clint Cooper, and McAfee? Are they dead or alive?

More than likely, *they have been werewolves all along.* Just like Glass-Eye Eddie. The teenager's cloistered lives are suddenly exposed to the harsh reality of surviving in a dangerous world full of uncertainty. A place with no guarantees.

The teenagers find themselves in the midst of a quantum growth spurt of maturity required for survival in a post-modern world punctuated by stress, desperation, uncertainty, and terrorism in all its forms. Tears for fears.

Outside in the cold night, it seems every wolf in Big Bend is howling in unison. How many are wolves, and how many are were-creatures?

The air in the vault is in short supply. It will quickly become carbon dioxide—poisonous and fatal. How can this kind of thing occur in such as nice neighborhood?

Darwin wonders to himself if the plan is in full swing. Are shape shifters methodically replacing humans one-by-one in every town and city in the world? Has the population of the earth come down a natural selection mandate? Has aggression been selected over negotiation? Perhaps Darwin's distant relative was wrong. The Sable experience suggests to Darwin a new mandate: survival of the fiercest, instead of the fittest. Considering all that's happening, are the lodgers witnessing the danger of complacency in a crowded world of special interests made crazy by the demands of hidden agendas?

49

CONFRONTATION

One thing is crystal clear: Someone has to leave the vault and fast. With every breath, it is becoming more difficult to breathe. A cell phone call has to be made—a call that seems a long shot amid the struggle of humans and their rivals, the shape shifters. If the cell phone works, there will be someone at 911 who can alert the Texas Rangers or sheriff's deputies to dispatch a snowmobile or helicopter to the top of Mt. Kyle. In anyone's wildest dreams could the experiences of the lodgers been foreseen to unfold as quickly and as deadly as they have? Now, time is most desperate for those trapped in the vault. A quick response from outside help appears to be their only hope. Outside, the lodgers are surrounded on all sides. It is also clear that Shadow Darwin is the person who must leave the safety of the vault and make the call. One call does all.

"Look guys, I'm going to dash over to the front desk ... I left my cell phone over there in all the excitement. We can't survive in here much longer. We'll suffocate. The wolf pack is closing in. If we die, we die trying. It's the only way to go," Darwin says in a determined voice as though the attitude of Americans to defend what they love and honor is bred into his bones. The kids nod. What else can they do?

"Jon and Trevor ... listen carefully ... if anything goes wrong out there and I don't return, you guys have to find a way to get yourselves and the girls out. All of you have a lot of living to do." Shadow looks away with his eyes welling with tears. He always wanted kids. He figured he had plenty of time. Facing the prospects of losing his life, these kids make him wish he had been more realistic in his timeline. In such a short time, bonding with them makes him suddenly realize why he had loved teaching all those young students and why he was somewhat saddened when they graduated. He loved the college life so much he never wanted to graduate. So, he did the next best thing. He became a professor and a professional student. Also, that explains why he always felt closer to the students than to his colleagues.

Jon and Trevor feel a deep pang in their abdomens, a sign of plunging serotonin, indicative of adolescent sensibilities drying up in the pit of their stomachs. There comes a time in every young person's life when he or she must be willing to turn loose of the adolescent trapeze, even though it's not clear who's the catcher on the other side. Will the catcher be in the rye? Will the parental safety net be removed? Perhaps young females are more fearless and make the leap sooner. Possessing the evolutionary means to carry life and give birth, no doubt, speeds the process of maturity and perspective.

Darwin puts the last two shells in the Josh Randall. He spins the chamber of the .38 to give the teenagers the impression it is fully loaded. With two shots of lead, the Bowie strapped to his calf, and a stomach full of acid, Darwin feels completely alone in his quest to survive. He sees in the young faces of Jon and Trevor a kinship all older males have with the new generation. It's a cruel reminder that everything in this world is temporary.

With a flick of the wrist and a spin of the locking handle, Shadow Darwin opens the heavy iron door of the only vault the great outlaws of the Old West failed to crack. He steps out into the lobby of the Sable; it feels cold and abandoned. The fresh air refreshes his lungs. The fire has burned dangerously low leaving weird shadows on the walls that appear to be long, wavy fingers pointing the way to his destiny.

More than anything, Darwin wants to see who is behind the strange occurrences of the weekend. He senses he is destined to meet the king of the shifters—the alpha shifter—face to face. Perhaps he has lived his entire life for this moment. Anyway, Darwin believes the alpha shifter is right around the corner in the *The X*. If he goes down, he goes down trying to depose a dangerous rival.

Darwin does not bother to make the call on the cell phone at the reception desk. He walks right past it on the way to his destiny.

In the darkened hallway, he approaches *X Marx the Spot*. He shudders in the cold air of the Sable. The once blazing hearth is now just a black hole in the brick wall containing a few smoldering logs. It has lost its life.

Darwin passes the hostess stand in the semi-darkness. He stops for a moment to stare at the last night of the full moon. He recalls the time he and his father viewed a full moon through his "new" Explorer telescope his dad purchased for him at a garage sale. They spent an hour or so exploring the heavens for star formations; they even found Venus. That evening is still one of the best memories of his childhood. Many years ago, Darwin decided to keep this experience with his father as a lasting memory when his father died. This time together away from the worries of the world would be his lasting impression of one of the people who gave him life. The simple pleasure of hanging out in the backyard with his dad seems such a distant event. The child in all of us must eventually give up and go ever so reluctantly down the road toward adult responsibilities. Looking down for a moment to gather his courage, he senses what surely lies ahead. *The X is dead ahead and the alpha shifter awaits!*

Sure enough, as he enters *The X,* a tall, shadowy figure stands behind the bar casually mixing a drink. Darwin figures the shape does not belong to Jill Frazier, the beautiful underachieving bar manager. He moves closer, gripping the Josh Randall harder. The empty .38 is under his belt mainly for effect. The Bowie is on his leg. He wants the best shot possible at the tall, shadowy figure.

With his back still facing Darwin, the shadowy figure speaks first. "Good evening, Dr. Darwin. I think you're looking for me." Under the dim mix of moonlight and shadow, the figure turns around. A familiar face appears.

"Peter Marx, what are you doing here? …. We thought you were in Lake Tahoe … We tried reaching you by phone, but …" Darwin's slight stutter increases.

"Come, now Dr. Darwin, don't embarrass yourself. You know I never left Mt. Kyle. How could I? My prize recruit was going to be right here in my backyard over the weekend. Come over here and have a seat. Let me fix you my specialty." With a crooked smile, Marx beckons to Darwin to join him at the bar.

Darwin moves toward the bar. In one of his sweaty hands, he clutches the Josh Randall with his finger on the trigger. Every muscle in his body feels like steel cables wound too tightly. He is trying to position himself to take his best shot with his small arsenal of weapons targeting the head and chest of Peter Marx, the alpha shifter.

Will gunfire be enough of a diversion for what must come next—a direct strike of the Bowie's seven-inch blade across the neck of Peter Marx, severing the head from the body of the alpha shifter?

50

LOOPERS

"Don't tell me you never suspected me of being the alpha. I'm going to feel badly if you never considered me," states Peter Marx, the alpha shifter. He never takes his eyes off Shadow Darwin, one of the few individuals Marx considers to be his intellectual equal.

Barely recognizable to Darwin, Peter Marx stands before him in the morph of the alpha shape shifter. He is dressed in black accentuating his shoulder-length blond hair and piercing blue eyes. Darwin and Marx have been friends for nearly eight years. On a regular basis, Darwin mingles with many of Marx's circle of friends. Now, with all he is about to discover Darwin wonders why the shifter pack had waited so long to make the move to "recruit" him.

Height-wise, Marx is normally about three inches shorter than Darwin, but not tonight. Marx appears taller, as though he's standing on something. He seems more muscular and powerfully built. His shoulders are wider. He looks invincible and seems larger than life. Morphologically, Peter Marx fits what Darwin always imagined the archetypal alpha shifter to be in full morph—tall, powerful, and indestructible. He did not expect cultured, intelligent, and impeccably tailored.

For sure, alpha shifters are certainly not hairy, foul-smelling wolves with blood-red eyes, oily fur, and long yellow teeth. Alpha shifters, as Darwin is about to learn, are successful entrepreneurs and high achievers in all walks of life—individuals who are *au courant* in popular culture. Cool is the only term for alpha shifters, Darwin is sorry to admit to himself.

The only evidence remotely attributable to wolfen characteristics is Marx's fuller lips and somewhat distended mouth, suggesting teeth that must be something to behold. An adversary would never want to see them in full grimace. Darwin correctly deduces the gums are protrusible from the lips as observed in grizzlies, and more recently in the omega looper, Glass-Eye Eddie.

In all respects, Darwin observes that the werewolf myth needs a major revision. Now at close range, Darwin, a human alpha male, and Marx, a wolfen alpha shifter, consider each other. Somewhat disheveled from his two-day encounter with the blizzard and the dangerous intruder (the recently deceased Glass-Eye Eddie Hawkins), unplugged from civilization, and practically buried alive in a blizzard atop Mt. Kyle, Shadow Darwin, looking weak and emaciated, is clearly no physical match for the powerful and confident alpha shifter.

Momentarily, the alpha shifter glances at the Josh Randall and the exposed handle of the .38 in the front of Darwin's trousers and behind his belt.

"I give you a lot of credit for being smart, Dr. Darwin. You must know your weapons are useless against me. They work well enough for the beta and omega loopers, as we refer to our mature subordinates and "lone wolves" respectively. Unfortunately, the loopers have yet to learn precisely the mechanics of morphing into the protective armor afforded by alpha status. Morphing—our major adaptation device—is still experimental to betas and omegas. Mr. Hawkins had a devil of a time with it. I suppose I knew he was destined to fail. Mr. Hawkins suffered from a number of major learning disabilities. The subtle art of morphing, an absolute requirement of our species, completely baffled him. Mr. Hawkins's delicate condition is one of the principal reasons why I never left for Tahoe. We have strong sensibilities to nature and all creatures around us. I sensed the weather would take a turn for the worse, which it did. I felt Mr. Hawkins might give away our little secret, which he did. No one but the most perceptive would have ever guessed the true nature of Mr. Hawkins's condition. With you here, that all changed, as I knew it would. My other little deception centers on you Dr. Darwin."

Shadow Darwin chose to ignore the reference to himself. He decided to gather more information from the loquacious alpha shifter, the most bad ass human-wolf in the world.

"You guessed correctly that the blizzard threw Mr. Hawkins for a loop. In reality, it's a hit-and-miss proposition for loopers. Since Mr. Hawkins could not overcome his omega status as a lonely human, why should he expect to be more in the shifter pack? Let's face it, lone humans become lone loopers. I intend to have words with the beta who brought Mr. Hawkins into the midst of our shifter pack. In all probability, Mr. Hawkins pissed off one of the betas and he just bit him. Like everything else these days, you have to be very careful whom you bite.

"I want to make sure you follow me so it's time for a little lesson in our lexica, Dr. Darwin. Beta shifters and omega shifters who make it into our pack are called 'loopers.' Our packs are elitist like your society, Dr. Darwin, so the lowly omegas seek respect by becoming betas and betas seek apex status by becoming alphas. Both groups must master the morphing process much like a person taking karate must advance though different colored belts.

"Unfortunately, omegas spend too much time at the extreme end of the continuum. They seem more comfortable as wolves. If I may intrude into your profession for a moment and 'read their minds,' I suspect they feel rejuvenated by their ability to aggressively take out their frustrations on others. Who knows, revenge for a lifetime of being shunned and ignored may be the sugar that traps the fly. Remaining in the wolfen morph too long has unfortunate side effects. In the wolfen state, loopers are the most vulnerable. New loopers are extremely susceptible to being killed as wolves. After all, morphing (like your species' adaptation ability) is an evolutionary mandate. It has taken our species over a million years to get it under conscious control to some extent. Omegas who fall between the cracks like Mr. Hawkins are a hazard to our species.

"Knowing you are an accomplished scholar with an insatiable curiosity, and before I reveal my plans for you, Dr. Darwin, I would like to give you a little history lesson," states the alpha.

"My plans fell through for the evening, so I'm all ears—sorry, no pun intended," replies Darwin.

"None taken," answers the alpha.

51

A Short History Lesson

"Coincidently, our species—the shape shifters—began with your species. Dr. Carl Jung who rightly theorized the significance of the collective unconscious explains the reason I know so much about my species from so long ago. I have inherited our entire history as you have yours, Dr. Darwin. It comes to us in dreams. The cradle of our intellectual history comes from the Greeks, who designated a god, Morpheus, to oversee this process in dreams. Yet, today, humans discount the power of dreams. However, it has been shown in hypnosis to be the main depository of all species' collective experiences. As you know, in any given eight-hour night of sleep, the sleeper becomes dreamer about four or five times. The first several dreams tap directly into the collective unconscious. Lucid dreamers have the most graphic experiences. Unfortunately, most humans view sleep as a passive, unconscious event centered on rest and rejuvenation. If they only knew what they're missing. Sleep is like a drive-in movie for dreams to project our primordial past. Primordial experiences comprise the content of *tableaux vivant* until the final dream of the night, which relates directly to everyday experiences. The last dream is the one most often recalled, yet it is the most insignificant one.

"The esoteric Dr. Jung found that in a dreamer's collective unconscious and archetypes, a rich and profound history lesson exists for those astute enough to decipher.

"Also, have you ever wondered why your paleontologists have failed to find the fossilized remains of the so-called missing link? Simple. There is no missing link. It's pure nonsense that lower forms evolve into higher forms. All species develop within their own species—human, animal, and shifter—as omegas, betas, and alphas. You must know *shifters are a sapient link to your species.*

Natural selection favored your species for adaptation abilities, as it favored ours with a more difficult assignment—morphing. I understand through the grapevine that two scientists have found my alpha ancestors in fossilized remains—one in Europe and one in Africa. You see, Dr. Darwin, unless omega and beta loopers master the morph—very few of our ancestors did, our species enters a kind of evolutionary cul-de-sac. We can't progress very far with loopers. We are in the midst of one of our looper cycles now. Some of our shifter historians refer to the time of repopulation of alphas as *alphabetization*.

"Historically, we lost huge numbers of our species due to glitches in the morphing process. Those who couldn't master its finer points fixate on the wolfen form too long. They were hunted and killed as wolves.

"Humans who seemed to vanish off the face of the earth were, more than likely, loopers. From the rich and famous to the faceless in all crowds, if a person vanishes with no trace, chances are great they were subordinate loopers."

Marx pauses to sip his Bloody Mary, the drink of choice for alpha shifters. He checks the time and frowns. It will be daylight soon. He continues.

"Dr. Darwin, morphing is similar to the human skill of adaptation. Your species survived the tortuous process of evolution because of your ability to build things as protection from harsh surroundings. Your species are creators and procreators—creating fire, securing shelter, preparing food, and giving birth to children, and then rearing them. But, your species are also destroyers—killing animals for food and garment, and each other for territory, passion, and revenge. We have survived for roughly the same reasons. We're both creators and destroyers. The act of morphing requires more mental concentration, focus, and experience than building a shelter or starting a fire. While our brains have always been sapient, our experiences in controlling the morph has been our real bug-a-boo. I shudder to think how many times our species tottered on the brink of extinction throughout our turbulent past. As I said, back a million years ago, morphing was very messy, a hit-and-miss proposition. Even 500,000 years ago, it was very unpredictable and unstable. Slowly, a select few of our species mastered the morphing process leading to alpha status. As alpha shifters, we are the last hope of our species. However, beta and omega shifters are everywhere. The world is full of Mr. Hawkins' types. You would be shocked to discover how many human neighborhoods are in actual shifter packs filled with omega and beta loopers.

"Throughout the centuries, we have survived due to sheer luck and, of course, our convenient human disguise. When loopers are found dead, we're either human or wolfen, never in-between. When the mature subordinates are killed toward the human transitional side, they die as a human. That way, no one ever knows our secret. However, if we're killed toward the wolfen state (I believe you saw evidence of that tonight), we die as a wolf with no human characteristics whatsoever. The carcass of a wolf is found.

"Throughout history, the loopers who had the most trouble with morphing become basket cases; they suffered mental illness. I believe psychiatrists diagnosed loopers as schizophrenics, or psychotics who suffer from hallucinatory experiences related to lycanthropic episodes. Many committed suicide due to the horrible nightmares they suffered, which were not nightmares at all; they were real experiences of morphing that seem like bad dreams. Night terrors, fugue states, and amnesia are directly related to the morphing experience as well.

"The Middle Ages were truly Dark Ages for our species. A large number of loopers spent most of their lives in lunatic asylums. Until the eighteenth century, close to 90% of all severe mental illness was due to the effects of sporadic and uncontrolled morphs, or the fear of it. We call the fear of morphing *morphophobia* in our psychiatric lingo.

"With the rise of psychology and psychiatry in the nineteenth century, alpha loopers applied science to our condition. For the past 350 years, we have come into our own. It has been a long and treacherous journey. Finally, we are learning to control the morph by understanding brain chemistry and the placebo affect. Ironically, the work of neuroscientists like yourself paved the way for our species to actualize. Unintentionally I'm sure, progress in your science afforded your unknown rival the final piece of the puzzle—a way to perfect the morph intrapsychically. Now, we're ready to take over as the dominant species. Our numbers are so great when you see wolves or humans, you have to ask yourself whether they're loopers or not," concludes Peter Marx.

52

THE HOUR IS GETTING LATE

The pensive Darwin is now ready for his two-cents worth. "I have two questions," inquires Darwin. "How do you identify loopers or alphas in everyday society?"

"Good questions," replies the alpha. "However, our time is running short. We need to conclude our business before daylight, so please excuse my hasty explanation," the alpha adds politely.

"Alphas have an uncanny clairvoyance with each other and for feeling the presence of loopers. Mostly, we can detect our species through eye contact. In human terms, alcoholics can spot each other at a glance across a large room of 300 or more nonalcoholics. It's the same principle. A huge downside to alpha paterfamilias is an entire cluster of shifter packs can loose wolfen, shifter DNA and become human when its alpha progenitor is killed. Amnesia for shifter status negates memory of their wolfen experience. Wolfen DNA is genetically connected to the alpha progenitor. So, alphas must be very careful not to be killed. We have considerable protection against such an eventuality.

"Alphas are ready to reverse the dominant species. We seek to demote the human race; we want humans to become omega and beta loopers." The alpha finishes his Bloody Mary. Once again he glances at Darwin's handguns.

"For alphas, it takes an elephant gun, a hand grenade, or a bazooka to slow us down. I see you have only 'pop guns' instead. Our ability of *morphallaxis*—rejuvenation of tissue—is a great advantage. The ability was there all the time. Neuroscience showed how this process can work more reliably as mind over matter—due to the placebo affect. Now it is our most sophisticated tool of survival. Our injuries heal almost as fast as they occur.

"Before you could pull the trigger on one of your 'pop guns,' your head will be in your lap. So, Dr. Darwin, please relax. We have great plans for you," states the alpha as though he is meeting a client for drinks.

For a moment, Shadow Darwin imagines he sees the alpha's plan for him in his icy blue eyes.

"Peter, I have to level with you. I'm tired, hungry, and sleep-deprived. This is just a little too much for me right now, but somehow I knew you would be here. So, why me?" asks Shadow Darwin.

"I have wanted you on our side for a very long time. The Desert Estates has become too large for one shifter pack. You did know our neighborhood is entirely wolfen, except for the juveniles," inquires Peter Marx with a gleam in his eyes.

"So you want me on your side—meaning you want me to become a beta looper and eventually an alpha?" inquires Darwin.

"Absolutely. I could not have phrased it more succinctly. We need intelligent human alphas just like you. You will master the morph in a few months under my guidance. While the Eddie Hawkins type in your world is merely unfortunate, in our world they are a major threat to extinction. Tell me, Dr. Darwin, do you know the difference between intelligence and being smart?"

Darwin decides to wait for an explanation.

"As humans, the brain is the source of brilliance and intellect, even if a person doesn't recognize it as such. On the other hand, the habits formed early in life and continuing make a person smart or not so smart. Among loopers we lose many of our ranks due to the casualty of morphing, while humans lose a lot of your members due to the inability to see beyond their own noses. How many emotional dropouts have you observed? As you know, people may be brilliant, but mostly dumb, if you understand my logic. It all boils down to habits. I believe the behaviorist B. F. Skinner identifies behavior that can be either smart or dumb as emitted behavior. Smart people watch for feedback; they know how to interpret useful feedback and ignore the rest. Individuals with a lack of perspective or immaturity are too self-absorbed and boxed into the small circle they inhabit. They miss opportunities everyday. They become self-absorbed, addicted, and useless to themselves and others.

"On the animal level, wolves, like humans, are creatures of habit. Wolfen brains may be smaller but their superior habits make up for lack of cerebral hemispheres. As shifters, we possess the very best of both species—human with a huge cerebrum and neocortex—and wolfen—with instincts, sensibilities, and the superior habits of wolves.

"If nature allowed wolves to utter humanoid sounds at the operant level, they could use speech, language, and their vast store of mental lexica just like humans. As it turns out, although wolves are not as brilliant by nature as humans, they're a lot smarter. That's critical for living in the real world. Alphas share the wolf's basic instincts as well as the *Homo sapien's* larger cerebrum, frontal lobe, neocortex, and propensities for rapid learning.

"The world is not an ivory tower, Dr. Darwin, it's a jungle. The jungle is the place wolves have learned from experience to survive. It's time for the best of the wolfen species and human species to step forward and command a role-reversal with the brilliant, but not so smart humans. In fact, the survival of your species might actually depend upon our success. The world is no longer a safe place; in fact, it really never has been.

"It's been in the myths for a long time. Now, it's scientific fact. Shifters are the next step. As a Darwin, Shadow, you should know that more than anyone; it's in your heredity and in your blood."

A measured bit of silence follows. Shadow Darwin is the first to break it. "Actually, Peter, you were 1 (a) or 1 (b) on my list. Your biggest competitor was of course Glass-Eye … I mean Eddie Hawkins," reveals Darwin.

The alpha stands in silence observing every aspect of the brilliant scientist. The best of one species analyzes the best of another. He feels he is addressing Mr. Charles Darwin himself when he speaks.

"As you have no doubt guessed, Julie and Jill are my beta loopers. They have been with me for some time. I wish they could become alphas, but it's not possible in our species. I asked them to wait at my place until this little matter between you and me is resolved. They are excited about you joining us. I'm sorry to tell you that you shot your friend McAfee a few minutes ago. Mr. Clint Cooper, another of my loopers, hoisted him out into a mound of snow. As you know, loopers do not regenerate like alphas. With the pack always near, nothing but a few bones is left behind after the pack devours the carcass. Carcasses of loopers are a rich source of food due an excess of protein in their muscles. Both Mr. Hawkins and Dr. McAfee are quite dead.

"For all purposes, their deaths will appear as freak accidents, unavoidable in such a remote region caught unaware when the blizzard descended. It will appear as though they were attacked and eaten by a pack of disoriented and hungry wolves. Naughty, naughty, naughty."

"Are there any more alphas in this vicinity?" asks Darwin in a somber demeanor.

"I will leave that to your intellect to decipher. As soon as you become an alpha, you will know. So, I won't spoil it for you. But forget what you have read in the myths. Alphas perpetuate the myths since they were all wrong. It helped to preserve our species over the centuries. Wolves and shifters are much better parents to their pups and juveniles than most human parents, who often wear their dysfunction like merit badges. We don't become alcoholics, drug addicts, wife beaters, pornographers, child molesters, or pill poppers. You'll find far fewer psychiatric problems in our packs.

"Occasionally, an omega will go ballistic—like the unfortunate Mr. Eddie Hawkins—and must be driven out of the pack or killed. I think human omegas are personified in the likes of Charles Manson, Ted Bundy, and Jeffrey Dahmer. On the other hand, I believe Jack the Ripper was in reality a very accomplished beta looper.

"Since we reanimate tissue, we can disappear from one place as we age and we can reappear in another place at any age we choose. Pretty cool, huh? But, enough is enough. It's time to take care of business, Dr. Darwin. I think you know what I mean," concludes the alpha with a wink.

53

BLOOD BROTHERS

"I have one more question … if you don't mind," requests Shadow Darwin politely.

"By all means," said his soon-to-be blood brother.

"I can't deny my academic curiosity from your unique perspective regarding characteristics among wolves, humans, and shifters," implores Darwin.

"We have plenty of time for cross-species analysis, but I know you academic types. You love to compare and contrast, analyze, and write your nosologies, and study your taxonomies. Let's just say this is Orientation 101 into species differentiation with a three-dimensional analysis. Unfortunately, last Friday evening you missed my lecture on the social order of wolves at the last meeting of the animal preservation society. It's rather ironic, don't you think, with all you know now?

"It's obvious that human society, like wolf packs and shifter packs, is elitist. First, alpha males and alpha females are the leaders across human and animal groups. Female alpha shifters are missing in our species due to brain chemistry. We prize nurturing from females as much as fierceness in males. In human society as well as in wolf packs, the alpha pair comprise the power couple. In human society, alphas are assertive, self-educated beyond formal education, unabashed, and self-motivated. The 'alpha mindset' often produces wealth. They are the artisans, politicians, and CEOs—the ones who lead corporate America. They often marry wealth so they can perpetuate control. When two human alphas marry, which they often do, they become the high-profile power couple known throughout popular culture. They are affluent professionals who live in the best neighborhoods and send their kids to the best schools. They are intrepid in the face of existential living—knowing success in life has little to do with liking and a lot to do with doing.

"In the psychologist Rotter's view, they are the internal LOCs—individuals with an internal locus (focus) of control. They believe in themselves and it shows. Sustained effort and focus produce positive results. In the interpersonal psychologist Sullivan's taxonomy, they are syntaxic thinkers—able to leap beyond logic and imagine aftermaths of behavior with astounding accuracy. They apply psychology everyday. Although compulsive to a fault, they exhibit remarkable flexibility—they strategize, look before they leap, and are intellectually fit. Human alpha males and females survive young adulthood with family in tact; they understand the difference between sex and intimacy. They communicate; they listen; they work things out; they are good judges of character; they don't display nervous, inappropriate laughter, which communicates insincerity to those smart enough to notice.

"Next, beta males and beta females are normally the mature subordinates across all three groups. In humans, however, the most diversity exists in betas observed across a wide continuum from radiant health on one side to severe disorder on the other. Usually, dysfunctional betas suffer from lack of effort toward fulfilling active imaginations. They wish to be more assertive, but talk is safer than action.

"They watch for any opportunity to join the ranks of alphas, but seldom make it due to self-imposed limitations, jealousy, infighting, and self-sabotage. They are not trustworthy due to their limited perspective and immaturity. They are often backstabbers, and they harbor hidden agendas. They are always searching for something, and they feel empty with results. Psychiatrically, they suffer from personality disorders, especially of the borderline, histrionic, and narcissistic varieties, and eating disorders. Due to immaturity and lack of perspective, they often flunk out of college as though they are supposed to, and they accept menial occupations that lead to a dead end, disappointment, and frustration —the making of victimization.

"Among humans, many betas need to become alphas with a healthy dose of self-efficacy, focus, and hard work; but, fundamentally, they can't see beyond what's right in front of them. Down deep, they don't know the first thing about themselves. Down deep they are afraid someone will discover the truth—that they are as hollow as a common straw kids use to drink milk through.

They have allowed others to direct their lives too long. They do not have their appetites under control. In Rotter's view, they are the external LOCs—they believe luck or chance is behind most achievement, and in Sullivan's view, they are parataxic thinkers preferring bias and convoluted logic. Due to these deficits, many betas become functional alcoholics, drug addicts, and the 'pill poppers' in human society."

Peter Marx pauses. He looks deeply into Shadow Darwin's eyes. In his clairvoyant ability, he sees many instances of individuals crossing his path as greedy social modelers. Marx knows they secretly admire Darwin but dare not let a single person know.

"Fundamentally, betas lack mental discipline. The betas who accept their flaws and strive to overcome them make huge contributions in human and wolfen groups by accepting their subordinate role. Few betas ever rise to the ranks of alphas. It takes great effort, focus, sacrifice, and perseverance—qualities that elude them. The few human betas that assume the place of alphas become self-actualized and work tirelessly to become their own person.

"Similar to shifter and wolf species, the omegas of human culture are often the outcasts—the antisocial misfits—who live in a scary inner world. In severe forms they are the predators of human society—the murders, child molesters, and stalkers. No myth or legend can rival human omegas as the true monsters of society. Their dysfunctional genes need to reach an evolutionary cul-de-sac—the end of the bag.

"Finally, the pups, or the young juveniles, round out the packs. They are the offspring who prosper with leadership of alphas and mature betas across all three species. Among shifters, a juvenile has to be over twenty-five years of age before looper status is considered. By that age, most are so disillusioned with hypocrisy observed in society that the change is an easy sell."

"Interesting," reacts Darwin as though he has been contemplating some of the finer points of the alpha's presentation. "Something just occurred to me. How does a human become a shifter in the first place?"

"I thought you would never ask," answers the alpha with the wide eyes of a child.

54

CONVERSION CRITERIA

Peter Marx seems to relish the opportunity to share his intellect on the delicate point of conversion. Never complacent, he seeks to match wits with his human Romulus, Shadow Darwin.

"Again, forget what you read in the books. There are only three ways a human becomes a looper. The first way, the old way, is to be bitten by an alpha, or a looper. The second way is by inheriting the shape shifter genotype. It can skip generations like most chemical disorders do. The third way is being pricked—pricked by the needle hidden inside my clever little necklace. My alpha blood is in the cylinder. One dip of the needle and one little pinprick, and that's all it takes. Alpha wolfen DNA is more powerful than pure testosterone. One drop in the bloodstream and the person becomes a looper within hours." Marx holds the amber glass and silver-ribbed cylinder between his oversized thumb and long forefinger.

Shadow Darwin observes the necklace and then looks away from the alpha. "I have one request before you inject me or infect me, whatever you are going to do. I want the kids to be delivered safe far away from this place."

"I'm ahead of you Dr. Darwin. Jon and Trevor will make terrific loopers one day soon, and so will the girls. But they have to be old enough. I want them in my pack. In the meantime, my private helicopter should be landing any minute to provide safe transport of the juveniles to Jon's mother's home deep in the valley. They will be safe there until we can dig out Mt. Kyle and things return to normal. I have already left messages with the kids' parents. I know them all. They trust me explicitly to do the right thing."

No sooner did the words leave the mouth of Peter Marx than the sound of a helicopter's powerful blades pierce the cold night.

Shadow Darwin and the alpha shifter have struck a blood bargain. *They are about to become blood brothers.*

But first, the juveniles have to go.

INTO THE LAIR OF THE ALPHA

Final good-byes are not easy, especially with all Shadow Darwin knows. He has a heavy heart. But, he has to work fast. He retrieves the teenagers from the vault.

"Am I crazy, or is that the sound of a helicopter outside?" asks Jon Marx, as the teenagers emerge from the vault giddy from oxygen deprivation.

"Jon, I had enough time on the low battery of the cell phone to contact your father. He brought me up to speed on arrangements he made from Lake Tahoe hours ago. He is sending his private helicopter to rescue us. The chief, your friends, and you must go first. I'll come along later on the second flight." Shadow found it much easier to lie with everyone scared, hungry, and tired.

"I have to find Julie, Jill, and our good nurse. I suppose McAfee and Mr. Cooper will turn up too. They are probably out looking for the women as we speak," speculates Darwin. "Jon, you and Trevor help me wheel the chief into the 'copter. You girls can wait by the door."

Loading up the chief was not a problem. One of the two husky helicopter pilots came in handy.

As he ducks under the powerful blades of the craft, Shadow is mildly surprised when Jon and Trevor extend their hands in friendship before they board the 'copter.

"Take care, Dr. Darwin, thanks for all your help and for keeping your cool. If more adults were like you, kids would have no excuse but to be normal ... I guess. Thanks for saving our lives. Trevor and I have some great material for term papers," Jon Marx jests.

Gable and Ashley embrace Shadow with a group hug, also a surprise.

"I guess you kids aren't going to the dogs like everyone thinks."

"No, we're just going to the wolves," quips the smart mouth of Jon Marx.

Shadow could only shake his head from side to side. *You may be right*, Shadow thinks.

With the door secure and seatbelts in place, the 'copter revs up her engines. The craft makes a swift ascent into the safety of the dark sky.

Within a few seconds, the Aerospecial is completely out of sight. But, the silence is short-lived. First one wolf then another interrupts the stillness of the night. Presently, the lodge seems surrounded by a huge wolf pack. Again, Shadow Darwin finds himself in the company of wolves.

Shadow braces himself against the cold. He enters the front door of the lodge and heads into the lair of the alpha. He is uncertain whether or not the blizzard, a freak accident of nature, has shaped his destiny. The theoretical prospect is intellectually delicious but it must wait. He files it away for future reference ... if he has a future.

As he enters *The X* the number of patrons has grown arithmetically. His glance falls on the missing lodgers—Julie, Jill, Susan Newby, and Clint Collins. They sit leisurely at the bar talking barely above a whisper. The bartender is Peter Marx, the alpha.

"Beside water, I always wondered what werewolves drink," Shadow remarks.

"We're partial to Bloody Marys," answers Julie radiating femininity in her beta looper morph.

"With salt on the rim, garnished with lime. A long-stemmed cherry has to be floating on top," adds a more voluptuous Jill Frazier in full blush as a beta looper.

There's no denying that female beta loopers might fulfill every requirement of companionship and nurturing complementing fierceness expected in beta and alpha male shifters. Gender—the behavior expected of a male or a female in a given society appears clearly differentiated in shifter society.

"May I?" Shadow pulls out a barstool. He sits down beside Julie.

"Peter, are you familiar with the mythical founders of Rome?" Shadow asks as he bellies up to the bar. "I think I'll take one of those Bloody Marys. I have an awful thirst." Shadow makes himself comfortable.

"Of course—Romulus and Remus—they're in all the mythology books. It's standard reading in high school," replies the alpha.

"Tell us," requests Julie. She glances at her pack members—Jill, Susan, and Clint. They indicate they didn't know the story.

"May I?" asks Darwin, seeking permission from the alpha.

"Knock yourself out," grants the alpha.

Shadow gulps down half of the best Bloody Mary he has ever tasted. Then he begins his story.

"The twin sons of Mars and the Vestal Virgin, Rhea Silvia, were Romulus and Remus. They were the mythical founders of Rome. Placed in a basket and set afloat on the Tiber River, the basket came to rest at the grotto Lupercal.

"There, the twins were saved from starvation by suckling a she-wolf. A shepherd family finds the twins completely unharmed. They raise them as their sons. As young men, they are strong and handsome, and blessed with visionary gifts. So, they decide to establish a city.

"After studying meteorological signs and geological landmarks, they determine a portion of two sections of the proposed city would be under the providence of each of them. A deep furrow is cut in the earth to mark the two boundaries. It is discovered that Romulus' section is about twice the size of Remus' section. Remus, motivated by jealous rage, jumps over the furrow and lands on his brother's side. This sudden and unprovoked action regarding the disproportionate share prompts Romulus to kill Remus. Interestingly, another version of the story by the poet Ennius has Remus simply disappearing during a storm, possibly a blizzard. Undaunted, Romulus builds the city of Rome. According to the myth, it is named after him. He is later deified."

"Entertaining story, but what's the point?" asks the stuffy beta looper, Clint Cooper.

"The point is one of derivation and description I believe," answers Darwin. "The myth failed to identify Romulus and Remus as alpha shape shifters. The myth is actually a metaphor of revenge and survival. I think the story of Cain and Abel in the Old Testament involves a similar theme of jealousy, conflict, and ultimately survival. Mythmakers had no idea Romulus and Remus were descendants of shape shifters from millions of years ago. You left out this little bit of history, Peter. Apparently, an alpha descendant of Romulus was discovered in Africa and an alpha descendant of Remus was found in Europe. How many alphas are left?" Shadow pauses, half expecting an answer. Then he continues. "I guess I can answer my own question ... only time will tell," concludes Shadow Darwin half to himself.

"Thus you see, ladies and gentlemen, the worth of Dr. Darwin to our cause," replies the alpha.

56

THE BARGAIN

"The matter of our little bargain must now be addressed," says Darwin. He makes deliberate and constant eye contact with Peter Marx. "I haven't been completely honest with you Peter." He gulps down the remainder of the Bloody Mary and puts it aside on top of a cocktail napkin.

"We have no more time for smoke and mirrors, Dr. Darwin. We have our bargain and my agenda. Let's get on with it. You have a lot of training in store," replies the alpha matter-of-factly. He comes from behind the bar and stands close behind Darwin. The alpha senses the new recruit will present more difficulties than anticipated. Apparently, he's not just going to roll over and become wolfen.

Shadow Darwin, a human alpha male and distant relative of the man who spent more time studying species—both human and animal—than anyone else in the world, stands up and turns to face the powerful alpha shape shifter. He lifts his leg to the height of a bar stool, rests his foot on the seat and leans against it. His trouser cuff still hides the Bowie's leg strap.

"Peter, I'm not going out with a whimper." Suddenly, in one swift motion he pulls the Bowie knife from his leg strap under his trouser leg. His lightning speed and fluid motion is reminiscent of gunfighters of the old West. He aims at the right eye of Peter Marx. Like the slow-motion scene in the movie *The Matrix*, the knife is perceived by the alpha as a projectile in slow-motion flight. With plenty of time to snatch it out of the air in mid-flight, he avoids serious injury. Peter Marx's expression never changes. Nor does Darwin's, who does not seem the least bit surprised.

"Hit or miss, I've wanted to do that all night," says a smiling Darwin.

Alpha shape shifters are fearless predators. Since their wolfen

DNA configures their skin, bones, connective tissue, circulatory system, and vital organs to be practically invincible, a deathblow is practically impossible. Yet, alphas possess an Achilles tendon—one fatal flaw. The only way to kill an alpha is by decapitation—the evidence clearly apparent in the fossil finds of Dr. Zander and Dr. Martine. No rejuvenation is possible when the head is severed from the body. Alphas cannot morph into any other forms when the spinal cord is severed. The shape shifter looses its Mojo, and it dies. Instinctively, alphas have knowledge of this fatal flaw. With this in mind, they are aggressive from start to finish. They tear into the flesh of competitors with their powerful jaws, teeth, and claw-hands. Massive bleeding follows and that's usually the end.

Sensing the resistance of Darwin, Peter Marx grabs him by the lapels of his jacket and throws him across the room. Darwin slams into the wall bearing the great Shield of the Warriors and the double-edged tomahawk. Both come crashing down inches from Darwin. Displaying the athleticism of a younger man, Darwin retrieves the razor sharp warrior's tomahawk from the floor and in one motion, hurls it at the head of the alpha, who momentarily glances away from the fray to register the admiration of his loop-ers sitting at the bar. His look of narcissistic arrogance is quickly replaced by goggle-eyed surprise when he turns to face the whirl-ing tomahawk *vis-a-vis*.

The momentary lapse in the alpha's concentration allows the accuracy of Darwin's throwing skill to register a direct hit. The sharp blade of the hatchet separates the head from the body of Peter Marx. To the amazed onlookers, the ancient struggle from millions of years ago is over in the blink of an eye with the sever-ing of Peter Marx's head. For the future of *Homo sapiens*, the hatchet fell into the right hands and across the right neck. The carcass of the instantly dead alpha falls to the floor. Concomitantly, the demeanor of the former loopers—Julie, Jill, Susan, and Clint change immediately to the complete surprise of Darwin. Thank-fully, it is true that betas lose their enhanced looper status and wolfen side with the death of the alpha progenitor. *Homo sapiens* may just have caught a lucky break. If true, Shadow suspects the Desert Estate recruits of Peter Marx will never again recall their lives as loopers in any way except in dreams and nightmares, a safe refuge for imaginings.

Without a shadow of a doubt the secret is safe with Shadow Darwin.

57

Good for You

Sunday

All things considered, including sleep deprivation and REM rebound, Shadow Darwin feels revived and strong enough to walk outside and greet the cold morning sunrise on the front wraparound porch of the Sable. Practicing yoga and staying in good shape for most of his life helped his body and mind recover from the stress and trauma of the life-or-death encounter with the dangerous alpha and his shifter pack.

He wraps himself in a quilt, which has been warmed by the fire. He finds one of the large wooden rockers to sit in and think. He suspects the shifter pack of the Marx Desert Estates will, like loopers Julie, Jill, Susan, and Clint Cooper, return to complete normalcy courtesy of retrograde amnesia due to neutralized wolfen DNA upon the death of Peter Marx. Darwin feels somewhat confident there are no more alphas in North America, Africa, or Europe. For the rest of the world, especially in the Middle East, he is not so sure.

It is what he understands to be an existential condition of life best exemplified at birth by infants who are surrounded by smiling faces and all the infant can do is cry. Maybe infants have prescient knowledge about the harsh realities of living than adults give them credit for.

The Tahoe celebrants return soon and make their way up the north side entrance. The roads are remarkably clear as the temperature returns to the mid-40s. No doubt everybody will go outside and play in the snow and make snowmen surrounded by snow family members.

Just as the sun clears the horizon, Shadow's concentration is disturbed by the faraway sound of a helicopter. He glances back to the Eastern sky and sees a tiny dot just under the line of gray clouds, the exit point of the storm. If the 'copter belonged to Peter Marx, it is strange that it is returning so soon.

Sure enough, as it approaches the Sable's front lawn, Darwin glimpses Peter Marx's logo—ME—on the side of the Aerospecial helicopter, one of the most expensive jet helicopters in the world. He recognizes one of the pilots from last evening.

He stands to his full height and lets the quilt fall to the wooden floor of the porch now wet with melting snow. He feels strong legs under him. He moves close to the passenger side as the blades of the magnificent craft idle. The lone passenger opens the door. Jon Marx invites Darwin into the 'copter.

"Jon, what are you doing here? Where are your friends?" asks Darwin over the sound of the slowing blades.

"They're fine; they're with my mom in the valley. I arranged to return with the pilots. I came back to make sure everything worked out all right," replies Jon Marx.

"Why don't you come into the lodge, Jon? I have some rather unnerving news to tell you," Darwin says.

"Not as unnerving as mine," answers Jon as his eyes glow red, the sign of of a juvenile looper, yet another alpha in training. Wolfen DNA obviously had not skipped Jon's generation.

Shadow's heart sinks. He jumps almost head first out of the 'copter as it suddenly ascends. Darwin falls to earth with a thud.

Jon Marx settles back into the plush seat of the craft as it hovers over the head of Shadow Darwin. He reminisces over his newfound liberation as he pushes in Third Eye Blind's track of *Good for You*. He is pleased with the prospects for the future. With the death of Peter Marx, obviously known through the clairvoyance of his son Jon Marx, disheartening questions remain: Will Jon Marx learn the complicated nuances of looping by himself? Or, is an alpha mentor somewhere nearby? Or, will Jon decide to remain human and ignore his wolfen side, an option always open to those who inherit wolfen neurochemistry? Many options face individuals regardless of their species of origin.

Returning to the warmth of the lodge with a weary heart, the experience with Jon weighs heavily in the mind of Shadow Darwin. Recalling the poem *Richard Cory* by Edward Arlington

Robinson, obviously, Jon's not the happy-go-lucky rich kid; he has a darker side.

58

AFTERMATH

In the years that follow in the wake of the Sable experience—the fateful weekend when courageous lodgers in West Texas forestalled a looper uprising against their human rivals, the teenagers forge a lasting bond. They share the secret of that weekend with no one else. Who would believe them anyway? Jon, Trevor, Ashley, and Gable go their separate ways and flourish in college. Jon moves to New York for a while to pursue a writing career in horror fiction, but subsequently moves back home to the Desert Estates, and shares his former home with his mother. Under her guidance, Marx Enterprises continues to prosper, especially in the specialty restaurants of *X Marx the Spot*. Everyone there, sooner or later, discovers they have something in common, but they can't quite figure out what it is.

Jon establishes several endowed chairs in higher education. He eventually receives his masters degree in anthropology. He continues to write for pleasure and occasionally publishes short works of fiction. Recently, he submitted a proposal to David Pike, an associate editor at Kendall/Hunt Publishers, for publication of a novella recounting the fictitious experiences of four teenagers trapped in a hotel during a blizzard marked by strange occurrences in far West Texas.

Trevor is playing college football and aspires to be a professional athlete. Occasionally, he has nightmares about the night he and Jon confronted Glass-Eye Eddie. But he's a big boy now and that's all in the past. Through the years, the nightmares slowly disappear from his dreamscape. Healing is all about closure and then staying busy.

The once academically insecure Gable Jordan is in medical school at the University of Texas, Southwestern Medical School in

Dallas. She discovered a love of science can take the place of cheerleading with a little effort, inspired teaching, and the encouragement of Susan Newby her new mentor. However, she can still do a back round-off, back flip-flop and she expects to do it in her own backyard trampoline with her children when the time comes.

Ashley is a psychology major at Sul Ross State University. Her faculty advisor is Dr. Shadow Darwin. Her modeling career takes her to Paris and Rome during her summers and spring breaks. She has her sights set on a Ph.D. in clinical forensic psychology, regardless of how much success she experiences in modeling. She is intrigued by the brilliance of brain chemistry and how strategy, focus, and perseverance make individuals smart.

In their own way, each of the lodgers succeeds in adjusting to the events of the Sable Lodge during one of the worst blizzards in Texas history.

Dr. Shadow Darwin led police to the spot outside *The X* where hair and tissue samples gathered at the scene, along with a few large bones and teeth, proved conclusive when matched to dental records. Officially, the deaths of Peter Marx, Dr. Wells McAfee, and Eddie Hawkins are ruled accidental—attributed to a freak accident of nature, and its deleterious effect on a pack of disoriented and hungry wolves. After all is said and done, the blizzard is to blame for the strange occurrences of the Sable experience.

According to an animal psychologist, the destructive force of blizzards disorients wolves. In their heightened state of awareness, exacerbated by hunger and fear, they often attack any available food source.

A judicial hearing followed in subsequent months and concluded that a reasonable man could not have foreseen such an occurrence; hence, the deaths were ruled accidental. Wolves have been known to attack humans in the past and there's no guarantee they won't do it again in the future.

Brewster County sheriff's deputies find the body of Mr. Laurence Harvey, the former math teacher of Mt. Kyle High School, mid-day on Sunday. They attributed the cause of death to a freak accident due to the sudden appearance of ice and snow, causing the road to be too hazardous for safe travel.

Chief Jake Munoz makes a full recovery. He retires with a full pension and moves to a few acres near Alpine, Texas. Julie Quixotica becomes the new police chief of Mt. Kyle, and wins many accolades for meritorious service.

A segment of the television show, *Unexplained Mysteries*, tries to explain the fateful weekend at the Sable with a piece entitled: *Fable at the Sable or Reliance on Science?* Animal control groups volunteer to investigate whether or not wolves overpopulate the Big Bend area adjacent to Mt. Kyle. The report shows a very small wolf population manageable under normal circumstances.

Animal behaviorists launched a new web site with the latest findings from Mt. Kyle targeting homeowners who live in areas populated by wolves. To protect residents in the event of such a devastating meteorological reoccurrence, new guidelines become operative, warning residents of the dangers of disoriented, hungry, and frightened predators of the wild.

Dr. Shadow Darwin returns to his duties as chair of the neuropsych department at Sul Ross. He gathers enough data from his experiences at the Sable to revise myths relating to wolves and the reality that myths associated with shape shifters is completely false. Still, it is common knowledge that everybody trusts their beliefs and biases more than they do science. While Darwin's views should be revolutionary, they probably won't change a thing.

Revenge on rivals is as ancient as time. Darwin's theory of revenge may prove to be more applicable to modern times than anyone imagined.

The myth that alpha wolves are bad, evil, or demonic no longer jives with the new insights gained from Peter Marx's analogies of wolves, shifters, and humans. It is possible that one species can benefit from the experiences of another species and be better off for having the experience. Why not take all that's good about the wolf pack and incorporate those qualities into human families? The wolf pack nurtures and takes care of their juveniles. The value of an *eclectic perspective* is perhaps the best argument parents should use in persuading their juveniles to pursue a college degree. Everywhere in nature there are valuable lessons to learn. Unfortunately, human families have nothing to give back to wolves as a *quid pro quo*. When humans nurture their young, wolves are already doing it. When humans are abusive, neglectful, or harmful to their young—any behavior that's detrimental to healthy development—the wolf pack has already rejected it. Wolves have survived so long due to their human quality of being brilliant due to chemistry and being smart due to good habits. They didn't ask to be born, so they do what comes naturally: They love and care for their young and try to survive another day in hostile surroundings.

As for Jon Marx, he is fully aware he has choices to make not open to most people. He has reached a fork in the road. As a looper, with his human and wolfen disguises, he can travel down the human alpha road, or go by the way of the shape shifter. Choices require decisions.

Also, Jon Marx has the friendship of Shadow Darwin. Darwin decides to leave the decision in Jon's hands. Let him make the first move. Slowly, Darwin comes to the conclusion that Jon is making the right decision—to traverse the *Homo sapien* road of adaptation and not the looper's way of morphing. But, time will tell. It always does. In the meantime, Shadow Darwin does what he does best—observes human behavior and personality. When he meets someone new or has a conference with a new student, he always asks himself the question on the mind of every psychology major, "I wonder what this person is *really* like?"

59

POSTSCRIPT

Seven years after the Sable experience, Shadow Darwin is in his office overlooking the western part of Sul Ross. It is a beautiful spring afternoon the likes of which only West Texas weather produces. Most of the students have left for the day. He is sitting alone in quiet contemplation. The events surrounding one of the worst blizzards in West Texas history lingers in his thoughts. As he approaches forty-two years of age, he is contemplating whether the events of the Sable experience have altered his philosophical views. He is reminded of Jean-Paul Sartre's existential literature. According to Sartre, we must find happiness and contentment in an uncertain and ambiguous world—a tenuous world characterized by behavior, responsibility, and consequences. Nothing comes free. He wonders why parents shield their teenagers from this reality for so long.

He is reminded of Sartre's little play *No Exit (Huis Clos)* about three people who discover they are trapped in Hell. When alive, the characters lived amid insincerity. They were incapable of making *authentic decisions*. Now, they dare not redefine their lives, even in their current predicament. Confronting the future is unbearable without maintaining the bond to the past. When a journalist asked Sartre to provide a short explanation of his play he responded—

> ...A vast number of people in the world are in Hell because they are too dependent upon the judgments of other people. What I am implying is that many people are encrusted in a set of habits and customs. They make judgments about people that make themselves and others suffer. THEY DON'T EVEN TRY TO CHANGE. Such people are to all intents and purposes dead. They are dead in the sense that they cannot break out of the frame

of their worries, their concerns, and their habits. Therefore, they continue in many cases to be the victims of
judgments passed on them by other people ... I wanted
to show the importance of freedom to us—the importance of changing acts by other acts. No matter what
circle of Hell we are living in, I think we are free to break
out, and if we don't break out, we are staying there of
our own free will.

Darwin wonders what the outcome of the Sable experience
would have been had he not entertained the possibility that an
alpha shape shifter was behind the strange occurrences set in motion by the blizzard. Regardless, he has never been dismissive of
determinism with its limited menu, or behaviorism adhering to
cause and effect, or Sartre's view of freedom, none of which he has
decided is contradictory. The menu is intact and freedom is there
for the taking. We have to find the courage to admit that exercising
choices is often scary. We can't beat ourselves up when we're
wrong. We just have to keep trying.

Like the stoic Epictetus, Darwin continues to live his life without worry for the things he has no control over. The government,
politics, and world affairs continue in their orbits regardless if he
worries or not. Like Voltaire's *Candide*, Darwin finds peace in tend-
ing to his own garden—reading, teaching, writing, targeting his
Bowie, practicing his yoga postures, and being decent to others.
Lately, he's been thinking a lot about settling down with a wife
and a family. After all, you don't actually have to settle down that
much, just rearrange priorities.

On the seemingly common occurrence of freak accidents, he
analyzes a common example. Suppose a motorist is driving down
a narrow country lane, a winding kind of road with no shoulders.
It is early in the morning and very dark, a time when animals are
still foraging for food. The car speed is about 40 miles-per-hour,
and the headlights are on full beam. Suddenly, a few feet in front of
the car, a squirrel darts out from the thick grass-lined road. The
driver sees the squirrel, but is it too late? In a split second, both the
driver and the animal have options. The driver can apply the
breaks and try to steer away from the animal, or he can speed up,
or he can simply continue at the same speed with no adjustments.
How much of what the driver does prevents or contributes to the
animal's fate? We must not forget the animal has options too. He

can dart up or down, or he can dart sideways. He can stop on a dime or attempt to run back from where he came.

In this *confluence of events,* will he survive or will he become road kill? If the animal reacts in the wrong direction could it have been avoided? Or, is any action on either side simply too late? Whose fault is it?

Philosophical *determinism* is the academic egg that hatches experimental scientists like Shadow Darwin. In fact, determinism underlies all science. By this method, antecedent events (past experiences) set up narrow "menus" of "selection." The menu appears as "choices" related to capricious *free will.* Proponents of determinism argue the "choices" we make are really the only "choices" we could have made given the limited menu.

The scientist speaks of *contingencies of behavior* that sets up the menu directing subsequent behavior as cause and effect. In behavioral science, examples of determinism are psychological profiling, developmental stages, criminal behavior, and personality development.

Returning to the squirrel and the car analogy, the way the squirrel darts is based upon antecedent events of similar occurrences in the past. If darting to the left produces another day of life, the squirrel will be expected to dart that way in the future. Or, due to time compression, the squirrel may become disoriented and dart in any direction. It's a toss up whether or not it survives. Clearly, behavioral contingencies from the squirrel's prior "darting behavior" will be a factor—*if he has time and is not disoriented.*

If an unforecasted blizzard blows into town causing an unintended morph in a dim-witted looper and in the process uncovers an entire community of beta loopers masquerading as humans, is the confluence of events simply accidental? Eventually, would the charade have been discovered?

Perhaps it all boils down to the fact that we are simply *too late* or *too disoriented* or, in Sartre's view *too dependent* on other's views, stereotypes, or biases to avoid catastrophic outcomes. Hence, for the sake of authorities who have no clue of what really happened the events end up being labeled freak accidents.

The Sable experience solidified Darwin's philosophical views, rather than diminishing them. Paraphrasing the great sophist, Protagoras, how each person turns out in life is a measure of that person's own self-worth and ability to get things done.

Eventually, college students learn that success in college has nothing to do with liking it; rather, success in college has everything to do with simply *getting it done*. Like wolves, sophisticated individuals wise in the *ways of the world* may have the best chance of avoiding self-sabotage, major disappoints, and ultimate disillusionment.

Hoping no one sees us as we clear the lump from our throat and tears from our eyes contemplating underneath all the harsh realities life throws at us a fundamental truth resides: There is so much beauty in the world. Evidence is startling and everywhere. Look no further than music, children's faces, and the embrace from those who care so much for us—the same ones we met in a hospital room long before we could walk. Like defensive drivers, we must watch others like a hawk. We must wade into relationships, not fall into them. You never know when a looper may be looking our way.

60

THE HITCHHIKER

On a cold December day on the way to Mt. Kyle to visit an old friend, Shadow Darwin takes the high road along a mountain trail using his four-wheel drive Jeep. Far below on State Highway 118 he notices a lone hitchhiker, wrapped in a long black coat with a black knapsack on his back. He is walking along State Highway 118 in the midst of Big Bend National Park. The events of the blizzard at the Sable Lodge are now a distant a memory. It is near dusk. All deserts are known to lose heat rapidly at sundown. During the day the temperature barely climbed into the fifties, so the mid-forties feel much colder with the steady wind. The hitchhiker walks casually along the side of the road with his back to the passing cars heading into Mt. Kyle to the west. His left hand is down with the thumb up indicating his interest.

Presently, a 1966 candy apple red Mach 1 Mustang roars by. About fifty yards down from the hitchhiker, the red taillights blaze, suggesting the driver is stopping to offer a ride. The hitchhiker breaks into a laconic jog and catches up with the waiting car. The loud rumble, rumble, rumble of the car indicates a large engine displacement. The driver invites the hitchhiker into the sleek "muscle car." The car speeds off, laying twin tracks of rubber and blue tire smoke.

About ten miles past the point where the hiker made his hitch, the car weaves into the oncoming lane and the back again several times. Then, just as quickly, it comes to an abrupt halt on the side of the road. The passenger side door springs open. A large gray wolf jumps out. It heads into the dark woods of Big Bend. The sound of a howling wolf ignites a chorus of wolves in the vicinity of Mt. Kyle and beyond. The car's engine revs up. The driver continues up the steady grade leading into Mt. Kyle.

192

Shadow Darwin continues his ride along the ridge of the mountain with a new perspective. He pats the Bowie strapped to his leg for assurance. Up ahead is the Sable Lodge and Mt. Kyle, Texas.

This time around the events that are sure to unfold will not be attributable to freak accidents atop the Mountain of the Ghost.

NO SHADOW OF A DOUBT

Author Commentary—Chapter Notes

FRIDAY

1—The Find

The name "Max Zander" is in reference to the second philosopher from the Milesian school of Greek philosophy, *Anaximander* (circa 546 B.C.) and rhymes with it. Anaximander believed both animals and humans evolve. This view anticipates the thesis and worldwide recognition of the Englishman, Charles Darwin, a distant relative of Shadow Darwin. The find of the millennium by a renowned scientist sets the tone of *anticipation* and *authentication* with a fossil find that *may redraw the human family tree.* Authenticated by a renowned scientist, suspense arises over the identity of the find and why it was *decapitated.*

2—The Rival

Continuation of suspense regarding the fossilized remains of "the creature." If Dr. Zander's fossil proves humans have a *rival* (two distinct sapient creatures evolving from about the same timeframe in evolutionary history), what is it? How did it cleverly disguise itself? Since there are two distinct lines (two species), there is a shift away from evolution of species from lower forms to higher forms to *development within separate species as an adaptive mechanism* in line with survival of the fittest.

3—Wells McAfee

Dr. Wells McAfee stands for *allegiance to scientific inquiry,* professional integrity, and loyalty to students in the college experience. He is the antithesis of childish "turf wars" and rivalries observed among the pedagogically contentious. (However, competition between disciplines is not an altogether unhealthy condition. It can stimulate higher quality teaching.) The Foreword to Shadow Darwin's book *Reinventing Myth* introduces the place of *myth* in a world facing modern problems, *existential concerns,* and *post-modern sentimentalities*. A reoccurring theme in the novel relates to existentialism. A twentieth century philosophical movement, existentialism centers on the psychological problems created by individuals facing an unfathomable universe and the stress caused by shouldering the ultimate responsibility for actions without certain knowledge of what is right or wrong. The postmodernist may wish to return to more traditional perspectives, but have traditional methods proved effective lately in solving the scope of and intensity of modern problems? Perhaps the track record of tradition may not permit such nostalgia. *Post-modern* refers to reactions against philosophical practices of modern movements and a desire to revive tradition.

In a world of modern problems, the tendency is to be dismissive of myth as too extraordinary, favoring instead the skepticism of science. This chapter first mentions *freak accidents* as powerful, life-changing experiences possessing the strength to diminish truth, beliefs, and faith. The central question woven throughout the novel is one fundamental to the human condition: Can a freak accident erase a carefully constructed system of belief or change our *teleological* persuasion? Apparently, it depends.

4–Shadow Darwin

A "shadow of Darwin" is reflected in the name of the protagonist Dr. Shadow Darwin. He stands for the *results* of academic pursuits, expression of the *scholar mentality*, success as an intellectual *survivor* amid mediocrity, and rejection of complacency as an option. The virtues of Shadow Darwin include *critical thinking*, the use of *reason* and methodology in times of stress, *loyalty* to a trusted mentor, and the *care and nurturing* of students. Insight into a part of himself, his fatherly side, is suggested throughout the novel, evidenced by his care and concern for the teenagers. Introverts like Shadow are often misread as extraverts. This misperception often leads to the perception of *ambivalence* in close relationships. A theme barely suggested is Darwin's inner struggle of caring for the emotional health of others while trying to overcome an emotional distance due to his introverted nature. Interestingly, a similar conundrum underlies the practice of clinical psychology and psychotherapy. Curiously, target practicing with a Bowie knife brings relaxation—a still mind and steady nerves. Knife throwing displays his proactive quest for perfection (accuracy) at hitting the bull's eye (solving problems). His love of music is introduced with reclaiming an old hobby—playing the alto saxophone, and his preference for alternative rock music.

Darwin's theory of *revenge* explains why individuals act out inappropriately in society trying to solve their own inner demons. This sets the stage for impending future events. In what context will we next see revenge?

5 —Revenge

The necessity and practicality of *theoretical reasoning* is displayed in this chapter. Renowned colleagues embrace Darwin's theory and Darwin himself as an intellectual equal. The fostering of a proactive intellectual climate presents the antithesis of negativity, contentiousness, and complacency—anti-intellectual inertia—from those who have abandoned the high ideals of academia.

6—Cradle of Intrepidity

The geographical setting of the mysterious Big Bend region of West Texas is in itself a *central character* of the novel. In this context *appearances are deceiving,* leading to a foreboding of what lies behind deception. Contrasts and similarities between civilization and wilderness comprise the remaining portion of the chapter. Readers are asked to decide on which side of the fence resides the most dangerous predators—the civilized side or the wild side.

7—Desert Wax & 8—Not in the Forecast

The bounty of all deserts, which appear to be nothing more than a vast expanse of wasteland, is presented in Desert Wax. Actually, Big Bend is teaming with life. But what kind of life?

One of the central themes of the novel is *lack of preparation* and the *consequences* that follow. Can unforeseen events catch up with us because we let our guard down *inviting misfortune to derail our plans?* Aren't we capable of seeing potentially harmful things coming our way?

9—The Shadow Archetype

The Shadow archetype sets a foreboding tone. What do we have to be afraid of? What is coming that we have not anticipated? What strange occurrences lie ahead for the lodgers? What part does learning play in producing fear? What part does nature play in what we fear?

10—Mr. Laurence Harvey

Criticizers of education, of students, and of pedagogy—the art and science of teaching—in all its variations and across all academic levels are embodied in the persona of Mr. Laurence Harvey. The name derives from the Lithuanian actor who became a British film star in the 1950s and 1960s after producer James Woolf of Romulus Films discovered him. He depicted emotionally aloof characters amid the chaos of modern problems offering no solutions for those writhing in emotional pain.

Specifically, modified curricula, compulsory testing, athletics, attitude of students, and any extracurricular activities not tied to academics flow through this character. He represents the "old school" of education that ignores learning styles, learning disorders, and extraneous social influences that threaten to derail the focus of modern students. Mr. Harvey's complacency is perhaps more damaging than his detachment and contentiousness. Today, extracurricular *psychosocial activities* are known to round out a student's perspective and may actually enhance learning and the motivation to graduate.

The death (retirement) of Mr. Laurence Harvey (the sobriquet of "Mr." denotes a desire for respect where none is given) may be taken as the end of negativity from the "old school" anti-computer, anti-Internet, "the students are always trying to get away with something" mentality to a wider acceptance of the continuum of learning styles, academic performance, and the diversity of issues facing students today. Mr. Laurence Harvey actually turns students off to the prospects of education or makes their exit from his influence into higher education more rapid.

11—Peter Marx, Alpha Male

Rich and powerful, the archetypal alpha male, Peter Marx signifies the things money and influence can buy in the YAAVIST-driven culture of North America. The *leader of the pack* (a reference to 1960s rock music) and those who seek the material status of his ambition symbolize Peter Marx. We suspect somewhere in his fondness for the past between his "muscle car" collection, his love of surf rock, and his desire for material wealth, Marx's fatherly, nurturing side is suppressed. We wonder what kind of relationship Peter has with his only son Jon Marx. Is it as detached and aloof as Mr. Laurence Harvey's relationship is to students?

12—Animal Activist & 13—*Canis Lupus*

Thinly veiled reference of things to come. What is the significance of the animal preservations society? With all their wealth, why are they so interested in preserving wild animals? How come there is no mention of house pets so common among individuals with visible wealth? The wolf symbolizes order, intelligence, and learning capability amid chaos in the wild. Throughout the novel, the constant theme of *survival* is personified in the wolf and the grizzly. Due to sheer survival, they are serial killers. The question begins to slowly surface: Besides the blizzard, what else must the lodgers survive? What else is coming that none of them see?

14—"Muscle Cars"

A study in *psychological contrasts* highlights this chapter—the high-performance, nostalgic "muscle cars" from the 1960s and 1970s versus the *au courant* automotive models of today offering less horsepower and less character in exchange for punitive safety features. Modern cars seem perfect symbols of living in a metal enclosure of false security with no "horse sense" to get out.

Jon Marx is introduced as a typical teenager who simply *does not think ahead*, a common denominator of all college-bound students who find themselves in academic trouble because they did not see what was coming. Due to his actions, what lurks about to *derail his plans?*

15—The Creature

Early in the novel, this pivotal chapter displays how *different levels of meaning and comprehension* may be interpreted. Students entering the college experience must discern *metaphorical* versus literal meaning. Some kind of creature forces Jon Marx's car off the road minutes from the front door of the safety of the Sable, a place of *great familiarity* (contrasting high school as familiar with college as unfamiliar and uninviting). What kind of creature attacked Jon? Is Jon's trouble due to a freak accident, or could he have avoided the creature in the first place? What is the nature of the creature he could have avoided?

16—Male Bonding

Male bonding is an issue related to *adaptability.* Perhaps young girls tend to bond faster to their parents, peers, and friends than young males, but we must be careful of *stereotypes.* Young sons who do not bond to their fathers early may find it difficult to make male friends later in the well-known example of *problems with authority figures* observed in middle school and high school when the number of male teachers finally catches up with female teachers. Distant fathers may produce the need of a father figure by proxy as observed in coaches or teachers. A close buddy may likewise function in the role of a surrogate parent. Throughout the novel, we follow the status of Peter and his relationship with Jon, Jon and his relationship to Trevor, and the teenagers and their relationship with Shadow Darwin.

17—The "Darling Dart"

Other than sports, few avenues exist for young teenage males to forge a bond of friendship. A foreboding of what lies ahead occurs in this chapter: What is in store for the two friends that will call on their bond of friendship to help them survive? Survive what?

18—Late-Night Call

Apprehension re-enters the picture with the failure of Jon Marx to arrive as scheduled at the Sable. Apparently, Jon is in serious danger, but from what source? Since his trouble occurs so late (at night, recalling the Shadow archetype), do others who might intercede on his behalf have time? On another level, do parents, friends, teachers, or counselors have time to fix problems teenagers get into due to their *lack of being proactive*?

19—The Search & 20—The Attack

The chapters of *search* and *attack* display *psychological double entendre*. We are all familiar with soul searching when confronted with new challenges. How can we be up to the challenge of a new undertaking if we don't take the time to prepare? Looking (analyzing and strategizing) is preferable to leaping (impulsively acting without considering consequences). Jon is missing. Can he also be missing foresight, strategies, and maturity? A grizzly attacks the chief. Has it already devoured Jon? Can lack of preparation "devour" us? With dangerous elements swirling around Jon (lack of preparation), is the appearance of a wild and dangerous condition foreseeable?

21—Reverse

Jon wakes up (from his miscalculation). Does he have time to reverse his inexperience and lack of perspective? Can he help his friends see the error or his lack of foresight? Aren't friends supposed to help each other by recognizing their mistakes?

22—West Texas Grizzlies?

A short history of grizzly bears is presented for those who may have the misconception of the grizzly as just a dumb animal. Animals have to be smart in order to survive. Again, things are not what they appear to be.

23—Tahoe X

Change of pace and scenery occur in this chapter as the action shifts to the inaugural celebration at the Lake Tahoe X *Marx the Spot*. But Peter Marx cannot be found amid the proceedings. Where is he?

24—Resident Grizzly & 25—Research Implications

Darwin's revelation of the grizzly bear project at his Sul Ross campus gives the lodger's real cause for alarm. Do they have the means to defend themselves from a hungry, rampaging grizzly?

Physiological secrets of the grizzly may unlock some of the secrets to medical ills such as eating disorders, gallstones, and kidney disorder. The mission of science is to discover ways to improve the quality of our lives even if it means introducing a wild animal into the mix. Could it have been foreseen the grizzly might escape?

26—Something Strange

An action-packed chapter, physical evidence now exists in the savage attack on Chief Munoz and Jon Marx that points to a grizzly threatening the lodgers' lives along with the blizzard. Times are getting worse with the real possibility of a sudden attack looming heavy in the air of the Sable. Bad things continue to come the lodgers' way. Could they have averted any of it?

27—Glass-Eye Eddie & 28—One-Eyed Sentry

Glass-Eye Eddie Hawkins is introduced in these related chapters. The name derives from Screamin' Jay Hawkins, a pioneer of rock and roll. Glass-Eye Eddie is a colorful character who loves "muscle cars, " C&W music, and hunting. A man like Glass-Eye Eddie provides utility to residents who have more money than time. He is a bit dimwitted and strange but does he fit into the formula of the Marx Desert Estates? But what formula?

29—The Plan

The lodgers finally get a break when they discover a way to survive an attack by the grizzly courtesy of the impenetrable Union Pacific Railroad walk-in vault, a vault so safe it withstood the great train robbers of the Old West. Shadow Darwin hatches a plan for a night watch of around-the-clock surveillance.

30—The "D Spot" & 31—A-n-t-i-c-i-p-a-t-i-o-n

Perhaps the common observation of teenage *angst* is really not a dangerous mood condition after all. Perhaps it is a *symptom of longing*—a desire to fit in, to be accepted, and to have a meaningful relationship with someone who is not a parent or sibling. These chapters offer a glimpse into such conditions exacerbated by fear of new experiences (sexual tension) and the stress associated with not having all the answers. Why must some teenagers use alcohol or drugs in order to become intimate with each other? What kind of intimacy develops from drug-induced states? Is intimacy too threatening when individuals are sober?

The need to exchange tender emotions is a salient human trait. This need has always existed as an expression of female nurturing. It has remained one of the major gender divides between the sexes. Males have similar needs but seem always tongue-tied in their expression—to the vast disappointment of females. With little perspective and life experiences, what do teenagers have to offer each other?

32—Second Watch & 33—The Creature Invades

With the conclusion of Friday evening and Friday night's events, a foreboding occurs when the Sable's lights are extinguished permanently and Julie experiences a nightmare due to the stress of their predicament.

SATURDAY

34–Cabin Fever & 35–Survival Plan

Reality sinks in. What will the lodgers decide to do about it? When emotions wear off, exposing the cognitive reality of problems (referring to reason and judgment), what strategies follow?

36–Bonzo

The worst fear of Shadow Darwin is now realized. The lodgers' problems are far more serious than originally expected when they discover Bonzo never left the observation quarters at Sul Ross. *Fear of the unknown* enters the psychological perception of the lodgers. Yet, we discover Shadow Darwin had already anticipated it.

37–Serious Conditions

This chapter is metaphorical for how imaginations run wild when truth is unknown. So much time can be lost "shadow-dancing" around the truth.

38–Four Facts

This chapter is a metaphorical example of the process of critical thinking and the elements of empiricism—objectivity, observation, and the willingness to use speculative empiricism to find answers not immediately suggested by science.

39–Inspiration & 40–Fact Four Takes Shape

That other individuals we are romantically attracted to can be inspirational is well known in psychology. Excitable emotions can be motivating and can lead to achievement (as in declaring a major, the focus of one's academics in college). Giving an identity to a problem can help solve it regardless of how preposterous it sounds (such as the unmistakable evidence of an alpha shape shifter observed by Darwin).

41–Preposterous

The lodgers sit in disbelief as Darwin, the scientist, suggests possibilities that seem far-fetched to individuals with closed minds. Personal biases, stereotypes, rigid beliefs, and hidden agendas have long been *rigor mortis* to intellectualism. Do we have to observe something for it to be real? Does faith have a place in science? Does science have a place in faith?

42—The Alpha Has the Scent

How is myth to be interpreted though the critical eye of science and, on a more personal level, through everyday experience with modern problems? Can animals smell fear? Can humans effectively hide their fears?

43—*Homo Morpholupus*

Now, empirical evidence exists from two documented sources validating the existence of a parallel link and rival to *Homo sapiens*. Are there more links?

44—Girl Talk & 45—Darkness Descends

Talking about feelings is the traditional gender benchmark of females, while males often suppress feelings or act out in inappropriate ways. Fear of the unknown is expressed by Ashley who symbolizes ambition and the determination to overcome obstacles. On the other hand, Gable symbolizes insecurity and fear of change related to future academic expectations. Psychological darkness descends on those unprepared for potential outcomes through lack of foresight, planning, and failure to anticipate consequences.

46—The Real Glass-Eye

The true identity of Glass-Eye Eddie Hawkins is finally disclosed. The liberal use of personality *personas* (false fronts) today often confuse us to the ever-present issue of one's true identity. Can we believe what we see in others? Can we ever come to know our true selves and others? Does radical change create a monster? In academia, what do we call this monster?

47—The Josh Randall & 48—Pandemonium

When things get completely crazy, how will we handle ourselves when things are spinning out of control? What resources can we call upon when things get really bad? Shadow Darwin appears throughout the novel as a safety net for the miscalculations and problems of others. The absolute necessity of strong adult interventions in the lives of teenagers is portrayed by the actions of Shadow Darwin in the lives of the teenagers lacking perspective and maturity.

49—Confrontation

Because Shadow Darwin finds bonding with the teenagers to be so rewarding, he puts his life on the line. Or, does he do it just because he is a caring, thoughtful person? Confrontation in this chapter is metaphorical for confronting the reality of *facing life without adequate preparation.*

50—Loopers

Loopers exist as a *form fruste* of maturity; loopers are synonymous with *change* and the absolute necessity of *rapid adaptation* required in many experiences in life.

51—A Short History Lesson & 52—The Hour Is Getting Late

These two chapters are pivotal to the story regarding the extent of *antecedent events* (such as a psychosocial history in clinical psychology or a student's high school track record) contributing to *behavioral contingencies.* How significant are antecedent events in predicting present and future events in the *empirical analysis* of behavior? A recurrent theme throughout the novel is *how much of what happens to us is accidental?* How much could have been avoided? How much is foreseeable? How much is completely unpredictable. Philosophical *determinism* sets up "menus" of selection. Does a person really exercise capricious free will in decision making or is freedom illusory?

Are the so-called "choices" individuals are presumed to make really choices? In reality, are the choices the only choices individuals could have made given past influences? The scientific analysis of behavior depends on discovering *behavioral contingencies* that lie behind "choices." Seemingly, the novel suggests *very few things occur completely due to chance* or due completely to freak accidents.

53—Blood Brothers & 54—Conversion Criteria

Kinship to each other and similarities, rather than differences, highlight these chapters. Akin to the concept of *Universal People,* many cross-species similarities exist such as feeding, breeding, caring for young, and surviving.

55—Into the Lair of the Alpha

Confronting our worst fears is the message of this chapter. As a proactive strategy in problem solving, confrontation may lead to quick resolution or other direct strategies such as *compromise.*

56—The Bargain

The willingness of Shadow Darwin to face one of his worst fears leads to resolution. In this regard, given his options, Darwin's decision is kept secret until the final showdown. He stands firm on his decision after analyzing the up side and the down side suggested by options. He displays characteristics of an individual with an *internal LOC* (locus of control), sure of his abilities and confident of the outcome.

SUNDAY

57—Good for You

Near the end of the novel, the exhausted, but renewed Darwin, hopeful their troubles are over, is disheartened when he discovers that Jon Marx is a juvenile looper. Growing close to the teenagers during the ordeal makes this realization particularly disheartening. The theme of *existential reality* woven throughout the novel finds full expression in this chapter. Living in a world full of disappointment and uncertainty, how can we overcome negativity with hope, resolve, and dedication?

BEYOND

58—Aftermath

Instead of closure (or resolution), the novel ends unresolved where *options* remain open—like they are in real life. Reality is presented as a condition of *existential* design as events unfold at the Sable. In reality, the novel is about the dynamics of change, adaptability, and the flip side—complacency and not seeing what's coming in time to successfully adapt. If we're not careful, we can get comfortable with underachievement, negativity, and codependency.

The reality of finding solutions to the many options we face living in the real world leaves but one conclusion: Answers do not always come neatly packaged and the results of our efforts may not be satisfying. Furthermore, decisions are not guaranteed. Hesitating to make decisions set up by options *still results in a decision*. Existentially, we live in *a world of decisions set up by options,* and we may not like any of them.

Living in the real world of *existential reality* means we can be amazingly sane or incredibly insane. Being able to analyze options, calculate the up side versus the down side, make decisions, put the past into *perspective* and *move on to new challenges* offered daily is a benchmark of maturity, organization, and perspective. Psychology majors are taught to face the facts of reality and make appropriate decisions.

In the final paragraphs of the novel, Shadow Darwin is hopeful Jon Marx opts to avoid the path of the looper. Darwin believes Jon has chosen the path of the sapient—to become a young, alpha male who decides the path of least resistance may not be the wisest one to take. Will Jon Marx be successful? Or, will he decide when the going gets tough to take the avenue of least resistance—the one he seems destined to take? The existential answer is always the same: *Trust your gut feeling as time will tell.*

59—Postscript

To the best of their abilities, scholars attempt to understand the events that impact our lives. The perspective of empiricism (observation, objectivity, and experimentation), determinism and its menu, and freedom for the taking are tools Shadow Darwin uses to analyze freak accidents for meaning. He settles on two characteristics that make them so potentially deadly given a specific confluence of events. The events are both related to the perception that occurs due to *time-compression*. The first one is the sudden awareness of *not having enough response time to avoid making the BEST decision,* and second is becoming *disoriented*. Rapidly unfolding events often produce the catastrophes observed in freak accidents. Not enough time remains to make the best response.

60—The Hitchhiker

The novel ends on an *ambivalent* note, reminiscent of the events at the Sable Lodge. The well-known Mach 1 Mustang of Jon Marx pulls over on State Highway 118 and a mysterious nighttime hitchhiker is offered a ride. Down the road toward Mt. Kyle, the car pulls over and a big gray wolf emerges in full gallop. What does this mean? Who is driving the car? Who is the hitchhiker?

Ambiguous endings can be summarized in one sentence: We have to learn to live happy and prosperous lives in a world fraught with uncertainty and ambiguity. We must not shun problems that block us from being successful and prosperous in life.

We try to set good examples for our children and others. We work hard and sleep well. We strive to see the beauty of the world knowing it can change at any moment. We seek to enjoy every moment of time we have with our loved ones. Focusing on the lessons from Mt. Kyle, we learn our lessons and we move on and keep learning. In the end, time will tell how smart we have become.

FOCUS GROUP QUESTIONS

Directed Study of Freak Accident Relating to the College Experience

SHORT ANSWER

1. Name three expectations high school graduates may *not see coming* in the college experience.

2. When students are successful in the *first two years of college* (usually the hardest years) *what percentage* (50-50, 80-20, for example) is due to strategic organization, focus, and preparation? What percentage is merely accidental?

3. Name five *scholastic qualities* characterized by the personality of Shadow Darwin.

4. Regarding the *shadow archetype*, what do students have to fear in the college experience?

5. What is the possible significance of the colors used on the front and back covers of *Freak Accident*?

6. Give five instances of *metaphor* in *Freak Accident* as they relate to success (or failure) in the college experience.

7. What condition in the college experience could stand for *werewolves* in the novel?

8. What five conditions of pedagogy (teaching methods) are presented in the persona of Mr. Laurence Harvey?

9. Name three potentially injurious academic habits personified in the character of Peter Marx.

10. Pertaining to the college experience, what is a *shape shifter*?

11. Name three characteristics of a post-modern society.

12. Draw an analogy between Jon's late night encounter with the shape shifter and what might await him the first semester in college.

13. Why is the use of metaphor such an effective device for learning?

14. College faculty, student services, and counselors often exist as *safety nets* for students heading for academic trouble. Name three instances in the novel when the teenagers were in danger and Shadow Darwin acted as a safety net.

15. As the blizzard and the attacks on Jon and the chief add more tension and drama to the novel, what metaphorical situation does this suggest in the college experience?

16. The Union Pacific Railroad vault is metaphorical for what building on all college campuses?

17. When the teenagers decide to be alone in the X, how does this translate to college?

18. When Shadow Darwin finally shares his fears regarding the identity of the creature, what parallel situation in the college experience is suggested?

19. What is the possible meaning of the color black presented as darkness and white presented as snow in the context of fear, dread, and uncertainity in the novel?

20. What is the metaphorical significance of the Josh Randall, Darwin's Bowie knife, and the Shield of the Warrior and the tomahawk?

21. As the lodgers confront the reality of their desperate situation, what is a parallel to the college experience?

22. What is the metaphorical significance of *loopers* to higher education?

23. What is the significance of Darwin's various observations of the *creature* that stalks the lodgers?

24. The *existential component* of the novel relates to *options* that set up decisions we all face in everyday living. How does this relate to the the college experience?

25. Is there a final resolution to *Freak Accident*? It ends with *options*. Is this more like real life?

BURNING QUESTIONS

1. In the context of the Sable experience, how can the events be characterized as existential issues?

2. Psychosocially, what is the significance of the following names: Darwin, Marx, Lennon, and Lemark?

MATCHING

Match *academic qualities and roles* suggested from the following characters:

_____ 1. Shadow Darwin
_____ 2. Wells McAfee
_____ 3. "Glass-Eye" Eddie Hawkins
_____ 4. Chief Jake Hoover
_____ 5. Deputy Julie Quixotica
_____ 6. Peter Marx
_____ 7. Jon Marx
_____ 8. Ryan Trevor
_____ 9. Ashley Cox
_____ 10. Gable Jordan
_____ 11. Clint Cooper
_____ 12. Susan Newby
_____ 13. Jill Frazier
_____ 14. Mr. Laurence Harvey

a. nurturer
b. academic counselor, advisor, protector
c. degreed underachiever
d. insightful scholar
e. academically insecure
f. ambitious
g. registrar (enrollment)
h. loyal friend (colleague)
i. opportunist
j. wise mentor and teacher
k. typical teenager
l. academic critic (criticizer of college major)
m. campus security (authority figure)
n. undeclared major (major always "changing shape")

SHORT ESSAY

Bring a well-developed two to three page essay as a writing sample to your focus group. The title should be *Freak Accident: Metaphorically Speaking*.

ACCORDING TO FREAK ACCIDENT

Ten Ways to Achieve Collegiate Success

1. **Show Up Prepared**. Attend class. Listen to your instructor. If it sounds important, it probably is important. If you're not getting it, *talk with your professor.* Your best asset is *your personality.* Use it and develop it. You must learn to become an effective communicator in the college experience.

2. **Be a Long Liner**. Start the semester strong and *finish strong.* Avoid the tendency at midterm to coast. If you coast, you may be toast. Stay on top of your deadlines to avoid fading at the stretch. Your full-time job for the next four years is college. *Your job description: studying, taking exams, and writing papers.*

3. **I. D. Yourself.** Introduce yourself to your instructor in the *first three weeks of class.* Drop by for a few minutes' visit during office hours and chat for a few minutes. *Do not avoid authority figures.* Pretend all instructors are like Shadow Darwin, approachable, intellectual, and interested in your welfare.

4. **Note It, Don't Float It**. Make a note of all significant dates (deadlines, exams, papers) on your personal calendar. Don't float it in memory, or it may sink you.

5. **The 3 Rs: Read. Read. Read.** If you don't like to read, get over it! Find books by authors or subjects you find interesting and read every night. It's unimportant whether or not you like the content of textbooks; just comprehend what's in them.

6. **You're Already Brilliant, Now Be Smart.** Shadow Darwin offers proof of how this works. Go to www.freakaccident.info for evidence. Develop strategies *for balancing your life.* Working part-time and partying the rest of time will land you on academic probation.

7. **Work Yourself into College Not Out of It.** Expect to be financially uncomfortable while you're in college. Financially, you're not supposed to be comfortable. You're supposed to hunger and thirst for knowledge. You *just get by*, which you will.

8. **Close the Circle.** Hang with friends that support your choices. Say good-bye to your partying chums. You have plenty of time to catch up with revelers when you graduate. Make a new circle of colleagues. *Colleagues are defined as smart friends.*

9. **Copy Down www.freakaccident.info.** Go there often to check out the official website of *Freak Accident. Ask Shadow Darwin questions* about the college experience and what to do when you're stumped. He will respond immediately.

10. **Get Yourself Connected.** The writing's on the wall; rather, the writing's on the diploma. The only name to appear on your college diploma is your name. College is not about liking (as in liking all your courses), it's about doing.

DIRECTED STUDY COMPONENT

An additional academic component, directed study, allows students to study the novel as they go. Reading several chapters of the novel at once (three or four are suggested) and then referring to the authors' commentary comprise the first two steps of the directed study component. Answering study questions at the completion of the novel is the final element of directed study.

Students are not expected, necessarily, to comprehend the possible metaphorical meanings of the novel on the first reading. The fact the students don't see the metaphorical side is the point. *Not being able to see what's coming and how it applies to the college experience* is precisely why the novel is assigned as a focus group activity during college orientation. Additionally, the existential component of the novel—the necessity of living amid uncertainty and ambiguity in a world with little or no guarantees—will be addressed in focus groups.

The importance of metaphorical over literal meaning is presented in the final academic exercise beginning on page 209. In **Part I**, simply answer the study questions found in the directed study section that reads: Complete when you finish the novel. **Part II** is a continuation of study questions entitled Burning Questions. This section allows students to take notice (and notes) for use in the focus group session of college orientation.

Part III requires students to match academic qualities observed in higher education represented by the main characters. **Part IV** requires students to write a two- to three-page writing sample entitled *Freak Accident: Metaphorically Speaking.* To receive full credit, students must bring the writing sample to the focus group and submit it to the discussion leader. By completing the orientation (by attending fish camp or taking it online at www.wcfish.net), submitting the writing sample of *Freak Accident,* and attending the focus group, one hour of college credit will be awarded each participant.

Finally, students may go to the **official website** of *Freak Accident, www.freakaccident.info,* to make comments or ask questions of Dr. Shadow Darwin at anytime during the reading of the novel.